The Mean Girl's Murder

Afterlife Calls

K.C.Adams

broke the curse. That was a rare skill, though, so I really hoped that wouldn't happen in our lifetimes. He'd done enough damage to our family in the few weeks he'd been in our lives.

'*Do the police have any idea what happened to her?*' asked the presenter.

The reporter shook his head. '*Not that they're saying, no. All we know is that they believe the circumstances surrounding her death to be suspicious.*'

Which meant they definitely knew more than they were letting on.

I massaged my forehead, the latest mystery in our lives making my headache worse. A weird, disjointed whistling sound had kept me up overnight. I'd woken up with a horrible headache that I hadn't managed to shake all day.

'Suspicious usually means it looks like murder and they don't want to risk any leaks in case it harms the investigation,' said Ben.

Tilly gave up trying to console Edie and joined Ben and me on the sofa instead. We both reached over and she automatically leaned into me, exposing her belly for a rub. I wasn't sure who was more predictable – the dog or us.

'At her age, it's bound to be treated as suspicious until they have more details. Maybe she had an underlying heart condition. You never know,' I said. I hoped.

'Or she didn't have a heart,' Edie mumbled. I tried not to laugh. Edie looked horrified at herself. But, after all the horrible things Tessa had said and done…

1

Niamh

'*The body of a teenage girl was found on the outskirts of Hucknall today by two dog walkers.*'

I looked up at the TV screen. We lived in a relatively quiet suburb of Nottingham. I'd never heard of a body being found like that before, let alone one of a teenage girl. Hadn't we had enough drama lately, what with a psychopathic necromancer trying to absorb the life essences of every magic user in town?

The TV cut to a field reporter. '*Police are investigating the suspicious death of seventeen-year-old Tessa Barker, whose body was found this morning.*'

I leaned closer to the TV. 'Oh my god. Edie!'

Ben turned from his spot on the sofa beside me. 'What? What is it?'

'What?' echoed Edie, stomping down the stairs with Tilly and Spectre in tow. Tilly's white tail wagged with excitement. Spectre furry grey figure floated on to the sofa behind Ben and me, turning his attention to the TV. Edie watched, waiting to see why I'd called her. A photo of Tessa posing in front of a park filled the screen. 'Oh my god.'

The news report didn't give much away about Tessa's death, which, I supposed made sense. Anything they shared could harm their investigation. But still, I wanted to know.

Edie put her hand to her mouth. Tessa had been bullying her for months with no repercussions. She'd even stolen Josh, Edie's boyfriend and former best friend, from her.

All right, fine. It was more complicated than that. But Edie didn't see it that way.

They were all due to take their A Level exams in just a few months' time. And now Tessa would never get the chance.

Edie sat on the armchair in front of the sofa, her face in her hands. Tilly jumped up at her, but Edie ignored the little dog.

'You OK?' I said.

'I don't know. What am I even supposed to think? She was a horrible person, but to die so young? Nobody deserves that.'

The news shifted to show the reporter standing in front of a police cordon, a white tent in the background.

'Why aren't they saying what happened to her?' Edie leaned back in the armchair as the screen switched to show the anchor on one side and the reporter on another.

Death had become a weird topic in our house, especially since Dominic had found out about Edie's necromancy powers and manipulated her with his good looks and charm to get her to do what he'd wanted. After tricking Edie into hurting people with her powers, he'd killed me.

She'd resurrected me, but she hadn't forgiven herself. It didn't matter how many times Ben and I told her it wasn't her fault, she was convinced it was because she'd fallen for his manipulation in the first place. She'd always thought she was too smart to fall for a guy like him. But was anyone ever as smart as they thought they were?

Her ability to give and take life was rare. It also came with huge consequences.

Dominic had been a necromancer too, choosing to use his powers to heal himself of an terminal illness. Of course, it never lasted. Magic couldn't stop hi body from turning against him.

When Ben's sister, Lindsay, had found out what was doing, she'd cursed him, taking away his ac powers so that he couldn't hurt anyone else. H killed her in return, breaking Ben's family apart convincing Ben his witchcraft was useless incapable of helping others.

It was only because Dominic had killed me t my useless powers that Edie had realised he rea a monster. Dominic had been convinced that rid of me would make Edie more loyal to h that my powers would sustain him for longer of my heritage. But it wasn't that simple.

Edie had turned the very powers he' against him, stealing his life essence unt barely alive. Then, we'd cursed him.

Now, he was in a state of suspended inside an Ancient Egyptian sarcophagus fe eternity. Or until someone else sensed he

'They'll know more than they're saying,' said Ben. 'This feels more like the start of an investigation than a memorial.'

Edie turned away from the TV so that she was facing us. 'I hope she's not a ghost. Is that bad of me to say?'

'No. She wasn't a fun human. Can you imagine what she'd be like if we were the only ones who could see her?' I shuddered. Even though I hadn't had the pleasure of Tessa's company as much as Edie, I knew enough to not want it.

'I can't believe she's dead,' said Edie. 'Just like that.'

'I can't either,' I said. 'So young.'

'Everyone at college is going to be super weird tomorrow.'

'You think?'

The news, out of nice things to say about Tessa, moved on to another story.

Edie nodded, rubbing her hands together. 'She was Little Miss Popular. Everyone knew who she was, even if she didn't know everyone. Not to mention it happened so suddenly and so close to exams. It's going to be the talk of college. I can't see anyone getting any work done.'

2

Edie

I didn't have any college lessons that morning, so I got to avoid the initial discussions of Tessa's death. Given my dislike for her, it was probably a good thing. Most people would've probably been crying and talking about how sad it was. While I wouldn't wish anyone dead, I didn't have the energy to pretend I'd miss her. She'd been horrible to me for no reason. Would I miss that? No, no I wouldn't.

I really, really wanted a lie-in, but my brain wouldn't let me have one. It was too busy thinking about Tessa. Or, more specifically, her death.

So I spent the morning reading anything I could and what had (maybe) happened to her. The circumstances around her death were so unusual, it'd made the national news, but they still hadn't revealed her cause of death. All we knew was that she'd been found in a local park. Nothing mentioned her suffering from any sort of chronic illness, or hinted towards her having mental health issues. The police may not have announced an official cause of death, but the subtext was clear: *she was murdered*.

Every street I walked down, it seemed like someone was talking about Tessa's death. People huddled on front porches, keeping away from the draughts; they stood outside coffee shops, smoking a cigarette and talking loudly about how sad it was someone so young was possibly murdered; they walked down the street with dogs in tow, saying how pretty she was and how it was such a shame.

Several of the people I walked past mentioned the M word. I really hoped they were wrong. And I was reading the police subtext wrong. Murder meant unfinished business, and the only way to solve that unfinished business meant becoming a ghost. Frazzle.

When I reached the brick steps of college at lunchtime, a gaggle of press had gathered outside and were trying to interview students. As I walked past with my head down, they were interviewing someone from Josh's art class.

Away from the cameras, some people were sombre and barely speaking, dabbing at their eyes with mascara-stained tissues or scrunching up their faces to hide tears. Everyone else was gossiping.

The fact that the police still hadn't released Tessa's cause of death just fuelled the rumour mill more. Almost everyone was adamant she was murdered by a disgruntled ex or a jealous classmate. One person I walked past even suggested Josh. I curled my hand into a fist, resisting the urge say something. He'd never do that! Even after being tortured by a demon. He was too broken after being tortured; he'd never physically hurt another person after that.

I walked through the front doors, avoiding eye contact so that nobody would talk to me. Not that they ever really did anyway.

Given everything Tessa had done to me, from damaging my coccyx to stealing my boyfriend, it was safe to say we'd had a complicated relationship. Even though Mr Hazelock, the head of college, knew what she'd done, she'd got away with it. Just like any other child of rich parents got away with just about anything. It infuriated me, but there wasn't much I could do, and I'd had bigger problems to deal with. After facing a demon, saving Josh and Maggie from a curse, and taking down Dominic, Tessa and her attitude had seemed way less important.

And, thankfully, Tessa and I had seen each other less since the countdown to exams had started and the pressure had begun to mount. It felt like college wanted us to revise, do coursework, do mock exams, and start planning for our future, all at the same time. As if being a teenager wasn't stressful enough already.

What was the point in me planning to go to university like everyone else seemed to be? Did they teach courses in necromancy? The kinds of lessons I needed no traditional university could teach me. While I adjusted to my powers and the right ways to use them, it made more sense to stay at home and use my pre-existing support network who already knew about what I could do, even if their powers weren't the same.

I hadn't told Mum about my decision yet because I knew how she'd react. She hated the idea of me putting my ghost hunting or necromancy above a 'normal' life, but if Dominic had taught me anything, it was that my life would never be normal.

'Hey,' said Melanie, falling into step with me as I walked through the front doors. Up until recently, she'd been one of Tessa's best friends. We'd developed a mutual understanding after my mum, Josh, and I had exorcised a ghost from her. Tessa seemed to forget about her soon after, when she'd started going out with Josh. Things had been complicated between Josh and me ever since.

Dominic tricking me into using my powers to drain Josh's life essence and heal himself had made things even more complicated. Josh didn't know what I'd done, and it wasn't like I could easily hold a conversation with him yet. Me telling him would've just made him hate me even more.

I still felt guilty, though. I wasn't sure how much long-term damage I'd done to Josh, if any. So I mostly avoided him. He didn't seem to mind. It probably made it easier for him to avoid me.

'Hey,' I said to Melanie.

The beige corridors were relatively empty because everyone else had gone out for lunch. A couple of groups stood in corridors or sat in classrooms, eating sandwiches or drinking bottles of pop.

'It's weird, isn't it?' said Melanie, shaking her head. Her long, dark brown hair tickled her shoulders. 'Usually by now you'd hear her cackling.'

'Yeah.'

Tessa's laugh had always carried through the corridor. She was one of those people whose voice, and laugh, travelled. Whether you liked her or not, you couldn't avoid her presence.

'How are you?' I asked.

She sighed. 'Like…I don't even know. Tessa and I have been friends since we were five. And I know she ditched me for Josh, and she could be a total bitch, but it still hurts that she's gone, you know?'

'Yeah.' Sort of, anyway. I wanted to be as supportive as possible, but it was hard for me to imagine being friends with someone as petty and conniving as Tessa.

We didn't have a guidance counsellor or anything like that to help us with what was going on. The closest we had was Mr Hazelock, the head of the college, and he wasn't exactly approachable. He usually lurked outside the front doors, watching. Silently.

He wasn't there now. Was he in some sort of emergency meeting? Did the press want to talk to him? They always interviewed people who'd known the person who'd died, and they always talked about how lovely and kind and intelligent the person was, even if that person was actually horrible. Because the public would feel more sympathy and be more inclined to help if a nice person had died so young.

What would people say about Tessa?

She was selfish? Manipulative? A bully?

Please. They never said anything like that on TV.

We walked past Mr Hazelock's office. Voices echoed from inside it, but I was too short to see through the window in the door to find out whose they were.

I didn't need to, though. As we walked past, the door opened. Curiosity getting the better of me, I turned around.

Tessa's parents walked out, followed by Josh. Then Tessa.

Wait? *Tessa?* Tessa was dead. It couldn't be…

My back stiffened. There was definitely someone else with Tessa's parents and Josh. Her parents had shifted, though, so I couldn't see if my instinct had been right. They were blocking the other person's view, which was not a good sign. Either her parents really hated that person, or they didn't know said person was there…

'You all right?' said Melanie, watching me with narrowed eyes.

I grabbed her arm and pulled her into an empty classroom. 'I think…no. It can't be.' I shook my head, as if that would make it all go away. Nope nope nope. This was not happening.

Melanie wrinkled her brow. Of course she was confused. I was acting like a weirdo. 'What?'

'I think I just saw Tessa.'

'Her *ghost?*'

'Shh!' I said, flapping my arms like an idiot.

Just because we were in an empty classroom, that didn't mean someone couldn't hear us in the corridor.

'Sorry!' She covered her mouth with her hand. 'Are you sure?'

'Fairly. But I don't want to go out there and check.'

Melanie lowered her hand. 'If I could check for you I would.'

'Thanks.'

It was a sweet offer, but we both knew there wasn't much Melanie could do. She couldn't see ghosts, she just knew about them and wasn't totally freaked out by them. At least I had someone at college I could talk to about it, I supposed.

Taking a deep breath, I peered into the corridor, trying to act normal. Josh and Tessa's parents were still outside Mr Hazelock's office, talking to him. Tessa hovered around them, shouting and waving to get their attention. It didn't make a difference. If it wasn't for how much of a bitch she'd been, I'd have felt sorry for her. Well, a part of me did. She looked so helpless. I still hated her.

Melanie joined me by the door, peering over my shoulder at the group. 'Is it her?'

'Unfortunately,' I said through gritted teeth.

We stepped out of the classroom and stood in the corridor, me with my back to the wall so that I had something to prop myself up with, and Melanie facing me. And Tessa just to my right.

'Well damn. Now what?'

'I give her and her parents a wide berth. Then I don't have to see her. Problem solved.' I put my foot up against the wall, trying to look casual while I talked to Melanie.

Every so often, I glanced over my shoulder at Tessa's parents. Everyone else was watching them, too,

And OK, there was probably some magic involved, too. That was the only way the so-called surgery could've been done, really.

Ever since we'd mummified and cursed Dominic, Ben and Fadil had been looking after Dave. It was a temporary measure before we gave him to Tobias, but before we did that we wanted to make sure Tobias hadn't tricked or double crossed us somehow.

Mum had wanted to look after Dave, since Dave knew me and we already had a dog-friendly house. But he didn't like other dogs so he and Tilly clashed. Meaning he'd ended up with Ben and Fadil instead. I think Fadil was growing quite fond of him.

'I've been reading online about what people think happened to Tessa,' said Fadil. He unfastened Dave's lead. Dave trotted into the living room. When he saw Tilly, his back arched.

'Dave, *no*,' I said in my best dog training voice. Dave looked at me, glared, then trotted over to the far side of the room and lay down. Other dogs aside, he was a pretty apathetic and low maintenance dog. It also helped he knew me and apparently respected me enough to listen.

'What did you find?' I asked Fadil.

Mum waved from the kitchen then returned to whatever she was doing. Tilly danced around Fadil, demanding his attention. She ignored Dave, likely remembering their previous interaction where he'd tried to pick a fight with her, and not wanting to repeat it. Smart dog. Fadil picked her up and hugged her, then put her back down again.

'Since it was a closed crime scene, not a lot. There's a rumour she was dismembered. Some people are suggesting she was beheaded. But no one really knows anything,' said Fadil. 'Do you think she remembers what happened?'

'Dunno. Either way, it's not my problem,' I said. 'I don't care so long as the police get answers ASAP so that she can cross over.'

Fadil opened his mouth to reply. Before he could utter a syllable, Spectre jumped through the wall.

'Argh!' Fadil jumped so high I thought he was going to headbutt the ceiling.

'What?'

Fadil stared at the large, grey ghost cat, blinking rapidly as if that would make him disappear. 'Is that… your cat?'

'Wait. You can see Spectre?' I said, looking between them. Since when could Fadil see ghosts? That was new. And completely terrifying for him when he wasn't used to seeing them.

Fadil nodded slowly. He rubbed his face. 'Apparently.' He turned to me, his eyes wide in terror. 'What is going on?'

I guided him to the armchair by the window.

'I'll get you a drink,' I said, going into the kitchen.

Mum turned around when I walked in. 'What's up?'

I walked over to Mum, and whispered: 'Fadil just saw Spectre.' I didn't want Fadil to overhear; he seemed freaked out enough already. Hearing it might freak him out even more.

'Fiddlesticks.' She shook her head in frustration. 'You go keep an eye on him, I'll bring him a drink in.'

'Thanks.'

When I went back into the lounge, it looked like Fadil was trying not to hyperventilate. His life was just getting back to normal – or as normal as it could be for someone who was four millennia old – and now everything was changing again. No wonder he looked freaked out.

Tilly sat at his feet, staring up at him. There wasn't much she could do, but she'd probably keep an eye on him until he left now. That was the Nurse Tilly way.

Fadil turned around to see if Spectre was still there. The cat remained on his perch on the top of the sofa, oblivious to the chaos he'd just caused. Like any other cat, probably.

Mum came in and put a cup of tea and a plate of biscoff biscuits in front of Fadil.

'Biscuits?' said Fadil.

'Comfort food. Maggie and Abigail made too many so gave us the leftovers,' said Mum with a shrug.

Fadil took a biscuit from the plate, dipped it in his tea, then munched on it. The caramel and tea flavours seemed to soothe him a little. I didn't blame him. They *were* good biscuits.

'Much as it pains me, there are only two people who might be able to answer our questions about what's going on,' said Mum.

'Who?' I said.

'Since Fadil couldn't see ghosts prior to the transplant, Tobias, as he's the one who did it, and my mother.' She sighed. 'Mum!'

'Yes?' said Gran, appearing instantaneously.

Fadil jumped again, almost dropping his biscuit and spilling tea all over his lap. 'Dammit.'

'I'll go get a cloth,' said Mum, going back into the kitchen and coming back with a tea towel and some kitchen roll. She passed it to Fadil and helped him clean up the mess.

Gran approached Fadil, her eyes narrowed. 'You jumped when I appeared.'

Fadil's back stiffened. He refused to look at Gran.

'Are you making yourself visible to him?' I asked, trying to deflect the attention away from him.

'No,' said Gran. 'Do I know you?' she asked Fadil, still not looking at me. Charming.

'It's Fadil, Gran.'

'The *mummy*?'

'I am *not* a mummy,' said Fadil, looking into his lap as he continued to pat at his damp jeans with some kitchen roll. Mum wiped the armchair with the tea towel.

'You can see me?' said Gran.

'Yes,' Fadil confirmed through gritted teeth.

'What did you do?' she said to Mum accusingly.

Mum turned and glared at Gran. 'What makes you think *I* did something?'

Gran raised an eyebrow. 'You're usually at the centre of things.'

'Actually, I don't mean to sound bigheaded, but it's usually me,' I said. I really hated how Gran blamed Mum and made out like things were her fault all the time. If she wanted someone to blame, she really should've looked in the mirror – assuming they were a thing on the Other Side – since she was the one who'd kept all the secrets that had caused a lot of the chaos over the last few months. Anyway. 'It was my idea. The reason he can see ghosts, I mean. We didn't know it would be a side effect.'

'Explain,' said Gran.

'Fadil and Dominic swapped skins,' said Mum. She flipped the towel over her shoulder then looked out through the window. There was no one there, and it was pretty dark out anyway. While our lights were on, nobody outside would know we were talking to a ghost. To most people, we'd look like a perfectly normal family sitting in their lounge, talking. Sometimes I missed being normal.

Gran didn't know much about Dominic, but she knew he was a necromancer. I was too embarrassed to tell her that he'd tried to use the very tools she'd given me against me. If she didn't know, I wasn't going to fill her in. She nodded in a kind of 'I see' sort of way to what I did tell her. 'I'm impressed. High quality of work.'

Fadil shook his head, still squeezing his eyes open and shut but refusing to look anywhere but straight ahead, at the wall or switched off TV.

'Could it be a side effect of the, um, surgery?' I suggested.

Gran tilted her head. 'Well, the skin is the largest organ in the body. I've heard more ridiculous theories that have been proven to be true.'

Fadil's jaw dropped. We'd never considered that as a side effect, nor had Tobias mentioned it. Did he know it would happen?

'Is it permanent?' Fadil squeezed the bundle of kitchen roll in his hand into a tight ball. 'Why wasn't it instant?'

Gran shrugged. 'The best person to ask is the person who did your surgery.'

Fadil sighed, as if accepted he wouldn't get any more answers.

'Do you think he could experience any other side effects?' I asked, refusing to accept Gran's answer. It was something we hadn't explored enough at the time because it'd all happened so fast and our options to help Fadil had been limited.

'Of the donor skin or the powers?'

'Both.'

Gran pursed her lips. 'How long has it been?'

'A week,' said Mum. It felt like longer.

Gran pursed her lips, crossing her arms over her brown cardigan. 'Have you experienced any side effects so far?'

'Other than being able to see you and the cat?'

'Yes,' said Gran.

'Not that I'm aware of.'

'Very curious.' She narrowed her eyes, taking a moment to study Fadil. 'I would've thought you'd have experienced them by now if you were going to. But I can't be sure. I think monitoring the situation is best.'

4

Niamh

'Got everything?' said Ben.

'Think so,' I said, picking Dave up and placing him into the boot of my car. We'd packed up the few things he'd had at Dominic's, and that we'd bought for him, and were taking him to his new home. I felt kind of bad, giving him to the alchemist, but we'd agreed to let the alchemist have him as payment for helping us. We couldn't really say no when we needed him on our side so that he kept our secret. Given that alchemists were known to be shady, I figured he'd probably done a lot worse than strip someone's skin and give it to someone else, but still.

'You know, I think Fadil is really going to miss him. He seems to like the company,' said Ben.

'At least now he can go out a bit more.' I closed the boot then slid into the driver's side. Ben got into the passenger side. Dave started crying. Because of course he did.

I sighed, turning the engine on. 'It's all right, Dave. The drive isn't far,' I said in my calmest, deepest voice. It didn't make much of a difference. So I chose to ignore him instead. I always felt guilty, ignoring an anxious dog, but I knew that comforting him could feed his anxiety and make him worse. Dog training wasn't the same as raising a child, even if many people saw their dogs as their children, too.

Yes, me included.

'Hasn't he been in a car before? I don't get why he's so anxious,' said Ben.

'He's been in one a couple of times with us, but he was in the back with Edie. Maybe he's not used to being in the boot and unable to see.' I'd hoped it'd make him calmer, but obviously not. 'I still feel weird taking him to the alchemist. What if he's going to experiment on him? Or dissect him?'

'Do you really think he'd do that?' said Ben.

'I dunno. I don't know anything about him other than that he's seriously dodgy.'

'Well, if we get any red flags, we'll take Dave and leave,' said Ben.

There wasn't much traffic on the roads, but I tried to be extra careful just in case because the setting sun was blinding me and I had a headache that made the sun that bit more annoying.

I scoffed. 'You think he'll let us walk out that easily?'

Ben took his glasses off and cleaned them on his blue plaid shirt. 'Between the two of us, I think we could take him. He doesn't exactly look that physically fit.'

'No, but it wasn't a weakling's job to do what he did to Fadil and Dominic. I don't trust him. I'm not sure how much of what he does is an act to throw people off how powerful he really is.'

Dave started barking. I flinched, his high-pitched squeak making my head twinge. Just a little bit farther to go. Hold in there Dave…

'Maybe it is. But we'll keep our promise until we smell something fishy. Hey, that can be our codeword: fishy!' Ben put his glasses back on, chuckling to himself.

I rolled my eyes. 'We're having a code word?'

'Well, yeah. How else are we going to tell the other person something is off without him knowing it?'

'Isn't fishy a little obvious?' I said, turning off the main road.

Ben shrugged. 'I'm open to other suggestions.'

'All right. Dolphin.'

Ben frowned at me. 'Dolphins aren't fish.'

'Exactly. But they're marine creatures. He'll never make the connection.' I smiled at my clever code word.

Ben laughed. 'All right. Dolphin is our code word. But what are we looking for, exactly?'

*

Ben attached Dave's lead to his collar, placed him on the ground, then closed the boot. I carried Dave's things in his battered plastic bed. It was a short walk through the frosty forest to where the alchemist lived, which allowed us to enjoy the atmosphere and not think about just how creepy the place we were visiting was. Even though the alchemist had never done anything against me, there was something about him that I found unnerving. I couldn't work out what it was.

Ben knocked on the wooden door. Dave sniffed the outside of it, then sat down. He was a lot happier out of the car.

The alchemist opened the door. 'Niamh. Ben.' He looked down. 'And Dave!' He crouched down and fussed Dave's furry brown cheeks. Dave leaned in to his hand. It was the happiest I'd ever seen him. His tail was even wagging! Well, that was unexpected. Weren't dogs meant to be good judges of character?

Dave licked the alchemist's hand. Did he know him already, or something? I'd genuinely never seen the two of them look so happy before. When they both came across as so immune to emotion, it was unnerving.

Ben handed the alchemist Dave's lead as we stepped inside. The alchemist's house had been cleaned and dog-proofed since we'd last visited. It no longer looked like it belonged in a children's horror movie. This time, it looked much more like a home someone actually cared about. There was a new dog bed in the corner, with a bunch of toys and a couple of food dishes beside them.

'I thought he could use a new bed. Stayed up all night to finish making it,' said the alchemist.

I put Dave's things down by the front door. The alchemist could sort through them later. 'You made the bed?'

He shrugged. 'I had a few bits of leftover fabric and padding lying around. Why let them go to waste when

I could make Dave a new bed?' He let the dog off his lead. Dave sniffed around the room, located the new bed, then settled into it and lay down. The bed was a quilted design, with several different plain and patterned fabrics stitched together. I wasn't sure what he'd used to fill it, but it looked pretty comfortable compared to the plastic thing he was used to.

'Looks like he approves,' said the alchemist with a smile.

'I didn't realise you were such a dog person,' I said. Ben elbowed me. I ignored him.

The alchemist smiled. 'Some of us are more comfortable around four-legged friends than people. I'm sure you understand.'

What was he implying? I mean, sure, I preferred Tilly's company to most people's. But how did he know that?

'Well, if you're both happy here, I think we'll be off,' said Ben.

'Are you sure you don't want to stay for a cup of tea? The kettle's just boiled,' said the alchemist. He didn't look like he really wanted us to stay, more like he was following what he felt like were social norms. But I was more than happy to get out of there.

Ben checked his smartwatch. 'Thanks but we have somewhere we need to be.'

'We do?' This was news to me. Was he making it up to get us out of there?

'Yeah. There's something I want to show you.'

*

'Are we actually going somewhere, or did you just say that to get out of there?' I asked as we drove away. Ben had said it in such a believable way that I really wasn't sure. I mean, it was a line people used in films to get out of a situation, right? But Ben wasn't the type of person to use a line like that.

'We're actually going somewhere. Can you park by Wilkos, please?' he asked.

'Sure.' I had no idea what his plans were or what he wanted to show me in town. He wasn't generally one for secrets or surprises, so this was a new side of him that I was intrigued by. What was he going to show me? Was it just something cool he'd found in a shop, or somewhere new he wanted to check out?

Who was I kidding? New places rarely opened up in town.

I pulled up in the car park a few minutes later and followed him through town. Near the edge of the town centre, he stopped outside a vacant shop. It had a large glass front with a blank, faded white sign above it. It was hard to make out what was inside, but the little I could see was messy. And covered in dust and cobwebs. Nobody had been in there for a long time.

Ben shifted his weight from foot to foot, looking like an excited child. 'What do you think?'

I lowered an eyebrow. 'To what?'

He gestured to the shop. I was still clueless. What did I think to an empty shop?

Someone walked out of the estate agents next door and over to Ben. The blonde woman shook his hand.

'Ben, it's good to finally meet you.' She turned to me: 'I'm Lauren, the estate agent.'

'Niamh, Ben's girlfriend,' I said. It felt strange, calling myself someone's girlfriend at forty, but that's what I was. And I was happy to be with Ben.

Lauren grinned. 'You make such a lovely couple!' She'd probably just said that to butter us up, but I'd take the compliment. She removed a bunch of keys from the pocket of her tan-coloured trench coat and used one of them to open the door to the shop. 'Now, there isn't much inside here yet, but that means you can do whatever you want with it. It can really be brought to life with a lick of paint and someone to call it their new business. You want to open a bookshop, if I remember rightly?'

I turned to Ben, trying to hide the surprise in my face. I'd had no idea he wanted to become a bookseller. It seemed like a logical career progression for him, but he'd never mentioned any desire to do it. Of course, a lot of people had hopes and dreams they never talked about, myself included.

Ben smiled at me, nodding as Lauren walked us through the premises. It was basically an empty shell. Lots of formerly white walls that hadn't been painted in a long time. A very fusty smell in the air. Quite possibly a family of spiders living in the corner that I was trying not to look at.

But it also had a big window to show people all the books they could buy as they walked past. A potential way to lure people in as they walked through town or headed to and from work, or to public transport.

There was a bus stop right nearby, too. It was in a good spot.

'I'll leave you two alone for a moment to discuss things and take a look around. I'll be outside if you have any questions,' said Lauren.

'Well?' said Ben once she'd gone, a hopeful glint in his eye.

I smiled. 'I think it's a great idea. Why didn't you say something?'

He shrugged, stuffing his hands into his pockets and looking away. 'It's something I've always wanted to do, but I guess I've never found the right time, or the right premises, or had the money, or something else has got in the way. But Dominic's diagnosis and Tessa's death reminded me that life can be short. We don't know how long we've got left. If I don't take Lauren up on this, and someone else turns it into something else, will I regret it? Will I wish that someone had been me?'

I put my arms around him and hugged him. 'You're right. If it's what you want to do, you should go for it.'

Ben grinned. 'Really? You think so?'

I nodded. 'I think you'd be a great bookseller. And I think you'd love doing it, too.'

He straightened up, looking around. 'Yeah, this place has a lot of potential. I'm excited to be the one who can give it some life again.'

5
Edie

'Happy birthday!'

I opened one eye to see Mum and Tilly bursting into my room. Mum was carrying a parcel and grinning.

'My birthday was like two weeks ago,' I said. And a day I'd rather forget. I'd spent it alone. Some eighteenth that had been.

Mum plonked on to my bed. Tilly jumped up to try to join us. 'We didn't get to do things properly then, so I want to change that now.' She put the parcel in front of me. 'Your present.'

I sat up, pulling the parcel closer and unwrapping it. 'Mum, you shouldn't have,' I said as the wrapping revealed a new laptop. 'I don't deserve this.'

'You need it.' She picked up a bouncy Tilly and placed her on my bed. Her tail wagging, she ran over to me. I rubbed her head.

I'd done some horrible things because of my powers. I still felt guilty for taking Mrs Brightman's life. Mum had bought me an expensive birthday present I didn't deserve.

'What you crying for?' Mum asked, passing me a tissue from the box on my bedside table.

I wiped at my eyes with one hand, still fussing Tilly with the other one. 'After everything I've done, people are still being nice to me. I don't get it. You should all hate me.'

Mum shook her head. 'You're my daughter. I could never hate you.'

'But, I mean…' I shook my head, my hair falling into my eyes. I really needed to get my bad dye job fixed. Every time I moved, I saw the bad blend of black/grey/ginger hair out of the corner of my eye, and it made me angry at myself. It also reminded me of everything Dominic had done, which then made me feel sick.

'No buts. It's time to stop beating yourself up and look ahead instead. Dominic took you and your powers for granted. But now you're older and wiser.'

I lowered my head. 'Am I, though? I still don't know what I'm capable of. If I could hurt someone.'

Mum put her hand on my knee. 'You wouldn't do that. That's not you.'

'But I did do it. Who's to say I wouldn't do it again?' I sighed. 'You have hardly any power, but you're always using it to help people. What good is my power if it just hurts people?'

'Edie, you used your power to save me. And to stop Dominic. You've protected a lot of people from him. How are those bad things?'

I flapped my arms in the air. 'If I didn't have these powers Dominic wouldn't have targeted me in the first place! Or anyone around me!'

Tilly nudged my hand as I lowered it. I wasn't allowed to wave them in frustration – I had to keep giving her head rubs. At least she knew how to calm me down.

'You can't change what you were born with, Edie. You just have to find a way to work with it. If you fight it…Well. You saw what happened to me.'

I nodded. She'd ended up married to Dumb Dan, pretending she couldn't see ghosts for seven years while she was with him. They'd divorced when he'd found out she could see ghosts. And it hadn't been a pretty divorce. It had been for the best, but if she'd been upfront with him in the first place, maybe we wouldn't have had to live with him for so long.

My phone buzzed. I checked it to see a text from Fadil, wishing me a happy birthday. So Mum had got him involved in her plan too, then. She did so much for people and never expected anything in return. She couldn't even use her powers properly because she was using them to help Fadil adapt to modern life. The only reason he could speak English was because Mum lived close enough that he could borrow her powers, like an ongoing spell.

'Oh my god.'

'What?' said Mum. 'What's wrong?'

I put my phone down. 'It's not that. Everything's fine. I have an idea.'

'What kind of idea?'

'What if I used my powers to help Fadil?' I held my hand up to stop Mum from interrupting me. 'Let me finish. Gran said that if I keep using my powers, it will become addictive, and it could be dangerous. To me and the people around me. But if I'm not as powerful, because Fadil is constantly borrowing my powers, I can do less damage to myself and the people around me. And you have more power to be able to cast spells and stuff.'

Mum pursed her lips. I could tell from the way she was hesitating that she knew I was right. It was the best solution for all of us.

'We don't fully understand your powers yet. But I'm willing to consider it as an alternative solution. You should talk to Fadil about it, too, as it directly affects him.'

I leaned over and hugged her. 'Thanks, Mum.'

Tilly climbed on to Mum's lap, insistent on joining in with the hug.

Mum massaged her left temple, closing her eyes.

I pulled away. 'Are you all right?'

'Mmm,' Mum half-grumbled. 'Still can't shake this bloody headache. It's probably just because I haven't been sleeping well. I'll be fine.'

Something about the way she said it made me feel like there was more to it, but I couldn't work out what it was. 'Are you sure?'

Mum closed her eyes for a minute, as if they were sore or the light was too bright. 'Yeah. Don't worry about me. I'll be fine.'

'You didn't have to go to all this effort for a day that isn't even my birthday, you know,' I told her. 'Especially if you don't feel very well.'

'Oh, we haven't even started yet.' She grinned. 'I think it's about time we fix that dodgy dye job of yours, don't you?'

*

I'd never been happier to spend a whole day in a hair salon. It took most of the day to blend in the stripes and patchiness of my bad dye job, but it taught me a lesson: never dye my own hair. Ever again. I'd save it for the professionals or not do it. I wasn't coordinated or patient enough to get it right. And naturally ginger hair was complicated to deal with.

Mum had done it for me in the past, but seeing how much better it was when done by a professional, I was never going back even if it meant getting it done less often.

The radio chatted away in the background, singing eighties tunes to itself broken up by random discussions and news updates. We weren't really listening to it – we were too busy talking.

'Did you hear about that girl they found in the park? It's so sad,' said Bianca, my hairdresser.

Mum exchanged a look with me in the mirror, but didn't say anything. She was sitting in the chair beside me, chomping away on a sandwich. She'd only needed a couple of inches off the bottom, so she'd had her hair cut, then taken Tilly for a walk and returned with some lunch for me. It was the first time I'd ever had to eat my lunch in a hair salon, but it was necessary. I couldn't keep wearing hats, didn't want to cut my hair super short to get rid of the dodgy blending, and I didn't have the skills to fix what I'd done wrong. It was a good job my mum's hairstylist was a colour specialist.

'Isn't she your age?' Bianca continued, oblivious to the atmosphere she'd created.

'Yeah,' I stared into my lap, suddenly finding the synthetic black fabric of the gown I was wearing really fascinating. 'She was in a bunch of my classes.'

'Oh wow. I'm so sorry.'

Nothing to apologise for. Not that I said that.

'It's scary that the police haven't found who did it yet, don't you think?'

'They haven't confirmed it's murder yet, either,' Mum pointed out. While I couldn't turn my head, in the mirror in front of me I could see her reflection's pursed lips. She wasn't comfortable with the topic but didn't know how to change it. Neither did I.

'You don't think it was?' said Bianca.

'I don't think we should jump to conclusions until we know,' said Mum.

Bianca continued to paint lightener into my hair, dividing it into minuscule sections I didn't have the patience to do. The way she did it was almost meditative. We sat in silence for a few moments, the only sounds *Last Christmas* playing on the radio and Mum eating her food.

'Did you hear the police found another body this morning?' said Bianca.

'*What?*' Mum and I chorused.

Bianca nodded. 'I drove past Dob Park on my way into work. They had one of those tents up.'

'Doesn't mean they found another body,' Mum said, her voice rising in panic.

'I saw it on the internet.'

'Could've been someone just making it up, scaremongering, you know,' I said. I hoped. The scaremongering thing was part of why I didn't have a lot to do with the social media side of the internet, especially with all the bullying I'd experienced in the past.

'The local paper wouldn't do that, would they?' asked Bianca.

'Wouldn't put it past them,' Mum mumbled. 'They need to get clicks and sell papers to make money.'

'True,' said Bianca.

Mum and I were shooting her down and being cynical, but it was because we were nervous. If whoever had killed Tessa wasn't just targeting her, we had much bigger problems to deal with.

'What if it's a serial killer?' said Bianca.

'Around here?' I scoffed. 'Have you been binge watching true crime documentaries?'

Bianca laughed. 'A couple. But what if it *is*? Who's next?'

*

'Thank you,' I said to Mum as we walked out of the salon, six hours later. My hair was now a dark, chocolate brown, with matching eyebrows so that I didn't look really washed out or need to constantly fill them in with pencil or gel.

Mum put her arm around me and kissed the top of my head. 'There's just one more thing.'

'After all that?'

'You must be hungry, right?'

'Starving,' I said.

'Good.'

We got into the car, then she drove me to one of the fancier restaurants in town. It was hard to park, but we found space on a side street, then walked up the hill to get to it.

Inside, the black walls were offset with white, modern art statues that were missing various limbs or had holes in their stomachs. It was strange and artsy, but I knew the food was good.

Mum gave the server our name, then we were taken to a table where Ben, Fadil, and Maggie were waiting for us.

'Happy birthday,' said Maggie, grinning.

My first eighteenth birthday had been pretty crappy, but my second one turned out to be pretty good.

6

Niamh

I was hoping Thomas or Gwendoline might have some insights in how to deal with Tessa that I could share with Edie. We didn't know how she'd died, but we didn't need to. It was the police's problem, not ours. What was a problem was that Edie couldn't escape her. So, I went to the graveyard Monday morning, after taking a couple of books from the library. For pleasure. And to see Ben.

Except Thomas wasn't there. There were no signs he'd been there, either. It was unnaturally quiet, even for a graveyard. I even went inside the church, but that was empty, too.

He could travel, he just didn't usually want to, so I went to see Gwendoline on the new housing estate. Maybe he'd gone to visit her?

'Hey, Niamh,' said Gwendoline, floating over.

I sat on the bench in the middle of the green. A dozen or so houses looked directly on to the circle of struggling grass, so I put in my hands-free kit, and made a show of tucking my hair behind my ear and resting my phone on my lap, so if anyone was nearby they'd think I was on the phone.

'Hey. Have you seen Thomas?'

'No, why?' She floated in front of me, her blonde hair flowing behind her.

'He wasn't in the graveyard this morning, but I've only known him to leave it to visit us.'

'That is odd. If I hear anything, I'll let you know.'

'Thanks.'

It seemed strange that Thomas had gone missing around the same time Tessa had died, but it seemed unlikely the two events were related. As far as I knew, there were no signs Tessa's death had been supernatural. Although it wasn't like the police were sharing how she'd been killed, or would notice if it *was* supernatural, so it was possible, just unlikely.

'Did you hear about the murder?' I asked Gwendoline.

'It's all anyone can talk about.' She gestured to the park, which was usually full of ghosts. 'When they're here, of course.'

'Where is everyone?'

Gwendoline rolled her eyes. 'Exploring, I suppose.'

Someone in the house opposite where we were talking screamed. A moment later, a ghost flew out from the house in question, cackling, before disappearing out of sight.

Gwendoline's jaw tightened. 'I don't tell them they can't leave the park, I just tell them to be careful. Unfortunately, some prefer to terrorise the residents instead.' She sat beside me, resting her head in her hands. 'Some of them like to materialise for a moment at the top of the stairs, spook people. That's what Stanley just did.' She shook her head, as if she was all but ready to give up. 'We haven't had any accidents yet, but it only takes one person with a heart condition.'

I wished I could reach out and give her a hug, but the most I could offer was a frown and some empathetic words. 'I'm sorry. That sounds terrible.'

'It is. They don't seem to want to listen to me anymore. It's like I've lost all authority and I don't know why.' Gwendoline had made it her mission to help the lost ghosts in town, so them not listening to her must've really hurt. All she ever wanted to do was help people.

'I'm sure they'll come around,' I said.

'I hope so.' She stared off into the distance, her gaze sad and vacant. It didn't seem like she wanted to discuss it any more, and it wasn't like I could do much, anyway. If they weren't going to listen to Gwendoline, they sure weren't going to pay attention to me when I barely even had any powers.

'Is it true the victim is a ghost?' Gwendoline asked.

'Yeah. She's haunting Edie's ex. They were classmates.'

Gwendoline turned to face me. 'Oh. I'm sorry.'

'They never got along, but nobody deserves to have their life taken away like that, let alone at such a young age.'

'No,' said Gwendoline, shaking her head. What was I saying? She was around Edie's age when the mine collapsed. Idiot.

'Sorry. That was stupid of me to say.'

'It's OK. I've had a long time to accept my fate. I feel like I'm living a second life, now. Guiding the community, helping you when I can. It's fulfilling. Much more than my life was when my heart was beating.' She fidgeted in her seat. 'When they'll listen.'

I smiled. 'That's good. That's really good. Mostly.'

A guy walked past the edge of the park with his dog. He looked over, seeing me talking to myself. I waved, gesturing to the earphone in my ear. He nodded, shifting his gaze and carrying on walking. I really hated those encounters. You could never be completely sure if people thought you were nuts or not.

Who was I kidding?

I *was* nuts.

My whole life was.

*

After an unhelpful conversation with Gwendoline, I went to Mrs Brightman's house. Something smelled pungent. I really should've cleared it of perishables the last time I'd visited, but I hadn't been ready to. Now, I didn't have a choice. A smell like that wasn't going to go away on its own. Served me right.

Holding my breath, I opened the fridge and chucked all the milk, vegetables, fruits, and meat into the kitchen bin. There wasn't much – she hadn't eaten much – but it was enough to create a smell.

I tossed the smelly bin bag into the outside bin, waving at a neighbour as he walked past. I didn't know him, but I was pretty sure he'd gone to church with Mrs Brightman, so he was no doubt aware that someone else owned the property now.

Clearing the fridge and freezer wasn't interesting work, but it kept me occupied. The near-silence of the quiet cul-de-sac was soothing, offering a little reprieve for my growing headache.

I met Edie at Ben's after she'd finished college. We were going to explain her plan to him and Fadil. It seemed like Edie had already made her mind up about casting the spell so that I got my powers back and she was less of a target. But it wasn't just up to her. I liked the idea of having more powers again, but I didn't like the idea of her having less protection. As a bigger target, it meant she needed more protection, not less.

Dominic hadn't been able to tell I was less powerful than my mother, he'd only known I was part of a powerful family line. I figured if someone targeted Edie because of her powers, they may not be able to tell that Fadil was leeching her powers, either. It would depend on their powers and skills, I supposed.

Ben's house was filled with the aroma of chicken casserole as I walked through the front door. Fadil had been learning how to cook, and he was pretty good at it. There'd been the odd failed experiment – like a chocolate yule log we weren't allowed to talk about – but even Maggie's cooking hadn't been perfect when she'd started out. Fadil was learning to cook with ingredients that hadn't even been around during his first life. So, based on that, he was doing pretty damn well.

'Dinner smells amazing, Fadil,' said Edie as she went into the cupboard to grab a mug. It was tea time, obviously. And we spent enough time there that we knew where pretty much everything was in the kitchen, so just helped ourselves. Ben did the same at our place.

'Thanks,' he said, a proud grin over his face. 'It's a new recipe, with a few experimental ingredients, so I'm a little nervous. But I'm hoping it will turn out better than the recipe.'

'I'm sure it will,' I said. My rumbling stomach agreed.

Conversation between the three of us usually flowed easily. This time, awkwardness hung in the air. I couldn't work out who it was coming from, but it meant we all stood there, not knowing what to say or do as the kettle whistled in the background.

'Anyone want tea?' Edie offered. She was technically already making us drinks, as she'd got the mugs out and filled the kettle, but I supposed she was trying to break the silence.

'Please,' Fadil and I chorused. It wasn't often we agreed on something.

Edie met my eye. Was she waiting for me to raise the topic? Nope, definitely not. That was for her to deal with. It was her idea, she had to talk to Fadil about it.

Once our tea was made, we went and sat in the living room. The awkwardness continued until Ben came home a few minutes later. He walked over and kissed me, then went into the kitchen. 'Wow, that smells good!'

When he returned to the lounge, the atmosphere was still there. He frowned. 'What's wrong? Did someone die?'

'No!' said Edie, jumping up. 'It's not that.'

'Then what is it?' He stayed standing, studying everyone, waiting until someone explained what was going on.

Edie rubbed her hands together, her eyes darting around the room as she spoke. 'OK, so I have an idea. And it's one that will help Mum, and probably me, and probably other people, as well.'

Ben adjusted his glasses, resting his weight on his right leg. He seemed confused. She was babbling slightly, so I wasn't surprised. 'Right…'

Shifting in her seat as if she couldn't get comfortable, Edie looked to me for confirmation.

I nodded, trying my best to encourage her to continue. If I seemed calm, I hoped it would help her feel it, too.

'As we found out recently, Mum's powers are wonky because Fadil is constantly using her powers as his own, magical, subconscious translator. So we never really know when Mum is going to be able to do something, or what that something will be. It basically makes her human.' She cleared her throat, settling on sitting on her feet. 'So I thought, since I'm stronger magically, but also my powers are dangerous, make me a target, and are more likely to hurt someone, I could help Fadil instead.'

'You mean you cast the translation spell instead?' said Fadil.

Edie nodded. 'Having more power means I can afford to lose some. And if I don't have as much, it makes me less of a target.'

I still wasn't convinced being less powerful made her less of a target, but I was going to let her continue with that logic until we could prove otherwise.

Ben nodded a few times, a pensive look passing over his handsome face. 'I think you're right. I'd like to contribute, too. That way, it will draw less of your power when you cast the spell.'

Edie shook her head, her hair falling into her eyes. 'While I appreciate your suggestion and input, I think it's better if I do it alone. Your powers are helpful. You've never hurt someone with a forcefield, and you're not tempted to cast a spell to hurt someone. It's getting harder for me to not use my powers, and the more frequently I use them, the stronger that lure is. So the less power I have, in theory, the easier it'll be to stop. And if I can't stop, at the very least I'll be able to do less damage.'

Ben crossed his arms. It was hard to gauge what he was thinking. 'You understand you could be sacrificing a significant portion of your power for the rest of your life? That's a long time to not be able to use it.'

Edie tensed, looking at Fadil. 'I can't think of a better use for my powers than to help Fadil.'

Fadil reached over and squeezed Edie's hand. She smiled, placing her other hand on top of his. It was getting easier and easier to forget he was a four-thousand-year-old not-mummy. He'd fitted into our lives so well and become an important part of Edie's life. I wasn't sure our little family would feel complete without him. Helping him adapt to the twenty-first century in any way we could was an important part of that.

Ben nodded again. 'As much as I dislike you being solely responsible for this, I understand what you're saying and I agree with you.'

'You do?' I said. For some reason, I'd expected him to be more against her idea.

Ben chuckled. 'You didn't think I would?'

'I thought you'd have a full pros and cons list or something.'

To be honest, I was kind of hoping he would. Edie was afraid of her powers and wanted to be protected from them, but she didn't know how to use them, either. Would there come a day when she'd need to use them but couldn't because she'd never learned how?

It wasn't like we could leave Fadil to learn English from scratch. We may also need him at some point. And there weren't many places that taught Ancient Egyptian to English and would allow him to adapt so quickly to modern life. He enjoyed his documentaries and was beginning to leave the house more and more now that he didn't look like he was four thousand years old. Could we really take that away from him and make him start all over again? *Again*?

7
Edie

'Do we have everything we need?' I asked, glancing around Ben's kitchen. The prospect of casting a life-changing spell made me nervous, but it was something I really wanted to do for all the reasons I'd already explained. I just wanted to make sure we got it right, especially when Mum didn't remember the spell she'd used in the first place.

'Yes,' said Ben. 'Are you sure you want to do this?'

He'd asked me repeatedly as we'd eaten dinner and planned everything we needed. I appreciated how considerate he was, but it was getting on my nerves. I just wanted it over with already.

I nodded. 'This isn't just about me. It's about Mum and Fadil.'

Ben walked up to me and smiled. 'You're a very empathetic young woman, you know that?'

I glared at him. 'Don't be condescending.'

He lowered his smile. 'I'm not! It's a rare trait in someone your age.'

'Yes. Well.' I tugged at the edge of my black T-shirt. Compliments were alien to me. So I just nodded, then grabbed the scrap of paper we'd written the spell on and went into Ben's living room, where Mum and Fadil were sitting on the sofa.

'Are you really sure it doesn't matter what the exact words of the spell I used were?' said Mum, looking up at Ben as he walked back in.

'It's the intention of the spell that really matters. Having Edie and me here will help, as that will give your reversal spell enough power to work,' said Ben. He addressed Fadil: 'You obviously know you won't be able to communicate with us for a few moments. I'm not sure if there will be any physical side effects this time, but I wouldn't have thought so. Do you have any questions before we start?'

Fadil swallowed. He wiped his palms on his acid-wash jeans. 'No.'

Even though he was four millennia old, in that moment, he looked like a nervous child. I knew he was doing this for Mum and me, because we'd done so much for him already. I bent down and hugged him, hoping that it offered him some reassurance that it would all turn out fine. Not that we knew that, but I was determined to remain optimistic.

We had no idea what would happen next, only that we were about to do something big.

Mum and Fadil got off the sofa and sat on the floor. Ben and I joined them, creating a triangle with Fadil in the centre. I was really glad Tilly was at home, watching TV, because she definitely would've wanted to interfere and flop over in the centre for belly rubs.

Ben laid out the paper we'd written the first spell on so that the three of us could all see it. We didn't need any fancy equipment or anything; it was all about our words and our intentions. Or so he said, and he was the most experienced spellcaster.

'Release my powers from this leech, full control of my powers I seek,' chanted Mum.

I hated Fadil being called a leech, but it was the technical term for what he was doing.

Mum gasped, jerking backwards. Fadil went wide-eyed, as if everything in the room was totally new to him.

'Mum, are you all right?'

Ben and I hovered over her. She looked awake, but disorientated.

'I feel…different,' she said.

'Different how?' said Ben.

'Stronger. More powerful. More…like myself. And maybe a little sore. Does that make sense?'

'I guess,' said Ben, helping her sit upright again. 'I mean, you technically are more powerful now.'

She nodded, then looked to me. 'Are you sure you want to do this? I can keep going if you'd prefer.'

I swear I saw a glimmer in her eye, as if she was hoping I'd say no because she was enjoying being more powerful again. Even though more powerful for her technically just meant more reliable.

'Stop asking me! Let's just do this,' I said.

While I appreciated her concern, it was getting irritating being asked every five minutes if it was really what I wanted to do. Of course it scared me, but the damage my powers could do to people scared me more. I'd seen Mum use her powers to help Fadil for weeks and had little negative side effects. If she didn't suffer that much, I doubted I would, since I had more power to give away than her.

I put my hand on Fadil's leg. He smiled, nodding at me. He was clearly anxious and didn't like feeling left out of the conversation. I had no doubt he was intelligent enough to learn English on his own if we gave him the time, but with everything else that was happening around us, we couldn't afford to spend the time helping him learn. If there was a magical solution that helped him as much as me, I wanted to use it.

The next step was on me, since I was the one whose powers Fadil would be using. Mum's grip tightened on my hand. I yanked it free in case the spell channelled her powers accidentally. Then, I recited the scrawled spell from the scrap of paper: 'Take some of my powers, my bandwidth, so that Fadil can speak our language.'

It felt like something was being pulled from me and flowing into Fadil. It was weird. Almost like the opposite of when I absorbed someone's life essence, but not as strong. Kind of like my breath was taken out of me by a desktop vacuum cleaner.

Mum went to reach out to me, but Ben stopped her. She knew that it would take her magic, too, if she intervened, didn't she?

The sensation slowed. I leaned on my hands, taking a few deep breaths. 'Did it work?'

'It worked,' said Fadil, smiling. 'Thank you.'

'How do you feel?' Mum asked me.

I stood up and looked around the room. 'It's weird, but I feel…lighter, somehow. Less tense and anxious. There feels like there's less darkness floating around me. I'm not even speaking sense, am I?'

Mum looked to Ben. It wasn't like either of them had a reference for this kind of thing.

'I suppose,' said Ben. 'Necromancy can be dark and draining. And you used it quite substantially in a short period of time. That's bound to have an effect.'

'I hadn't thought of that,' I said, sitting cross-legged on the floor. 'That explains a lot.'

'Like what?' said Mum.

'Like when Dominic had me using my powers more, I felt…jittery. More scatterbrained. And I kept thinking things that didn't feel like what I'd normally feel.'

Mum put her hand on my knee. 'Why didn't you tell me?'

I shrugged, looking away from her. 'I didn't want to worry you. You've got enough going on already.'

'You don't need to keep this stuff from me. I'm here for you.'

I put my hand on top of hers. 'I know. It was just… it's hard to talk about.'

'It might be that the two are linked in ways we hadn't considered,' said Ben.

'What do you mean?'

Ben pushed his glasses up his nose. 'Well, the necromancy itself may not have been affecting your mood, but because you were worried about the consequences of your powers, and what Dominic made you do, that might've been affecting you. If you don't have the power to do those things…'

'That makes sense,' I said. 'And who knows? Maybe now I won't be able to see Tessa anymore.'

I could hope.

8

Niamh

When Edie and I got home, I was knackered and really just wanted to settle in bed. But of course, as soon as I got into bed and felt my soft, silk pillowcase against my skin…I was wide awake. And my headache came back, more evil than ever. It rippled into the rest of my body, taking over any chance it got. No amount of pain killers or meditation seemed to make a difference.

I was really glad Tilly was in Edie's room because the last thing I needed was a westie massage. And, knowing Nurse Tilly, that was *exactly* what she would've done to try to make me feel better.

Edie knocked on my door. 'Mum? Are you all right? You're usually up by now.'

I smushed my head against the pillow. Hadn't I only gone to bed like half an hour ago? 'What time is it?'

'Eight.'

'Fiddlesticks.' At least I didn't have anywhere pressing to be, but still. I hated wasting my day.

Tensing, I inhaled through my teeth as I tried to sit up.

Edie pushed the door open. Tilly bounded in, jumping up at the side of my bed to get to me. She could probably sense I was in pain. It was part of how she was such a good/aggressive nurse.

Edie frowned. 'You look…not yourself.'

'That's one way of putting it.' I almost felt worse than I had when Dominic had stabbed me.

'What's wrong?' said Edie. She picked Tilly up, then the two of them sat on the bed. Edie kept hold of the wriggling westie so that she couldn't climb all over me, like she usually did when someone was ill.

'Head,' I mumbled as I tried to roll over to sit upright. It wasn't going well. I couldn't get out of the foetal position.

'What's given you a headache?'

'Wish I knew,' I said through gritted teeth, the vibrations from talking making my head hurt even more. I was glad I'd tied my hair up before going to bed because I'd woken up a sweaty mess and had no energy to shower. Sticky hair just would've made me feel even worse.

Had Edie resurrecting me done something to me? Was that why I had a headache I couldn't shake?

And if it was because she'd resurrected me, what did that mean for my future?

'What can I do?' Edie offered.

'Just let me sleep. I'll be fine.'

Edie fidgeted. She obviously didn't like my plan. 'I could call Maggie?'

'No!'

Things were still questionable between us. I didn't want to jeopardise anything by relying on her just yet.

'Why not?'

'Things are fragile. I can't risk bothering her with something like this. It might ruin what we've rebuilt. What's happened between us is hardly normal.'

Tilly tried to wriggle free, so Edie pulled her into a bear hug. Tilly relaxed into her arms. 'I'm pretty sure she'd understand. It's that or I call Doc.'

I flinched. 'What can Doc do?'

'He's the doctor, he'll know. Although I think Maggie is the better option.' Having decided on her plan, she stood up, leaving Tilly on the bed and making a beeline for me. I grabbed Tilly, keeping her to my side so that she didn't come too close.

'Edie, you really don't have to—'

My words were cut off by her walking out of the room. It was always nice to have a daughter who listened.

A few moments later, Edie re-entered my room looking accomplished. 'Maggie will be over once she's dropped Abigail off at breakfast club.'

I glared at her.

'She's better suited to helping you than I am.'

I shook my head, then regretted it, because it caused a pulsing in my head, like an electric shock to my brain. 'No one can help me with this. Right now I really just need to sleep.'

Edie's enthusiasm and energy seemed to falter. She lowered her shoulders and sighed. 'Fine. Do you want me to get you anything before I go to college?'

'Tea. And plain biscuits. Don't think I could stomach anything else.'

'Coming right up.'

*

I really hated that Edie had bothered Maggie with something so trivial. Things were still tenuous between us and I didn't want to risk any future friendship we may have.

Sure, we'd been friends for almost forty years, but her coma wasn't exactly a little hiccup in our relationship. She'd been tortured by demons who'd made themselves look like Edie and me. That kind of trauma didn't just magically go away. She hadn't even been able to look at me when she'd first woken up. It was too hard for her to tell what was real and what wasn't. Josh was still struggling, although he refused to talk to anyone about it.

I was just falling back to sleep when I heard a key in the front door. How had I forgot Maggie still had a key? Maybe the fact she hadn't returned it after her coma was a subtle sign there was hope for us, she'd just needed time. Or maybe she'd just forgotten and it was coming in handy now.

Tilly dived off the bed and ran down the stairs, excited to see one of her favourite people. I heard the clatter and shuffle of Maggie taking her coat off, putting her keys down, then make a fuss of Tilly. She came up and peeked her head through my open bedroom door. Tilly wriggled in her arms, licking her face to say hello. Maggie kissed Tilly's furry cheek.

'How are you feeling?' she asked me, walking farther into the room.

'Ngh,' I said, my face smushed against my pillow.

She hovered between the bed and the door, still being lick attacked by Tilly. 'I brought some chicken soup over. I know there isn't technically anything in it to help with headaches, but I know how much you love my nan's recipe.'

I smiled, adjusting my head so that I could see her properly and wasn't talking into a drool-covered pillow. 'I do. Thank you.'

She nodded, finally putting Tilly on the floor. The little dog continued to jump up at her, so she knelt down to fuss her. 'I missed you too, fluffball.'

Hearing her say that made me well up. I hadn't considered how being away from Maggie might impact the dog. Maggie was definitely one of her favourite people, and it wasn't just because of the expensive offcuts of meat that Maggie sometimes smuggled her way.

Maggie looked up at me, a rogue strand of brown hair falling into her eye. She tucked it behind her ear. 'Are you crying?'

'No.' I turned away, wiping at my eyes with the back of my hand.

Maggie stood up and walked over. 'Have you been sleeping?'

'Barely a wink,' I mumbled. 'And I think my head is going to explode. One minute it feels like I'm being punched by Thor's hammer, another it's pulsing like I'm being electrocuted, then it just…hurts.'

'That sounds tough,' said Maggie.

'Tell me about it,' I mumbled. 'I'll be perfectly fine tomorrow, I'm sure.' My words were optimistic, but the headache had been going on for several days. I'd hoped saying something positive aloud might convince me. It didn't.

Maggie frowned. 'Why don't you speak to Doc? See if he can at least give you something to help with the pain?'

'Not you as well.' Edie was still texting me about getting some advice or painkillers from Doc. 'I've seen him enough lately.'

Maggie rolled her eyes. Her expression quickly lit up again as another idea came into her head. Oh no. 'There is one other thing that might help. You won't like that suggestion either.'

'Why won't I like it?'

'It goes against everything you want to do right now.'

'Everything goes against what I want to do right now, because all I want to do right now is sleep.'

'Exactly. And one of the easiest and most cost-effective ways to deal with pain is mild exercise.'

'Oh, bloody hell.'

9
Edie

Ever since Tessa's death the end of the week before, there'd been a weird atmosphere at college. No one seemed to know what to say. Nobody had ever experienced the death of a peer or student in such a brutal way before.

More details had come out about what had happened, although many were still just rumours. The police had, at least, confirmed it was murder. Which meant the rumour mill was going mad, and the police had questioned Josh and Maggie. I'd only heard bits about what had happened from Maggie, but I did know the police had decided Josh was innocent, which was something.

Josh wasn't, however, entirely free. Tessa was still haunting him, and it was getting harder and harder for me to ignore her. English class was the worst. Josh didn't sit next to me anymore – because he'd moved after getting with Tessa – but it was hard for me to not look over at him. As much as I didn't want to, I still had feelings for him. He'd been my best friend for most of my life, and being in such close proximity but unable to talk to him, and now totally devoid of friends with Dominic gone, made me feel more isolated than ever.

Most of our lessons currently compromised of revision or mock exams, which meant the classrooms were quieter than usual. The lack of background noise just made everything that was going on in my head even louder.

As usual in English, Tessa hovered over Josh's shoulder, trying to tell him the right answers as he scribbled things on to his piece of paper. I couldn't tell what he was writing, but, judging from Tessa's tone, I had a feeling she disagreed with his answers. Even though I disliked her, I couldn't dispute how intelligent she was. She had to be: she'd wanted to be a lawyer.

Her hopes and dreams didn't matter anymore, though. Whatever they were, she'd never get to fulfil them.

Tessa reached out to try to grab Josh's pen. Her hand went right through him. He didn't even flinch. She looked so crestfallen, like she really just wanted to help him and all her ideas were backfiring. If I'd liked her, I might've felt sorry for her.

Mrs Mitchell, who'd been patrolling the class, pulled out the chair beside Josh. Tessa hovered over Josh's shoulder to listen in on the conversation. 'How are you getting on?'

'You know.' He shrugged. He'd never been that talkative with teachers. After everything he'd been through recently, he wasn't all that talkative with anyone.

Tessa shook her head. 'Ask her for help! You're never going to do well in exams otherwise!'

Some confidence she had in him. He wasn't *that* bad at English.

'Give me a shout if you need anything, all right?' said Mrs Mitchell.

Josh nodded but didn't look up.

Mrs Mitchell got up and walked over to someone else.

Tessa noticed the chair Mrs Mitchell had vacated was still pulled out. She went to sit on it, the same as she would've done when she was alive. And she went right through it, falling partially into the floor below before she could stop herself.

I scoffed.

Realising what I'd done, I turned away.

'Something funny, Edie?' said Mrs Mitchell.

'Just…uh…a bird flew into the window over there,' I said, sounding like a massive sadist. I figured they wouldn't believe me if it was the window to the classroom we were in because others would've heard it. But if it was in the corridor the classroom looked out on to, it would've made more sense if other people didn't notice it.

Mrs Mitchell just nodded and went over to talk to Melanie.

Tessa, on the other hand, looked up at me and met my eye. 'You can *see* me.'

I pursed my lips, turning away from her.

'I know you can see me.'

Keep reading. Make notes. Ignore her.

I really hoped that she didn't try to grab me or the pen I was holding. That would mean real trouble. She may not have been able to do that with Josh, but to me, she'd feel corporeal. Anything I touched was fair game to the ghosts who wanted to interact with me, annoyingly. Which meant Tessa could take hold of my pen if she wanted to. And I couldn't stop her without looking like a total freak.

Well, I'd look like a freak anyway. Either from trying to stop her from grabbing my pen or because she'd managed to take hold of my hand. What a scene that would cause in the middle of a quiet room where everyone was concentrating or trying to look like they were. I'd be shipped off in no time.

I was hoping she wouldn't want to risk embarrassing herself enough again in front of me to try it.

'LOOK AT ME!' Tessa shouted.

I had to admit, I was pretty impressed at my resolve. I was staring at my paper, totally ignoring her.

She moved from beside me, wedging herself between the chair in front of me and the desk. She knelt down, trying to force herself into my line of vision. 'Do you know who did this to me? Can you help me?'

I felt bad not answering that one. She deserved answers about her death, at least, so I gave a small shake of my head. Just once. Nothing anybody would notice. If they were watching me, it would've looked like I was flicking my hair out of my eyes.

Her lips curled into a snarl. 'I always knew there was something weird about you. You're a witch, aren't you?'

I sighed. Of course she'd jump to that, because apparently we'd gone back in time three hundred years.

Opting to ignore her instead of encourage her hysteria, I tightened my grip on my pen and continued to read my textbook.

'Witch! I'm going to tell everyone you're a witch!'

Well that plan had backfired.

Sigh.

I looked up and met Tessa's gaze, my eyebrow raised, challenging her to tell someone. Who would she tell? She could scream it, but the only people who'd be able to hear her were other ghosts and necromancers. And I was pretty sure they wouldn't care.

'Witch! Wiiiiiitch!'

'Excuse me? Mrs Mitchell? Could I go to the loo, please?' I said.

Mrs Mitchell nodded, gesturing with her hands to the door. She was busy helping Melanie with something and didn't want to be disturbed. It worked for me.

I jerked my head at Tessa, hoping she'd take the hint to follow me. The toilets were only a couple of doors down. I didn't know how far away from Josh she could travel, so somewhere that close felt like a good place to talk.

Thankfully, nobody else was in there when I walked in. I checked under the stalls just in case, but the only thing present was the faint aroma of someone's lunch disagreeing with them. Gag.

Crossing my arms, I leaned against the sinks and waited for Tessa. She floated through the walls and looked like she wanted to spit fire. Finally, I had the power over her. And it was glorious.

'Can you find who did this to me? *Please?*' It looked like being so polite to me was killing her. Again. But I was more inclined to be helpful if she was *trying* to be nice to me. At least she had enough people smarts to know that.

'I'm not a police officer or a private investigator. It's out of my skill set. I'm sorry.' Mostly.

She clenched and unclenched her fists. I really hoped she didn't plan to use them. 'Then why can you see me? What *are* you?'

'I'm a necromancer.'

It wasn't like she'd be able to tell anyone who didn't already know. It was surprisingly freeing to say it so bluntly.

Tessa laughed. Why was that less believable than me being a witch? 'Sure you are.'

I shrugged. 'Doesn't matter to me what you believe. Just leave me alone.' I went to push past her, but then realised I needed to give her a wide berth so that she didn't notice she was corporeal to me.

'Wait,' she said, a note of desperation in her voice. 'If you're really a necromancer – and I'm not saying I believe you – but if you are, does that mean you can bring people back to life?'

All right, now I felt bad for her. I uncrossed my arms and lowered my shoulders. 'In theory. I've only done it once.'

'So you could help me?'

'No.'

The anger was back. 'Why the hell not?'

'Because you were murdered. And possibly dismembered. The police have your body. Parts.' Gross. 'There's a media circus around your family. I couldn't get to your body to bring you back, and even if I could, it may not all be there. And it's not like you'd be able to go back to the life you once had on the off-chance I could resurrect you. You'd be poked and prodded and treated like a freak because you did the impossible. People would want to know how you did it to help other people, and if you didn't help them, they'd see you as selfish.'

Not to mention I wasn't sure if I could even do it anymore, now that Fadil was borrowing some of my power. Or the impact resurrecting her would have on my powers and psyche. But since she only cared about herself I didn't think that was worth mentioning.

Tessa lowered her head. 'I always knew you were selfish!'

That was rich, coming from her.

'Whatever.'

This time, I really did leave. Tessa chased after me, shouting things and trying to goad me, but I planned the rest of my day in my head to block her out.

The bell rang as I walked back into the classroom, so I packed up my stuff as fast as I could. Tessa was still trying to get in my face, but I continued to ignore her.

Before I could leave, Mrs Mitchell cornered me. 'Edie, have you thought any more about uni?'

'Um…no?'

Her face fell slightly, but she tried to hide it.

Tessa eavesdropped from just behind my teacher's shoulder. I tried not to look at her, but I really wanted to tell her where to go.

'You need to get your application in by the end of term. You know that, right?'

'But what if I don't want to go to uni? What if I want to take a gap year, or do an apprenticeship, or something else?'

Why was there so much pressure to have everything figured out when I was barely eighteen? Why couldn't I take some time to figure out my life? What was so wrong with that?

'It's still worth filling in an application, that way you at least have the option if you change your mind.'

Great. More stuff to do. 'I'll keep that in mind.'

She seemed to take the hint, as she returned to her desk without saying anything else.

Tessa sneered at me as I slung my bag over my shoulder. It almost looked like she was jealous of me. Could she really be?

After one last glare her way, I scurried out of the classroom to get to the opposite side of campus and as far away from her as possible. I just hoped that would be far enough away from Josh that she wouldn't be able to follow me.

10

Niamh

The downside to not having a set work schedule was that I could stay at home and watch daytime TV when I wasn't working. Or, more specifically, watch the news to see what the police had found out about Tessa's murder.

They weren't releasing much, which suggested to me that either they didn't know a lot, or it was worse than they'd originally thought.

Tilly woke from her spot beside me on the sofa and barked at the TV. Tessa's parents were being interviewed. Heh. She always had been a good judge of character.

Out of curiosity, I turned the volume up.

Spectre looked up from his spot on top of the bookcase and floated down, settling on the arm of the sofa beside Tilly. Curious cat.

'Tessa was such a wonderful girl. We'd raised her so well,' said her mum in between sobs. 'I don't get how anyone could hurt our girl in this way.'

Possessive, much? Tessa was eighteen; technically an adult. I did find it interesting that most of the press coverage had referred to her as a 'girl' instead of a 'woman'. The different connotations would've changed the thread of their media coverage and earned her less sympathy from the public.

'We have every faith that the police will catch the monster who did this to our daughter. For anyone who has any information that leads to his capture, we're offering a £500 reward.' Stingy considering I knew they both had well-paying jobs. And unlikely to get them very far. But I understood their desperation. I couldn't have put up a reward like that for answers if something had happened to Edie.

Then again, I could've asked Edie's ghost what'd happened to her instead.

*

Before I searched for other causes of my headache, I had to speak to someone to put my concerns to bed. I really, really didn't want to talk to her about it. But I didn't have a choice.

So I summoned my mother.

She appeared in front of me, hovering beside the coffee table in the living room. 'You look well.'

'Gee. Thanks.' I leaned forwards, resting my elbows on my lap and my head in my hands. I didn't have the energy for her passive aggression, circles, or riddles.

My mother narrowed her eyes at me. 'What's wrong?'

'Could my resurrection have done any long-lasting damage?'

'Like what?'

71

Tilly hopped on to the sofa and curled up by the arm of the sofa. I reached out and stroked her. Small comforts.

'Like I think my head is going to explode. It feels like I haven't slept properly in forever. This can't be normal.'

My mother pursed her lips, placing her hands in front of her. It was somewhere between a pensive and a defensive stance, and I didn't like where it was going. 'Have you been feeling stressed lately?'

Was she *serious*? Was I stressed? Was I bloody stressed? I knew she didn't follow my life that closely but she knew enough to know that even half of what'd been happening lately was going to make me feel stressed!

I waved my arms in the air. 'Stressed? Of course I'm bloody stressed!'

'There's no need to snap at me like that.'

'I wouldn't be this bloody stressed if it wasn't for you! If you'd have told me the truth about my heritage when I was younger, Dominic wouldn't have been able to manipulate Edie. We could've trained her how to use her powers from a young age and she wouldn't have had to go to a raging psychopath to discover what she could do!'

My mother adjusted her high bun, shifting away from me slightly. 'I didn't tell you what I felt at the time were irrelevant details. I had no idea Javier came from such a powerful lineage.'

I stared at her, deadpan. Did she really think I believed that? 'So you're telling me you never sensed that Javi's powers were bound? My seventeen-year-old daughter, who has only just tapped into her powers, can sense bound powers in a total stranger. Are you seriously telling me that you never sensed them in Javi? Despite how often you saw him?' I continued to watch her, daring her to lie to me again. If her body language was anything to go by, she knew she'd messed up big time and had to tread carefully.

'It's not like I saw him as often as you did.'

'That does not answer my question.' I crossed my arms.

Until she answered, I wasn't going to say anything else. She was going to tell me what I wanted to know if I had to wait in painful silence until she did.

My mother ground her teeth together, floating back and forth a few times as she tried to work out what to do. A part of me enjoyed seeing her so conflicted. It wasn't often she was backed into a corner like this.

Spectre watched from his spot on the top of the living room bookcase. If I thought cats could judge, I definitely would've called his expression judgmental.

Tilly was still beside me on the sofa. She'd adjusted herself so that her head was resting on her paws. Her gaze was fixated on my mother. What was she thinking? Did she dislike my mother as much as I did? She was probably the only person the little dog didn't get excited to see…

My mother lowered her shoulders, as if admitting defeat. 'I sensed something, but it was none of my business. When you're as powerful as me you sense a lot of things about people they don't necessarily want to know.'

I rubbed my face. 'You're unbelievable, you know that? Fucking unbelievable.'

'Don't swear at me like that!'

I stood, squaring up to her. I'd never been filled with more rage towards the woman in my entire life. 'After decades of your bullshit, I think I'm allowed. That's the really clever thing: you've never overtly lied. Instead, you've danced around the truth; you've left things out; you've done whatever you can to protect yourself first and foremost. It would be clever if it didn't make me want to punch you.'

She jerked her head back, as if I'd actually do it. I wouldn't, for the record. Nor could I, since she'd already crossed over. Surely she knew that?

I rolled my eyes. 'Please. You're not even worth it if I could punch you. Get out of my house before I do something else.'

Her eyes went wide. 'Did you just threaten to exorcise me?'

'No. You interpreted what I said as that.'

It felt kind of good to play her at her own game. I should've done it years ago.

*

'Niamh? What's wrong?'

'My mother!' I shouted down the phone at Maggie. My mother had gone, but her words – her excuses – were still very much in my head.

I slammed a mug on to the kitchen side, then changed my mind and shoved it back into the cupboard, closing the door with a semi-satisfying bang. While the angry part of me enjoyed it, the headachey part of my very much didn't. I leaned against the side for a minute, grinding my teeth together.

'What did she do?'

'Can you meet? I need to vent.' I tapped my foot against the cupboard door.

Tilly and Spectre will still in the living room, neither of them wanting to stay near me when I was in such a bad mood.

'I'm at work, sorry.'

Of course she was. I was such an idiot.

'No, I'm sorry. I shouldn't have bothered you.' I pulled my phone from my ear and reached for the end call button.

'Wait! Why don't you come over after work? I can feed you and you can vent.'

I nodded. Yes, that would help. 'That sounds like a good plan. What time do you finish?'

'In about an hour. So why don't you take Tilly for a walk, then take a *slow* drive over here?'

'Why did you emphasise the word "slow" like that?' What was she implying? I was always a careful driver!

'Because I know you,' she said vaguely.

'Meaning?' She so wasn't going to get away with not filling in the blanks. I'd had enough of that already.

'Meaning I remember not long after you passed your driving test you reversed your car into a pole because your mum stole your secret ice cream stash from the freezer and finished it off without telling you. So if you do that over ice cream…'

'I couldn't see the pole! My back window was too high up and the pole was too short and I had no rear sensors!'

'Still. You don't want to take your bad mood out on your car.'

My shoulders relaxed. Maggie wasn't the villain here. She was offering to feed me and let me vent. She was on my side. And probably right about the car. 'No, you're right. I'm sorry for snapping.'

'I'll see you in a bit, all right?'

'All right.'

*

I expected Javi to turn up while I was rage-walking Tilly, but to my surprise, he didn't.

Then again, he had the common sense to know that when I was in a bad mood, Maggie was the best person to calm me down. While he was good at making me laugh, he often said the wrong thing and made me more annoyed.

Not to mention it appeared that he now spent a lot of time with the source of my anger, making him an easy target if he did come near me.

Despite her hatred of walks, Tilly walked well, as if she sensed that I needed to get out of the house. I appreciated her understanding.

*

Usually I liked to listen to music or the radio when driving, but both made my headache worse so were out of the question. Even the indicators clicking caused me to cringe. I tried to block the clicking out, to focus on the road ahead of me, but it wasn't easy when light also hurt my eyes, even through sunglasses.

Maggie worked as a part-time chef at a fancy local place on the outskirts of Nottingham. When I pulled into the car park, I'd never been happier to stop the car and not have to listen to the humming of the engine any more.

The restaurant car park was moderately busy, but easy enough to find a space in. And, more importantly, quiet enough that Maggie and I could talk in semi-privacy.

When I went inside, the server showed me to a table that had been reserved for me. There was a handwritten note from Maggie, scribbled in her scruffiest handwriting, the style she only ever used when she was in a rush but really wanted to write something down. The note informed me that food was on its way and the bartender would make my favourite coffee when I got in.

I relaxed into the plush seat, closing my eyes to listen to the sound of people talking and the water feature on the other side of the window. The splashing water was soothing, helping me to block out the argument with my mother that was playing over and over in my head.

'Coffee?' said Maggie's voice. She sat opposite me, placing a mug of my favourite in front of me, then sitting opposite me with a cup of tea.

'Bless you,' I said.

She smiled. 'So. What happened?'

'I made the mistake of asking my mother for help, and she suggested the reason I haven't been sleeping is because of stress.'

A server placed two meals in front of us. 'Guinea fowl?'

Maggie gestured to me.

'You're feeding me guinea fowl?' I asked as the server put the plate in front of me and chuckled.

'Trust me,' she said. 'Unless you'd like to swap for my chickpea and quinoa salad?'

'I'm good with the meat,' I said. It wasn't that I had anything against eating vegan, but I couldn't angrily chop into grains in the same way I could meat and veg.

We thanked the server, then Maggie continued: 'You have been stressed.'

'And whose fault is that?' I picked up my cutlery and stabbed the guinea fowl. The metal knife clanged against the plate. 'It's hers.' I sliced into the meat, ramming my hand back and forth as fast as I could. 'If she'd told me the truth from the start—' slice '—Dominic wouldn't have been able to manipulate Edie —' slice '—because we would've known what she was capable of and could've trained her from the start!' My knife finished slicing through the bit of guinea fowl I'd been cutting, so I stabbed it with my fork. Yes, that felt better.

Maggie put her hand on top of mine. 'You're going to damage the plate if you keep sawing your food like that.'

'Sorry.' I tried to relax my grip on the cutlery, focusing on eating instead of attacking. The guinea fowl had a stronger flavour than chicken, but Maggie was right: it *was* nice. She'd picked well. Why was I surprised? She always picked well.

'It gets better,' I said, shovelling some cabbage on to my fork.

'Worse than her lying to you?'

'She knew Javi's powers were bound and never. Said. A word.' I punctuated the last few words for dramatic impact and with more – delicate – slices of roast potatoes.

'All this time? She *knew* and never told you? Or him?'

'If Edie can tell when people's powers are bound, there's no way my mother couldn't. Especially not with how much time Javi spent at ours when we were teenagers. She would've sensed it, even if she couldn't tell exactly what he was capable of.'

'Damn.'

'And she has the audacity to not realise she caused so much of my stress!' I put my cutlery down and waved my arms in the air. 'She's got no accountability. It's like she doesn't care and can't take responsibility for any of it.'

'Are you really surprised?'

I sipped my coffee. The sweet, acidic taste was exactly what I needed. 'What do you mean?'

'This is pretty standard behaviour for her, isn't it? The only difference is that the consequences are greater.'

I sighed. 'You're right. You're totally right. She's not acting out of character. I was expecting too much from her. More than she's ever shown herself to be capable of.'

'You were expecting her to be a good person,' said Maggie. 'It's not too much to ask.'

I scoffed. 'It is for her.' Shaking my head, I returned to eating my roast dinner. Maggie knew if I didn't eat I'd crash once the adrenaline wore off. That's why she'd offered to feed me.

'Thanks for having my back, Mags.'

'Any time.'

11

Edie

I didn't know how to handle seeing Tessa at college every day. When the corridors were crowded it was a little easier, but being in the same building, living in the same town, we inevitably crossed paths.

I should've gone to English, as Mrs Mitchell was going over some we needed to know for our mock exams, but it was going to be even harder to concentrate now that Tessa knew I could see her. It was bad enough with her talking over the teacher, then shouting out answers only I could hear. I should've stolen her answers. It wasn't like anyone would've known I was cheating.

And I so wasn't in the mood to face her, so I skipped English and went to see Fadil instead. I had a free morning aside from English anyway.

'Morning,' said Fadil, stepping aside to let me in. He wiped at his red nose with the back of his hand, then snivelled.

'Morning,' I said with a sigh. I sat on my usual spot on the sofa, resting my head in my hands.

Fadil sat beside me, a look of concern on his new face. Even with a new face it was an expression of his I was all too familiar with. Was I really that pathetic?

'What's wrong?'

'Am I that transparent?' I asked.

'Yes. What's wrong?'

'Are you OK? You seem snivelly.'

Yes, I was avoiding the question.

'I have a cold, but I'll be fine,' he said with a big sniff. What was it with the people around me insisting they'd be fine lately? Had Mum's attitude rubbed off on Fadil? 'Back to you: what's wrong?'

I shook my head. 'Tessa found out I can see her. And now I'm hiding from her like a baby.'

'You're not being a baby. It's a weird situation.' He pursed his lips. 'Can you stop twitching your leg, please? I feel like I'm in one of those vibrating chairs.'

'Sorry. I didn't know I was doing it.' Oops. I must've been more on edge than I'd realised. It was a subconscious habit I saved for when I was really restless. 'How do you know what a vibrating chair feels like?'

'Ben ordered one from the internet. He returned it pretty quickly because it sounded like a jet engine.'

I laughed. 'Ben ordered a massage chair?'

'Why is that funny?'

'Didn't see him as that kind of person.'

Fadil shrugged. 'I think it was a late-night impulse purchase to try to distract himself from his breakup with your mum.'

'Oh.'

He nodded, pulling his navy dressing gown tighter around him. He looked really cold. And ill. They were his first modern germs, so I supposed they would hit him a lot harder as he didn't really have an immune system yet.

I'd never thought about how their short breakup had affected Ben. Then again, I'd never really seen the impact on Mum, either. I'd been too busy getting brainwashed by Dominic. That had turned out well.

At least Ben had had the common sense to return the noisy chair when they'd both hated it. It showed how much he included Fadil as a part of his life now, too. It warmed my heart.

'Let's go do something,' I said, standing up. 'Once you've got another layer or two on.'

Fadil looked up at me. 'Like what?'

I put my hand out. 'I think it's time we introduce you to the tram.'

*

'I'm not sure this is a good idea,' said Fadil, wrinkling his nose to try to stop himself from sneezing.

'Relax, this is a quiet time of day,' I informed him.

We sat on the tram, facing ahead, ready to visit the city centre. Fadil hadn't left Hucknall since he'd been resurrected. If he'd still been using Mum's powers to understand English, he wouldn't have been able to since eight miles would've been too far away from her. But since he was using my powers now, it meant he could travel into town with me.

Going just after the school rush meant that hardly anyone else was on the tram. We practically had a carriage to ourselves. That would probably change as we got closer to town, but I doubted it. We'd definitely have our own square of four stripy blue chairs to ourselves. Even so, we chose to sit next to each other.

'I'll find a way to pay you back for my tram ticket,' he said.

I squeezed his arm. 'It's fine, really. It's only a few quid.'

'But I don't have any money! Or any way to earn it! I'm constantly sponging off Ben and I feel bad enough already.' He lowered his head, staring into his lap.

I'd never really thought about that before. I took having money for granted. I knew Mum worried about it, but she was conscious to not pass that worry on to me. Not thinking about money was probably a bad habit to have given that I was now eighteen, but I'd deal with that another day.

'How can I even get a job if I don't have a proper ID?' he asked as the tram pulled away.

'You have Dominic's,' I said, although I doubted it'd offer him much reassurance. 'Technically, you're him now.'

Doc had found a way to adjust Dominic's legal records and basically replace him with Fadil. It wasn't an ideal solution, but it was all we could come up with at such short notice.

Fadil cringed. I didn't really blame him. He was basically impersonating a power-hungry psychopath.

'We'll figure it out, it just takes time. There isn't exactly a roadmap for this.'

He shook his head. 'Yeah, you're right. It's just that every time I feel like I can do more, something else gets in the way.' He snivelled, wiping at his nose with the back of his hand. 'I want to carve out my own life, but it's hard when my only chance of acceptance in the real world is pretending to be *him*.' It was almost like Fadil couldn't bring himself to say Dominic's name, which was fair enough. He hadn't exactly been a stellar person, although technically he hadn't done anything to hurt Fadil directly.

In fact, Dominic had been the one to free Fadil from his sarcophagus and the blood curse that had incapacitated him…but only so that he could work out how to cast a blood curse on Maggie and Josh. He'd done a great thing to fuel a terrible thing.

I rubbed Fadil's hand in what I hoped was a supportive way. Leaning in to his ear, I whispered, 'There are cameras. Not sure if they can hear us, but maybe we should pretend you're auditioning for a role, just in case?' While I doubted they'd take us seriously, you could never be too careful. It was a quiet tram and a sensitive topic.

Fadil burst away from me, standing in the aisle of the tram and holding his arms out. 'How dare you accuse me of being melodramatic! I'll have you know I'm a terrific thespian.'

A few people on the tram looked over. Some rolled their eyes, a couple laughed.

Fadil bowed, returning to his seat and suppressing a cough before he spoke. 'How was that?'

'Pretty good. Had me convinced.'

He grinned. 'How are your mock exams going, anyway?'

Smooth change of subject.

I looked out of the window at the trees as we went past them in the rickety tram. They were evergreens, so still lush despite it being December. A couple of places had put up decorations or signs ready for Christmas, too. On top of the fence that separated the tram from the rest of the world, an inflatable crocodile wore a Santa hat, a *Merry Christmas* sign taped to his side. I was so drained that the absurdity of it barely even registered.

I'd been so wrapped up in my powers, Fadil, Dominic, Dave, mock exams, and now Tessa, I hadn't even had time to think about Christmas approaching. I hadn't even started Christmas shopping!

What was I going to get everyone?

'Edie?'

I sighed, turning away from the window to look at Fadil. 'Don't tell Mum, but not great.'

Fadil frowned. 'Why?'

'I haven't had enough time to revise. And to be honest, I don't have the energy. I'm exhausted, mentally and physically. It's like my brain just won't retain information. And the harder I try, the harder it is to even remember what the date is. I misspelled my own name the other day.'

'Damn,' said Fadil.

'Yeah. I just don't know what's wrong with me.'

'I don't know what's wrong, but I can help you study if you'd like? You know I love learning new things.'

'You'd do that?'

Fadil smiled. 'Of course I would. You, Ben, and your mum have done so much for me already. If I can return the favour, even in a little way, I will.'

I hugged him as my eyes filled with tears. 'You're the best.'

12

Niamh

Insomnia sucked. It was even worse with a pulsing headache. No wonder I couldn't sleep.

All right, I had a lot on my mind as well. I had my powers back, but I couldn't help but worry that Edie was more vulnerable now that she had less of them. I had to respect her decision, though. As much as I disliked it, I understood it.

Then there was the Tessa thing. The police and press had remained quiet about what had happened to her, and Tessa seemed more interested in pestering Edie than sharing useful information with her. Which meant she continued to annoy Edie when she was trying to concentrate in class. It wouldn't be long until her grades suffered as a result. No one could withstand that level of annoying forever.

Not wanting to waste reading time on tossing and turning, I sat up. Tilly, disturbed by my movement, opened one eye and glared at me. I smiled at her. She rolled over and fell back to sleep on her side, with her head hanging off the end of the bed. She always had loved sleeping at weird angles.

The house seemed different now that Edie was back. But in a good way. It had more life in it again. The energy had changed.

It was quiet, though.

That was why I'd chosen the house. It was a quiet area, where, when the wind blew a certain way, I could hear the motorway in the distance, humming like a lullaby.

It wasn't the motorway I heard this time, though. It was whistling.

Was Tilly snoring?

I reached over to lift her head and help her back on the bed, but as she woke up, I realised it wasn't her breathing. It was coming from outside. And it was getting louder, too.

It wasn't the first time I'd heard it, but this time, it seemed closer.

There was no particular tune or pattern to it. It was just enough to make the hairs on the back of my neck stand up.

The more frequently I heard it, the harder it became to dismiss it as a dream or auditory hallucination. Seeing Tilly react to it proved to me it wasn't just in my head.

I rubbed at my ears, in the hopes I was actually hearing things, but the noise was still there when I stopped.

Tilly stood, looking around. Her back arched. If she could hear it, there was no way I was dreaming it. But what *was* it?

We occasionally got drunken people talking or arguing or whistling as they walked past on their way home from the pub. But something about this felt different. Unnerving. Paranormal. I couldn't put my finger on why, but it gave me goosebumps.

I picked up my phone and called Ben. It seemed silly, but I needed to speak to a grown up right then. Even if it was three in the morning.

'Niamh? What's wrong?' He sounded alert.

'Can you hear it?' I held the phone out. The whistling continued.

'Hear what?'

'The whistling!' I whispered. 'Someone's whistling and it's getting closer.'

'I don't hear anything except our voices and Fadil snoring,' said Ben.

Great so I'd woken him up for nothing. 'Are you sure? It sounds supernatural.'

'What makes a whistle sound supernatural?'

'Like…it's close but not. High but low. No particular tune, but haunting.'

'You were probably just imaging it in your sleep,' he suggested, making me feel even more paranoid.

'Tilly heard it too!'

She was now sitting on the edge of my bed, her head cocked to one side, as if she was listening for the noise.

'I wish you were here right now,' I said. Even though he couldn't do anything, and I might've dreamt it, his presence would've reassured me and made it easier for me to fall back to sleep. Not because he was a male who needed to protect me, but because he was Ben. My Ben.

'Me too,' said Ben.

*

'Did you hear weird noises last night?' I asked Edie as we sat down to breakfast. The breakfast news played in the background, talking about nothing particularly interesting. Tilly lay at our feet, underneath the breakfast bar, hoping for a scrap. It never happened, but she continued to dream.

Edie sliced into her fried egg on toast. 'What kind of noises?'

'Whistling, I guess.'

I still wasn't totally sure what I'd heard. But whistling was the only word I could think of to describe it. And, despite what Ben insisted, I *hadn't* dreamt it.

'At first I thought it was Tilly snoring, but then she seemed to react to it as well.'

Edie shook her head, causing her freshly dyed brown hair to fall into her eyes. She tucked it behind her ear. 'No. But I slept pretty heavily last night. Was it loud?'

'Not really. But Tilly only settled down when it faded away. Ben couldn't hear it either.' I shifted in my seat, feeling uncomfortable that I'd mentioned him because of how much I'd wanted him to be there and convince me I was sane.

Edie looked up from her plate. 'Ben was here?'

'No. I rang him.'

'In the middle of the night?' She didn't try to hide her surprise, making me feel worse for waking him up over something seemingly stupid. But then, she seemed to switch tones: 'Maybe he was too far away to hear it.'

'Yeah. Maybe.' Although the phone hadn't picked it up, either, so I wasn't totally convinced. I pushed a bit of toast around my plate, nervous to bring up what I really wanted to ask her. 'Would you mind if he did stay over? Like, just in general. Not just when stuff is going on.'

Edie shrugged. 'Doesn't bother me. So long as I can still get to college on time.' She shoved a forkful of egg and toast into her mouth as if the topic was no big deal.

I sipped my coffee to hide my grin. 'Given how much you both love learning, I think he'd be the last person to hold you up.'

'That's true.' Edie's gaze turned to the TV. She grabbed the TV remote and turned it up. It had switched to the local news. Another body had been found. Not far from where we lived.

'Oh my god.'

'Do you think it's related?' Edie asked me.

'What do you mean?'

'The whistling and the death. Maybe it was the murderer you heard,' suggested Edie.

'Maybe,' I said. 'But that doesn't make sense. Why would a serial killer draw attention to himself like that? How many whistling serial killers have you heard of?'

I *was* starting to wonder, though. I'd heard the same tune the night Tessa was murdered *and* the night before we'd visited Bianca at the hair salon. The nights leading up to it usually had a different, but just as jarring and sleep-disrupting, tune. *Was* there something weird going on with what I was hearing?

Edie sipped her tea. 'They have to kill at least three people at different times to qualify as a serial killer. This guy just hit number three.'

Of course she'd know that.

'Still. I'm sure it's nothing to worry about. It's probably just a bunch of coincidences. I was probably hearing things and the murders aren't related. I mean, they all have different backgrounds, genders, races, jobs. There's nothing tying any of them together. The odds of a murderer targeting the three of them when they have nothing in common is pretty slim. It doesn't make sense.'

Edie smirked. 'So you *do* pay attention when we watch true crime documentaries.'

That was what she'd got from everything I'd just said? Sigh.

'Some of it has to go in,' I said. She made me watch enough of them. 'Let's just focus on getting you through these exams, yeah? Let the police worry about who's trying to kill people.'

'You don't think we're in danger?' said Edie.

'We're both better protected than your average person, don't you think?'

13
Edie

Why were mock exams even a thing? As if the pressure of an actual exam in a few months' time wasn't bad enough, I had to ruin Christmastime by spending the whole of December revising and doing exams. Festive cheer surrounded me, but couldn't enjoy anything without feeling guilty and like I was meant to be studying. It wasn't fair.

When the day of my English mock exam came, I wanted to go in even less than usual. Tessa would be there. And I really didn't want to end up doing badly because she was distracting me the whole time, just because she could.

To my surprise, when I got into class, she was crouching down beside Josh, giving him a pep talk. As usual, he was oblivious. He stared into his dog-eared copy of *Wuthering Heights*, taking one last look at the source material before he had to put it in his bag for the test.

I settled into my seat at the opposite side of the room, hopeful that Tessa would have forgotten that I could see her. It'd been a few days. She'd had other things to worry about.

I could dream.

'You've got this, Josh. Just remember what we talked about when we revised together a couple of weeks ago. Oh my god, was it really just a couple of weeks ago we were revising together in my bedroom?' Tessa started making crying noises. She was shaking, floating up and down frenetically, and looking generally distraught. She'd always been so put-together that seeing her like that was almost unnerving. Up until that point, she'd seemed to be handling her death well. Maybe it was all an act, both when she'd been alive, and now that she was dead. I had always thought she'd make a great actor.

The lights flickered a few times, reflecting her intense emotions. Everyone in the room gasped and mumbled.

'All right, all right, I'm sure it's nothing to worry about,' said Mrs Mitchell as she handed out the mock papers and began explaining the rules. They never changed – turn off phones, transparent pencil cases, blank copy of the book you're writing about in front of you, don't look at other people's papers – but she had to reiterate them anyway.

Once she'd passed the papers out, she glanced at the tinsel-covered clock. 'You've got two hours. Go.'

Go? My brain didn't want to go. But I turned to the first page anyway and skimmed the question. My brain didn't like the question. It didn't like Tessa's monologue in the background, either. She was still talking to Josh, trying to tell him what to write. Sometimes, if he wrote something she *really* disliked,

95

she'd throw a tantrum like she was two. But it didn't matter. I was the only person who could hear her.

I tried to concentrate, to write *something*. Something was better than nothing, right?

But Tessa's voice was the type that carried. It was hard to block out because she was loud and wanted to be heard. And of course, it wasn't like I could put headphones on to drown her out.

I looked up at the clock. Halfway through. How was it halfway through already? I was in so much trouble if I didn't get more writing done soon. But how could I with Tessa in my ear?

So far, she hadn't acknowledged me. That was good. Her acknowledging me probably would've been worse. But I was getting increasingly wound up by her screechy voice coming from a few feet away. If I didn't calm down soon, I'd be too wound up to concentrate.

'Excuse me, Mrs Mitchell? Could I got to loo, please?'

'Sorry, Edie. No toilet breaks allowed,' she replied.

Wasn't that just great? What kind of place didn't allow toilet breaks? What if I had IBS? Dysmenorrhoea? Ulcerative colitis? I didn't, but that wasn't the point.

Or maybe it was. If I had any of those things and she knew, she probably would've allowed me to go. I couldn't exactly tell her it was because of a ghost, though.

Ugh.

The tinsel surrounding the grey wall clock was old and threadbare. In its heyday, it had been blue and silver, but now it was more like a dusty, mottled grey. The sellotape that attached it to the clock didn't help, since it flattened some of it and would inevitably take some more tinsel with it when someone removed it after Christmas.

Oh my god, why was I analysing tinsel? I needed to focus!

I tried to write, but, at the end of the two hours, I knew I could've done better. It was too hard to ignore Tessa. She'd been shouting in Josh's ear towards the end. And she really wasn't happy with what he'd written. Nor could she accept that no amount of shouting at him would change whether or not he could hear her.

Frustrated at the end of class, I charged out, ready to go bury my sorrows in an expensive coffee.

'Edie, wait up!' a voice called to me as I ran down the stairs and out of the building.

I turned to see Melanie chasing after me, hugging a paperback to her chest. 'Hey, you OK? You rushed out of the exam pretty quickly.'

She was checking up on me? She'd never done that before. Maybe there was hope for our friendship yet, now that she was out of Tessa's clutches. It wasn't like she could have any other underlying motive. She'd mostly kept a low profile since Tessa's death, avoiding talking about it to pretty much anyone, even teachers and classmates. When the congregation of local press outside of the college had tried to talk to her, I'd thought she was going to break their cameras for a moment. She'd looked like a dragon ready to breathe fire. It was so different to everyone else – they seemed to seek out the media even if they barely knew Tessa.

I shook my head, trying not to cry. 'It was a disaster.'

'It's just mocks. I'm sure you'll do better in the real thing.'

'Not if Tessa's there.'

Frazzle. Why had I just said that?

Melanie froze. '*What?* Tessa's ghost was in there?'

I pulled Melanie into a corner, near the far side of the building we'd just vacated. I could see Josh inside the classroom we were near, talking to one of his other teachers. Tessa floated beside him.

'She's haunting Josh,' I said.

'What? No way! Does Josh know?'

'No,' I said. 'It's not really the kind of conversation that rolls off the tongue. Especially when he can't even look at me.'

'No, I guess not,' she replied. 'Where is she now?'

'Inside with Josh. I don't think she can go that far away from him,' I said.

'Can she see us? Could she come over here?' It almost sounded like she didn't want Tessa to do that, but that another part of her was curious. Who wouldn't be?

I looked back into the classroom. Tessa had disappeared from beside Josh. That was weird. I could still sense her nearby…

'*What* do you think you're doing?'

Ah, there she was.

'Hi, Tessa,' I said through gritted teeth. She'd appeared on my right, while Melanie was in front of me. So I looked at Melanie while I addressed Tessa. It would look more natural to anyone walking past, and annoy Tessa even more.

Melanie stiffened. 'She's here?'

'Of course I'm here! Tell her I'm here!'

'She says you look good,' I informed Melanie.

Melanie smiled. 'Thanks!'

'I did not say that! Hang on. Is she wearing my Ralph Lauren scarf? I can't believe she stole my scarf! Tell her she's a thief!'

'She says she hoped you did well on the exam,' I told Melanie.

Melanie laughed, adjusting the pink woollen scarf that was tied artfully around her neck.

'Hang on. That's *definitely* my blouse under that awful coat. What, is she trying to become me or something? Please. That colour washes out her skin tone so much she looks like she belongs on *The Simpsons*. And that neckline makes her neck look huge.'

I rolled my eyes. Had she been like this behind her friends' backs when she was alive? No wonder Melanie had been a lot nicer to me than I'd expected her to be after we'd exorcised her. She was probably grateful to have someone do something nice for her.

'She likes your blouse,' I told Melanie, a ripple of smugness flowing through me.

Tessa balled her hands into fists. 'Why are you not telling her what I'm saying?'

I glanced over my shoulder, meeting her eye for the first time, and smirked. Revenge was sweet.

Tessa tensed her shoulders then floated away. Oh no. How would I cope without her by my side?

'She's gone,' I told Melanie.

Her shoulders relaxed. She had a strange relationship with Tessa, one I really couldn't work out. Did Tessa's presence really put her on edge that much?

'You don't think she could haunt me, do you?' said Melanie.

I looked back into the classroom. Josh was packing his things up, ready to leave. Tessa was still glaring at me. I grinned back at her. Her nostrils flared, but she didn't come back over. Surprisingly.

I patted Melanie's shoulder. 'I wouldn't worry. Tessa won't be bothering you any time soon.'

14

Niamh

Ben's first sleepover. No big deal. Definitely no big deal.

Although the word 'sleepover' did make it sound like we were about fifteen.

With the fluttering in my stomach, I felt like I was. What was wrong with me? Butterflies hadn't swarmed in my stomach since I was a teenager. Since…since Javi.

I sat on the edge of my bed and sighed. Javi had made it pretty clear he was Team Ben – even though there was no Team Ben – but that didn't stop the guilt.

I'd planned to spend the rest of my life with Javi. When he'd died, I'd married someone else. Someone so different from Javi he'd ended up being completely the wrong fit.

But then, Ben wasn't exactly like him, either. He was more mature. And older. Barely, but still. Javi had been thirty when he was killed. Ben was thirty five.

Thoughts of Ben and Javi continued to torment me while I made dinner and as Edie and I sat down to eat in the living room. Usually, we would've had the TV on, but we didn't because of my headache. Edie had taken to wearing headphones more often so that she could still listen to music and TV while I got the quiet I needed. I hadn't asked her to do that, which showed how understanding she was. Despite her worries of her powers corrupting her, and what Dominic had tried to do, she was a good person, even if she didn't realise it yet.

'Are you sure you're all right with this?' I asked Edie for the hundredth time, pulling the cushion my plate was balancing on closer to me.

Edie rolled her eyes. 'The amount of times you've asked me, I'm starting to wonder if *you're* all right with it.'

Busted.

'It's just new. And different.'

Tilly watched us from beside the coffee table, hoping we'd spare her a mouthful of chicken. The fact I'd cooked her extra broccoli wasn't as important to her as the cooked chicken she wasn't allowed because it was slathered with onions.

Edie poked at a carrot baton on her plate, not looking up at me as she spoke. 'Do you want to be alone forever?'

Ouch. What a question.

'No. Of course not.' I rotated my fork against my plate, careful not to make a noise and torment my headache.

'Well then.' As if that was that, she got up from the sofa and went into the kitchen. A minute later, the tap started running to signal she was washing up.

Not in the mood to eat anymore, I followed her.

'Don't ask again,' she said as soon as I walked through the door.

I laughed, put my plate down, then hugged her. She squirmed, but also leaned into me.

'Thank you.'

'You're welcome.'

*

Ben came over shortly after we'd washed up. Edie went to her room with Tilly and Spectre, giving Ben and me some alone time. It really was like being a teenager again. Having him there made me feel calmer, which improved my headache a little. Well, that and the happy hormones released by certain activities…

When we were finally tired enough to sleep, Ben put some earplugs in. He said it was a habit from when he'd lived with his parents, because they'd both snored. Nowadays, it helped him switch off.

Was that part of why he hadn't heard the whistling the other day, or had he just been too far away? Why was that noise still stuck in my head, despite everything?

I lay on my side. Ben curled into me and wrapped his arm around me. It had been a long time since I'd spooned with anyone. It felt good. I fell asleep easier than I had in years.

*

I jolted awake, Ben's arm flying off me. There it was. That whistling again.

It was still dark outside. My bedside clock said it was 3:18am.

I nudged Ben. 'Ben. Ben! Do you hear it?'

His brown eyes flitted open. He squinted at me, taking out an earplug. 'What's wrong?'

'Listen!' I put my finger to my lips.

The whistling continued, although it didn't seem to get louder or quieter, like it had last time. It was just a constant, annoying note, playing over an over, as if whoever was responsible had half learned how to whistle but never bothered to learn how to do it properly. It was hard to pin down or explain.

It mostly consisted of a grating noise that made me want to burst my ear drums so that I didn't have to hear it ever again.

Oh my god, my head was going to explode if it kept going. Something about it was most definitely not normal. I just couldn't work out what.

Ben shook his head, removing the other earplug and placing both in the case on the bedside table. 'I don't hear anything.'

'How can you not? It's *really* loud!' And a bloody horrible noise, too. Could he really not hear it?

He grabbed his glasses and put them on so that he could see properly. 'Do you have tinnitus?'

'No my ears aren't bloody ringing! Someone is *whistling* outside!'

Ben got up and looked out of the window, opening it so that he could get a better look up and down the street. The street lamps created an eerie amber haze, casting giant tree shadows up and down the road. There were no signs of life, though. Not even the distant hum of the motorway that I liked so much.

'I don't see anyone, but there's a pub nearby. Maybe someone's on their way home late.'

I wrinkled my nose. 'The pubs closed three hours ago.'

Ben shrugged, closing the window. 'They might've come from town.'

'In the middle of the week?'

Ben yawned. 'I'm sure it's just the wind or something.'

A bird cawed. I joined Ben at the window to see a glowing raven fly past. A ghost raven? I hadn't seen one of those before, but it wasn't impossible.

'See? It's probably just the raven imitating something it heard.'

'They can do that?'

'Yeah.'

'But if it was the raven, wouldn't you hear it? It hasn't stopped.'

'Are you *sure* you don't have tinnitus?'

There was no way he was going to get it, so I stomped back over to my side of the bed and pulled the covers over me. Our first sleepover and he thought I was hearing things. Good start.

15
Edie

Ben sleeping over felt oddly normal. Although he did spend a lot of time at ours already, so I supposed the only weird thing really was that Fadil wasn't there. Based on the texts I'd had that morning, Fadil seemed to have slept well overnight and enjoyed having the house to himself for the first time. He had spent four thousand years on his own, so it wasn't like being alone bothered him.

'Look who it is,' said Tessa, appearing in my face as I left college that day. Thankfully, she was to my side, so I didn't have to barge past her to get away. If I did that, she'd know I could touch her. Which risked moving her torment to a whole new level. As if it wasn't bad enough already.

I kept my head down, looking anywhere but at her. If I acknowledged her, that'd only encourage her to keep going. Not that ignoring her seemed to work all that well, either.

'Did you find out what happened to me yet?'

Tiled floor. Feet walking along the floor. Gross things I didn't want to know what they were on the floor. Focus on those, not on Tessa. Focus. Focus…

I'd never had such an intense focus on the crappy flooring before.

Josh was a few feet away, walking away from me. I could tell it was him from his shoes and his walk. He was turned away, with his head bowed. Was he ignoring me, too? Or was he just being quiet because he was grieving?

Even though we'd known each other for so long, it was hard for me to figure out what was going on in his head. In just a few weeks, I'd gone from knowing everything about him to feeling like he was a total stranger.

Shaking my head to get rid of the building tears, I kept going.

'What's the matter? Disappointed he hasn't rebounded back into your arms? You obviously weren't as good as you thought.'

Don't punch her. Don't do it. Think happy thoughts. Think getting out of there. Don't punch her.

I sped up, charging towards the exit. Tessa cackled in my ear. Her laugh was even worse when she was dead because she was even closer to me.

'It's OK, there are places you can go to learn how to—'

Before I could punch her, or she could finish her sentence, she was pulled away. Thank god Josh had been power walking, so he was now far enough away to keep her far away from me.

What was Tessa's problem with me, anyway? She was dead! Shouldn't finding her murderer have been more important than bothering me? It felt like she just assumed I'd be figuring it out to help her even though she was still being a bitch to me.

Ugh.

*

When Fadil had offered to help me revise, I'd assumed it was a kind, but otherwise empty, gesture. I hadn't expected him to turn up at my door after college, a bunch of Ben's stationery in hand, and a huge grin on his face.

'What's with the stationery store?' I asked as I let him in.

'To help you study!' He was the first person I'd ever spoken to who sounded excited to study. I didn't get it, but as long as he was happy to let me, I was going to take full advantage of his enthusiasm. Maybe it'd rub off on me.

'Don't look so confused,' he said as we settled into the living room. His nose was red and he was snivelling pretty badly, but he seemed determined to help. Mum wasn't quite so interfering – she preferred to nag – and Ben stayed out of it. Fadil was taking a much more active approach to ensuring I studied.

And I supposed it did benefit him as well, in a way, since he'd get to learn stuff from my revision too.

Tilly was out for a walk with Mum, so, for once, he wouldn't get a westie face wash when he walked in. He'd get one when they got back instead.

'I love learning. This is another way for me to do that.'

'All right, I'll give you that,' I said. 'How's your cold?'

He opened the bag he was carrying to reveal a giant box of tissues. 'I feel terrible, but we have work to do.' He sounded weirdly enthusiastic about the prospect of revising. It was unnerving. 'How was college?'

I fell back onto the sofa with a thud. 'Confrontational.'

He sat beside me, his brow furrowed. 'That's not normally a word I hear associated with college. Not from everything I've watched, read, or listened to, anyway.'

'Tessa got in my face again.' I ground my teeth as I relived her crude comments. 'I don't get it. She's dead! Shouldn't she be trying to figure out who killed her?'

'She's haunting Josh, right?'

'Yeah.'

'She probably can't do much to solve her murder from there. Unless he can suddenly see ghosts too.'

I shook my head. 'No. Maggie is a chef and Harry is an accountant.'

Fadil tapped his foot against the sofa. 'Maybe what she's looking for is the same thing she was looking for in life.'

'Which is?'

'Connection. Affection. Love.'

I snorted. 'Tessa doesn't know what love is. She's too self-centred.'

'She has an idea of what it means to her, even if it's not genuine love. She chose Josh over her parents and other friends.'

I shuddered as I realised how right Fadil probably was. 'Josh is the first person she's felt truly connected to. That's why she chased him so hard.'

Fadil nodded. 'Seems likely, yeah.'

'It doesn't explain why she won't leave *me* alone. Even after she got with Josh she still made a beeline for me whenever she wanted to wind someone up. I'm tired of being her favourite target.' Crossing my arms, I slumped deeper into the sofa.

'Could it be more about her than you?'

Deja vu ripped through me. Dominic had said something similar. And while he'd had a reason to lie about most things, this didn't feel like something he would've lied about. Dominic had tricked me so easily because he was good at figuring people out. He could've easily been telling the truth about Tessa to earn my trust so that I'd do more for him. I felt sick.

Fadil didn't know what Dominic had said. But if two unrelated people who'd never spoken about it thought the same thing…

'Your family has been through a lot, and no family is perfect, but your parents – and even Dumb Dan – come across a lot more caring than her parents did when I saw them on TV,' said Fadil.

Dumb Dan came across as more compassionate than her parents? That was impressive.

'How did they come across?' I didn't have the mental capacity to watch people talk about how nice Tessa was every time she was mentioned on the news. It was too nauseating.

Fadil ran his hand back and forth over the arm of the sofa, caressing the worn fabric. 'They seem a lot like Tessa. They talk more about how their lives have been affected by her death than about how much she's lost. They also seem to be loving the limelight. It's all very self-absorbed. It makes me feel a little queasy.'

Of course. 'Entitled and selfish parents having an entitled and selfish child.'

'Is it just entitlement and selfishness?' Fadil asked. The conversation was getting deep. Did he want me to empathise with Tessa? That wasn't going to happen.

'If her parents are entitled and selfish, it probably means the love she got from them was conditional. That'd make anyone insecure and seek affection elsewhere.'

As much as I hated to admit it, I understood where he was coming from. Just not where he'd learned all this psychology. 'Where did you get all this from?'

He'd been comatose for four millennia, unable to even hear any outside conversation because his sarcophagus had been hidden deep in an Egyptian pyramid. There's no way he could've learned so much about people from there. Then again, he probably spent more hours studying per day than I did at college, and every week he had a new topic of interest.

He chuckled, a blush forming on his cheeks. 'I've been reading a lot of psychology books lately. And, uh, watching a lot of romance films.'

I nudged him, laughing. 'You softie, you.'

16

Niamh

I didn't actually like walking, I just saw it as a necessary evil to stay mildly fit and exercise Tilly. That was one of the main reasons we'd got a dog – to get us out of the house and exercising more. Little did we realise at the time we'd bought a dog who preferred to act like a cross between a cat and a teddy bear, wanting to spend her days watching TV and snuggling instead of out of the house.

As much as Tilly hated when I dragged her off the sofa, I knew she wouldn't get up off it all day if I didn't. And neither would I, to be fair.

So, I donned my biggest, darkest sunglasses and some noise-cancelling headphones, then headed out with my four-legged protestor.

We were walking along the main road, so Tilly was on her lead. Some days she was so adamant she wasn't walking she'd try to step in front of oncoming traffic in an effort to go home. The last thing we needed was to lose Tilly on top of everything else, so I kept her lead short but slack.

I was about to cross the road when Tilly started pulling me in the opposite direction. Unusual. Something had piqued her interest. She sniffed the ground, dragging me along with her surprising strength for a small dog. We reached some bushes, where she nudged them out of the way to reveal a hand.

My curiosity wanted me to see how much of a person was there, but I knew I'd never shake the image from my mind if I did. The rubbery skin, with its grey sleeve sitting just below the wrist, was more than enough for me to tell the hand wasn't fresh. Whomever it belonged to was definitely no longer alive.

And had clearly been there a while. Could his murder have coincided with the whistling I'd heard when Ben slept over? But why would a murderer whistle and draw attention to themselves? It didn't make sense.

What was worse? I could sense darkness. Something very bad had happened here. Murder wasn't common in the small town, despite the myths cosy mysteries perpetuated. They were even less likely because of the supernatural.

I called the police and waited in the freezing wind for them to show up. There weren't really any buildings to offer shelter from the elements, which was probably part of why the body had gone undiscovered for so long. So Tilly and I stood there, my hands going numb as we waited. Tilly refused to sit down as she didn't like cold floors, so she stared at me impatiently, her eyes burning into me with questions I couldn't answer in a way she'd ever understand.

People drove and walked past, oblivious to what was just a few feet away from them. How many people had gone past without noticing what was hidden just out of sight? How much longer would it have been before someone else found the body if I hadn't chosen that particular route that day?

While I waited, I tried to analyse the scene. There was something dark about it. The energy surrounding the scene called to me, trying to lure me closer. It was tempting, like alcohol after a long, rough day.

But I knew nothing good would come from giving in to that temptation. I took a few steps away from the scene until the evil energy lessened enough for it to be easier to ignore.

One thing the scene confirmed was that there was something paranormal about this murder. Someone – or some*thing* – using that much power left a mark. A presence. And this one had kick.

Did it feel stronger because I hadn't felt it in forever? Or was it really that powerful? Nobody knew about my ability to sense evil, so it wasn't like I could talk to anyone else to check. It felt like the wrong time to bring it up with everything else going on.

When the police arrived, they sectioned everywhere off, guiding me away from the crime scene to explain what'd happened.

Unfortunately, while I was there, an officer confirmed there was a body. In several pieces. It was really hard not to vomit.

Oblivious, Tilly asked every police officer who came near us for a head rub.

I told them what little I knew, took a card from them, gave them my details, and scurried off. The less I knew about that crime scene, the better.

On my walk home, I rang Ben in a panic. I didn't care that he was at work. He answered right away. 'I just found a dead body. In several pieces.'

'Slow down. What happened? Where are you?'

'Walking home with Tilly. Of course she sniffed it out,' I said, rolling my eyes. It was always the dog walkers. 'The police are dealing with it now. Unfortunately, I was around long enough to hear them describe some aspects that sounded a lot like what happened to Tessa.'

'So you think they're related?'

'Yeah. But if they are, it means Tessa wasn't your standard murder victim.'

Tilly and I needed to cross the road, but the light was on green. Restless, I bounced on the spot until we could cross. Tilly watched me, confused. I was acting out of character and restless to get home. Would anyone blame me?

'What do you mean?' said Ben.

The light turned red and the little cartoon man appeared on the pedestrian lights. We scurried across the road. 'I could sense the power. There was so, *so* much of it. It's not often I sense that much.'

'Do you think it felt stronger because your powers haven't been working for a while?'

'I did wonder that,' I said as we crossed another road, 'but this was different.' I almost said darker, but stopped myself just in time. 'Thinking back to the other times I've ran into powerful ghosts, the only other one who felt even close to this level of power was a long time ago. And this felt even stronger than that.'

'When was the last time you sensed a ghost this strong?' asked Ben.

I tightened my grip on Tilly's lead. 'The day Javi was killed.'

*

Ben was at my front door when Tilly and I got home. Without saying anything, he wrapped his arms around me. I rested my head on his chest, feeling safer in his embrace. I hadn't even known I'd needed a hug until that moment.

Tilly barked at us, then looked at the front door. She wasn't having any of it. She wanted to get inside, which meant we had to, too. We had been out twice as long as planned, and it was cold, so I didn't blame her.

I unlocked the front door, took off her lead, then began to remove my layers. Ben did the same.

'Did you leave work early for me?' I said as I removed my headphones. The sunglasses stayed on; even with the curtains shut the house was too bright for me in some rooms.

'You just found a dead body! Of course I left work early for you!' said Ben. 'How much did you see?'

'Just the hand,' I said with a shudder. 'It was pretty clear its owner wasn't breathing.'

Ben frowned. 'Did you see any ghosts?'

'No.'

'It's unusual for a murdered ghost to cross over, but not impossible,' said Ben.

'They don't always stay with their bodies, though. Look at Tessa,' I said.

'True,' Ben agreed. 'But maybe Tessa is a good place to start.'

'What do you mean?'

We went into the kitchen and sat down. Ben picked Tilly up and put her on the chair beside him. She sat down, nudging his hand until he stroked her. Little attention seeker.

'She knows you and Edie. She's going to be more likely to cooperate.'

I snorted. 'Wouldn't be so sure about that.'

'She's stuck around and she keeps asking Edie for help.'

I gave Ben an incredulous look. I wouldn't call what Tessa was doing *asking* for help. From what Edie had told me, most of it was ordering her to find her murderer or insulting her.

'Well, in between insults she's asking for Edie's help in the only way she knows how. It goes against her best interests to not cooperate if we ask her about what happened.'

I lowered my head. He was right. Of course he was right. But it was really not an idea I wanted to entertain, let alone actually act on. Ugh.

17

Edie

'Have you found anything yet?' Tessa asked, shoving her face into mine as soon as I reached the outside of college. I hadn't slept much and the caffeine hadn't kicked in yet, so I really wasn't in the mood to deal with her.

Josh was a few feet away, talking to some of his friends from art class. He'd been hanging out with them more since Tessa's death, I supposed because they were detached from Tessa and me so therefore devoid of negative associations for him.

I sipped my coffee, continuing down the corridor and ignoring Tessa.

She followed me, trying to get in my face again. I dodged her a couple of times so that I didn't hit her. 'Hello? Can you hear me?'

Rolling my eyes, I put an earbud in and tucked my hair behind my ear. 'Contrary to popular belief, I'm not a private detective. I am, in fact, just a student.'

She sneered. 'No one else here can see me. Something about you is different.'

'Doesn't make me a private investigator. Or obligated to help you. Let's also not forget that I'm not getting paid to do this crap.'

'I need to find who murdered me!'

'And I'm working on it.' Sort of. 'But it's not that simple because once we've found them, we need—'

Someone pushed past me, causing me to stumble in Tessa's direction. Luckily, she jumped back on instinct so I didn't fall into her.

I turned around, but the offender was scurrying off, totally oblivious to the problems they'd almost caused me. Git. 'I'm fine, thanks for asking,' I said, half to the offender and half to Tessa.

Straightening myself up, I carried on walking to my next lesson. 'I get that you're impatient, but I have a lot going on right now. So either you back off, or I'm not going to help. Understood?'

Tessa lowered her head.

'Good.'

*

When I got home, Mum was asleep on the sofa with Tilly. I crept past them into the kitchen. Ben was in there, making dinner.

'Hey,' I said. 'Not that I'm not pleased to see you, but shouldn't you be at work?'

He gestured for me to come closer, lowering his voice so that he didn't wake Mum and Tilly. 'Your mum found another victim earlier.'

'*What*?'

Ben nodded. 'She's pretty shaken up.'

Of course she was. She found a dead body! Who wouldn't be shaken up by that?

'And she thinks a ghost did it,' he added.

'What? But how? I thought only necromancers could touch ghosts.'

'It's complicated.' Ben stirred whatever was sizzling on the stove, then gestured to the breakfast bar. We both sat down. 'For the most part, yes, you're right. But as I'm sure you've seen or read about in some hauntings, there are times when ghosts can interact with objects and even people. It takes a lot of power. Generally, only poltergeists can touch people because anger is one of the strongest emotions. To sustain the amount of power required to kill and dismember a victim, it requires more than either of us have ever encountered before.'

'What about when Dad was killed?' I didn't know the full story, but I knew it had been at the hands of a poltergeist.

Well, now I did, anyway. Mum had originally told me he'd died in a car accident. I'd only recently found out the truth – because of Dominic – but I was over that now. Mostly.

'From what I know, it was a flash of power that flung your dad across the room. This is different. Long, drawn out, calculated. Cold.'

'So like a ghost super charged by how angry they are?'

'Basically.'

I picked up a blue fabric stress ball from the kitchen table and squished it in my hands. What could I say? What could I even think? Should I wake Mum up to check on her, or let her sleep?

'Could it be something else? Something that isn't a ghost?'

Ben tapped the side of the unit beside him. 'It seems unlikely. Gwendoline managed to get access to the victims' autopsies and their causes of death sound too much like they'd been done by a human. And their dismembered limbs are done with almost surgical precision.'

I shuddered, reluctant to hear the answer to my next question. But I needed to know: 'Does this mean we have a serial-killing ghost on our hands?'

'We believe so, yes.'

'Frazzle.'

'We also think the next step should be to speak to one of the victims,' said Ben.

I looked up and met his eye. 'So we'll start with the latest victim, right? Their memories will be freshest.'

'Actually, I think the best person to speak to first might be Tessa.'

I groaned. 'Why?' Anyone but her. *Anyone.*

'As far as we know, she's the only victim who's stayed behind. She's closer, and she's been asking for your help solving her murder. Personal issues aside, she's the most logical option.'

'I know you're right, but I'd just like it to be known I really hate this idea.'

18

Niamh

I woke up from my nap with an even worse headache than when I'd fallen asleep. Had someone hit me with a bag of rocks while I was asleep? There was a weird taste in my mouth, too. I needed something to get rid of it, but that required moving. Why couldn't my powers be more useful?

Why hadn't I taught Tilly to fetch my things for me?

Slowly. I needed to move slowly.

First, I swung my legs around. Then I paused, because my head was throbbing again. Nope, I wasn't going to keep going without more painkillers.

'Edie,' I croaked.

She appeared from the kitchen. 'How are you feeling?'

'Water and painkillers please,' I said. 'Why do I feel so terrible?'

'Do you remember what happened?'

I squeezed my eyes shut. The hand. The probably dismembered hand.

'I found…was it another victim?'

'Probably.' Edie leaned against the doorframe. 'Ben had an idea, before he left to check on Fadil. He thinks we should summon Tessa.'

I wrinkled my nose. Despite how much I disliked the idea, the more I thought about it, the more it felt like our only option. 'Do you want to summon her?'

'No, but I think we need to,' she said with a sigh.

'All right. Once I've had a drink we can get started.'

'You don't have to help. I can do this on my own, or get Ben to come over. You should rest,' said Edie.

I smiled. 'Thank you for worrying about me, but I'll be fine.' Probably.

*

While I didn't like the idea of summoning my daughter's bully into my living room, I was also aware that we needed to find out what she knew to get rid of her sooner. Talking to her with Josh around was out of the question, and the only way to temporarily break her tie to him was to summon her.

So, our options were limited. We moved the living room furniture out of the way, then created a thick salt circle around the room, just in case. And shut Tilly in the kitchen with a fish treat. I'd tried to kick Spectre out, but in true cat style he refused to move. So he floated above the sofa, watching us, instead.

'Are you ready?' I asked Edie.

She stood in front of the window – which had the curtains closed, obviously – while I stood opposite her. She took a deep breath. 'As I'll ever be.'

I nodded and we recited the spell.

Tessa appeared, looking around in confusion. 'Oh. I always wondered what your house would look like.'

She paused, studying our small living room. 'Not what I expected.'

I almost asked what she'd envisaged, but I honestly didn't care. Edie clearly did. 'What did you expect?'

'Something messier and more goth. Less grey. Did you know grey is the millennial beige?' She gave me a dirty look. Yes, I was an elder millennial. She could also kiss my ass. It was our house and Edie and I were happy with it.

I rolled my eyes. 'Would you like to continue insulting our interior decoration or would you prefer to find your murderer?'

Tessa studied her fake nails. Why I didn't know. It wasn't like the pink marble-effect gel nails would ever fall off now that she was dead. And she'd never be able to change the colour of them again. Or salvage her natural nails. 'I'm listening.' She couldn't have looked less interested if she'd tried, but I had a feeling she was putting on a front. People like her got good at doing that to protect themselves.

'Tell us what you know,' I said.

'Like what?'

Edie crossed her arms. 'It's a fairly simple question. What do you remember about your murder? Or do you just not want to find out who killed you? And continue haunting Josh for the rest of your afterlife, seeing him move on with someone else and being helpless to stop it?'

Tessa stiffened. Edie had clearly hit a nerve.

I was pretty sure she'd described what it'd felt like when Josh had moved on with Tessa, but I doubted she wanted Tessa to know that. Admitting that would've been a weakness in Tessa's eyes. And therefore more ammunition. Like she needed any more.

Tessa clenched her jaw and her fists, clearly arguing with herself about if she should help us.

'Just imagine: if you stay as a ghost, you'll have no one to talk to except for us and our friends,' I said, smirking. Being stuck that way would definitely bother her. Pretty much every ghost got bored of talking to the same people all the time unless they were deluded or loners. It was why most crossed over or became angry, and eventually, poltergeists. There were exceptions, of course, like Thomas and Gwendoline, but they were rare.

Tessa's eyes went wide. Gotcha.

'I don't remember much. It's all kind of blurry.'

'Start with what you do remember. Some ghosts find it comes back to them as they replay it,' I said.

Ghosts often suppressed the memories of how they'd died because it was traumatic. They blocked it out to protect themselves, particularly if they'd met a violent end like Tessa had. I didn't really blame them. But in this case, we needed something or we had no chance of catching her murderer.

'OK. Um…I was walking back from a party. It wasn't that late. Maybe just after one? I wasn't that drunk. There wasn't much alcohol there, and the stuff there was cheap and lame, so I just made out with Josh for most of it.'

Edie flinched. If Tessa noticed, she didn't react.

'Then I felt…something hit me. From behind. I face planted the grass.' She tried to spit, as if getting rid of the grass from her mouth. 'It tasted gross. But that wasn't the worst of it. He rolled me over. Then he started punching me, I think.' She froze, turned away, and curled into herself. It couldn't have been easy reliving all of that. We were hearing it, sure, but she was seeing and feeling it all over again.

'Thank you, Tessa. I know this must be hard for you.' Compassion was always important in a situation like that, even if the person receiving said compassion didn't know how to return the favour. Also it would calm her down enough to get her to answer my next question: 'Can you remember anything about what he looked like?'

She paused, turning back around. Biting her lip, she looked around as if she was a startled child. Her gaze landed on Spectre, who was hovering above the back of the sofa. 'You have a ghost cat?'

I shrugged. 'Came with the house.'

Her shoulders fell. 'Must be nice for him, living with people who can see him. I wonder how many houses are haunted by animals.'

'Not many, as far as I've seen. It's pretty rare thankfully,' I replied.

She nodded slowly, her eyes glazing over. 'That's good. That's good. The…the monster who did it was…I think…really tall.' Her nodding increased in pace as his image returned to her. 'Yeah. Yeah. He had on some sort of hat and an apron. Was this guy in fancy dress or something?'

We paused, not looking at her.

'Wait. Do people dress like that? Was the red stuff on his apron…was it…*blood*?' Horror flickered across her face.

'Maybe,' I said. Who *was* this ghost?

'Whatever. That guy was a psycho.' She shuddered. Whenever something got too much for her, she seemed to dismiss it as if she didn't want to think about it too hard. I didn't really blame her, but it did make me sad for her. 'Is that everything? I was helping Josh revise.'

Edie folded her arms. 'How? He can't hear you.'

'I managed to nudge a couple of pieces of paper like, a millimetre. I'm sure he noticed.'

Edie and I exchanged a look of doubt. I supposed Tessa had to cling on to something to keep herself going.

'If you think of anything else, and you really do want us to solve this, will you tell Edie right away?' I said. Even though it was clear Tessa disliked me, I was hoping she'd still been raised to respect her elders. Or at the very least care enough about herself to cooperate with the only people who could help her.

She nodded. 'Yes.'

*

'Well that was a waste of time,' said Edie, sinking on to the sofa after Tessa had gone. Spectre was still hovering above it, so she stroked him while we talked.

'No it wasn't. We have a better idea of what he looks like.'

She looked up, a frustrated expression on her face. 'How does that help us defeat him?'

'It doesn't, but it might help with identification. Maybe he was a doctor or surgeon or dentist or something. It narrows down our search. Until we know what we're looking for, we don't know what's useful.'

I went into the cupboard under the stairs and took out the vacuum to get rid of the salt before I let Tilly back in. I didn't want her getting the grains stuck in between her toes or pads, or spreading salt through the rest of the house.

Edie hugged her feet to keep them away from the vacuum. Once I was done, I let Tilly in, and the four of us sat on the sofa, Edie stroking our ghost cat and me stroking our dog. What a group.

'Do you really think it'll lead to us finding something?' Edie asked. Her tone suggested she thought it was a dead end.

'It's more information than we had before, and every piece helps us to form some sort of image of what we're up against.' I put my hand on her arm. 'We're a long way off from giving up just yet.'

'We can't give up! I wasn't suggesting that! If we give up, he could come after any of us next!'

I stroked her hair, pulling her in to me. 'It's OK. We're not going anywhere. He's not going to get us. We have a lot more protection than your average victim does.'

Edie seemed to relax at this reminder. 'Yes, you're right.'

But truth be told, I was just as worried as she was. After all, I'd been hearing whistling since Tessa's death, and he still hadn't come for me. Was I on borrowed time?

19

Niamh

I didn't sleep well that night. All right, so I wasn't sleeping well anyway. This time was worse, though. Every time I closed my eyes, I pictured a different poltergeist torturing us. Since we didn't know who it was, or what they did, my overactive imagination had serious fun. I did not.

The only thing we knew for certain was that the serial-killing ghost struck in the middle of the night, so at least I could still have breakfast with Maggie. There was no point disrupting everything in my life because of yet another ghost. If I did that every time a crazy came to town I wouldn't have a life.

So, I had a cold shower to wake myself up, then went to see Maggie. I'd missed her breakfasts.

'Did you see the news?' Maggie asked as she opened the door to Tilly and me.

'I was part of the news,' I informed her as I pushed my sunglasses up my nose. The media hadn't found out what had happened right away, so I'd left before they could descend, keeping me away from any interviews. I was pretty confident the police wouldn't give my name out as the person who'd found the victim's body, so I was safe from them trying to get in touch with me. The last thing I wanted was my face on TV or in the local paper.

Maggie gasped. 'Was it something spooky that killed him?'

'You could say that,' I replied as Maggie closed the door and I let Tilly off her lead. The little dog sniffed the shoes by the door, re-familiarising herself with her second family.

'Wait. It *was*? I was joking.'

'Well maybe don't joke. Cause you might just be right.'

Maggie pursed her lips, crouching down to fuss Tilly. 'Maybe we should talk more about this later. Abigail's not feeling too well so I decided to keep her home. I hope you don't mind if she joins us.'

My heart swelled. I hadn't seen Abigail in forever. She was the sweetest little girl and I'd missed her. Her kindness and compassion was beyond many children her age, to the point where she reminded me of Edie when she was five. 'Nope. Don't mind at all,' I said, trying to hide the emotions welling inside of me at the thought of seeing her again.

Up until Maggie and I had stopped speaking, Edie and I had spoken to Abigail at least once a week, sometimes more. When we'd moved back to Hucknall, it had turned into an almost daily occurrence. She was almost like a second daughter to me, and I was pretty sure she saw Edie as her cool big sister.

Maggie, now carrying Tilly, went into the living room. Abigail looked up from the sofa as we walked in. 'Auntie Neevie! Tilly!' She jumped up from the sofa, covering Tilly in kisses which Tilly happily reciprocated. Abigail then ran over to me, wrapping me in a bear hug. She rested her head on my waist and I put my hand on her back, feeling like things were back to normal now that the three of us could hang out again.

Having her in my arms again reminded me of how much I'd missed her, and of how concerned I was about her. She'd been possessed by a demon just a few weeks ago. We had no idea how long she'd been possessed for, or if it had caused any long-term damage.

Sometimes the damage done could take years to appear, just like with any other kind of childhood trauma. I couldn't handle it if something bad happened to Abigail because of that demon. A demon that had possessed her to get to Edie. At the time, we hadn't known why the demon wanted Edie. But now that we knew how powerful Edie was, it all made sense.

'All right, let Auntie Neevie go,' said Maggie, trying to prize her daughter away from me while still holding the dog. 'She's not going anywhere.'

Did what she was saying have multiple meanings? I was going to read into it and convince myself that that meant she was keeping me around, even if she only really meant that I was staying for breakfast.

Abigail ignored her mum and tightened her grip on me. I laughed. Then winced. Laughing hurt my head.

Maggie must've noticed, because she said, 'Auntie Neevie is poorly, too. You need to be gentle with her.'

Abigail looked up at me with her big, brown doe-eyes. She loosened her grip a little. 'Auntie Neevie? What's wrong?'

'My head is just a little sore, that's all. I'll be fine.'

Maggie shot me a concerned look. What? It was true.

Abigail let go and squeezed my hand instead. 'I'm sorry. Is that why you're wearing sunglasses and ear plugs?' She lowered her volume: 'Would you like me to whisper?'

I smiled. This girl was killing me with cuteness. If she carried on, my ovaries were going to explode. 'You don't have to whisper, just be gentle.'

'Why don't you play with Tilly while I finish making breakfast?' suggested Maggie.

Abigail grinned. 'Oh! Can I get Tilly her present, Mum?'

Present? What present?

Maggie looked at me to check it was OK. I shrugged. I didn't even know what it was, so how could I say?

'I think it's under the sink,' said Maggie.

Abigail scurried into the kitchen, ushering Tilly to follow her. The little dog was more than happy to do so.

'Abigail was really excited Tilly was coming over again, so I said she could get a toy I knew you'd approve of.'

A moment later, a larger-than-average tennis ball rolled into the living room. Tilly chased it, a giggling Abigail running after her.

'I thought with it being a bit bigger she couldn't chew it,' said Maggie. I'd missed her thoughtfulness. She really did consider everything.

'Thank you,' I said, my eyes welling with tears.

Maggie put her arm around my shoulder.

*

Breakfast with Maggie and Abigail was exactly what I'd needed. It was calming and healthy, distracting my brain from the flashbacks it was so keen on.

After we'd eaten, Abigail went for a nap, while Tilly fell asleep between Maggie and me in the living room. We were on our third cups of tea when the front door opened.

My back stiffened. Josh and Harry weren't so welcoming towards Edie and me. They still blamed us for everything that'd happened. They weren't technically wrong, but it was also a lot more complicated than that.

Either way, I had to face them eventually, I supposed.

Josh entered the lounge, Tessa close behind him. I tried my best not to look at her so that I didn't encourage her. We still hadn't told Maggie or Josh that he was being haunted by his dead girlfriend. While I hated keeping secrets from them, it was never something people wanted to hear. And they'd been through enough already.

Plus, knowing someone you couldn't see was following you around tended to freak people out and make them self-conscious. Especially when the ghost couldn't go that far away from whomever they were haunting, like Tessa couldn't.

When Josh saw me sitting next to his mum, he froze. His hands curled into fists. His jaw tightened. I didn't think he'd hurt me, but seeing the boy I'd watched grow up stand there, so angry at my presence in the same room as him and his Mum, hurt.

Tessa tried to mimic his posture. It didn't look threatening on her, it looked kind of sad.

Tilly looked up from her napping spot between Maggie and me. Spotting him, she ran over, jumping up and barking excitedly. He ignored her. Meanie. The dog hadn't done anything wrong. Why punish her?

'Are you kidding me? After everything they've put us through, you're letting her back in? Don't you get it? She's the reason everything that's happened to you, me, and Abigail, happened! How *could* you?'

I clenched my jaw.

Tilly, realising Josh wasn't going to give her any attention, returned to her spot between Maggie and me on the sofa. I rubbed between her ears.

'Be careful, your sister is asleep upstairs,' said Maggie in her best Mum Voice. 'And no, it isn't Niamh's fault. She's a friend, be polite.'

Tessa rolled her eyes.

While they were arguing about my daughter and me, this felt more like a mother/son argument, so I bit my tongue and let Maggie say what she needed to. Given how much Josh hated me, anything I said could make things worse instead of better. If anyone was going to win him around, it would be Maggie or Abigail, not Edie or me.

Josh crossed his arms. 'How can you say it isn't her fault? *Everything* happened because of them!'

It was so nice to know what he thought of Edie and me. He couldn't even say our names anymore he hated us so much.

'Niamh and Edie have names, Joshua,' said Maggie, her Mum Voice deepening. She didn't use it very often. Her children being so well-behaved, she seldom needed to. It was a shame she had to use now. I was almost honoured she was using it to stand up for me. 'Niamh and I have been friends for decades. This is the first time something has happened that's affected us because of what her family can do. So instead of blaming her and Edie, how about blaming Dominic instead? He's the one responsible for what happened to us.'

'I always knew that Dominic was a weirdo,' said Tessa.

I rolled my eyes. This was none of her business.

'Don't roll your eyes at me.'

Fiddlesticks. I hadn't expected her to notice.

Tessa shoved her face into mine. She had the height on me, since I was still sitting, but that was it. 'You're just a family of freaks.'

'*Exorcism*,' I mouthed. If I spoke it aloud, Maggie and Josh would've noticed I was talking to someone else. Although they seemed to be pretty engrossed in their argument, so maybe they wouldn't.

My threat worked. Fear flickered in Tessa's eyes. She backed off, hiding behind Josh. Ha.

Josh shook his head. 'I can't believe you're being this naive.'

'Don't talk to your mum like that!' I interjected. So much for staying out of it. But Maggie was no idiot. She knew what she was doing. I wasn't going to let Josh talk to her like that. 'Despite what you seem to think, she's an intelligent woman.'

'Oh I know she is. That's why I don't get why she's kept you around.'

Wow. Where had the polite, considerate young man gone? This was not the person Maggie had raised.

I was really glad Edie wasn't around to hear his words, because they were designed to burn. And they did.

'That's enough,' said Maggie. 'Go to your room until you find your manners again.'

'You'd better add bars and a letterbox to my door, then,' said Josh. He stormed out, slamming every door he could on his way to his bedroom. Tessa floated away behind him.

'I'm so sorry about that,' said Maggie. 'I had no idea he was coming home early. He usually goes to the library if he has a free period.'

'That's OK. It wasn't your fault.'

Maggie stared into her lap, shaking her head. 'Wasn't it? He's my son.'

Tilly nudged her leg, as if sensing she was upset. The cure for that, in Tilly's eyes? Fussing a cute westie called Tilly, of course.

'Yeah, but you can't control how he responds to what happens to him. Or who he blames for it.'

Still staring into her lap, she blinked back tears. 'I just wish he'd talk to someone! Alanis has tried, but he won't open up to her. Or me. Or...anyone. It's like he's put up a wall around himself. I've never known him to be so closed off.'

I put my hand on her shoulder. Tilly climbed on to her lap and licked her face. Maggie giggled, stroking the cream streak on Tilly's back.

'You can't blame yourself, Mags. It's not on you how he processes – or doesn't process – what he's been through.'

Maggie sighed. 'I know you're right. But that doesn't mean I have to like it.'

20

Niamh

'I'm sure Josh didn't mean it,' said Ben, picking up his chickpea wrap and biting into it. We were out for lunch and I'd just finished venting to him about what'd happened at Maggie's place. Hard as I tried, I couldn't get Josh's angry expression out of my head.

'I'm sure he did. He was just so *angry*. Like a totally different person.' My shoulders dropped at the memory of Josh's reaction to me.

Ben frowned. 'He's been through a lot and isn't emotionally mature enough to process any of it. Most of us wouldn't be. He just needs time.'

'Yeah, I hope you're right.' I continued eating my food without really paying attention to it. I was too focused on everything else going on to enjoy – or even really process – what I was eating. It was fuel, nothing more.

To distract myself from how Josh's words had hurt me, I eavesdropped on the conversations around us. A table of four people in suits were clearly talking about work. Yawn. A couple gazed into each other's eyes, lovingly discussing their upcoming wedding. I wasn't sure whether to find that one cute or nauseating.

But I didn't have much time to think on it, because I heard the table closest to us mutter the words 'serial killer'. Which gave me an idea.

'What about a seance? To summon one of the other victims?'

Ben nodded, taking another bite of his food. Once he'd swallowed, he said: 'It's a start. They might remember more than Tessa. Or something else that could offer us some new insights.'

'Let's hope so.'

Although, to be fair, being more helpful than Tessa wasn't hard. And everyone would remember something different, so it might give us more to go on.

After we'd finished lunch, we set up my living room, put Tilly in the kitchen, and drew a salt circle. Since we didn't know anything about who we were summoning, and there was a murderer on the loose, I wasn't taking any chances. The ghost appeared without hesitation. He was a middle-aged Pakistani man in a sharp, grey suit with a warm smile. But he did look very confused about why he was in my living room, which was fair enough.

'I was just about to strike a deal!'

'With who? You're dead!' Not my most tactful response, admittedly, but seriously. Who was he striking a deal with?

He straightened his collar. 'That's none of your business. Who are you?'

Unable to stop myself, I glanced down at his right hand. It looked a lot like the one Tilly had found, but less rubbery. I suppressed a shudder.

'We're trying to find who murdered you,' said Ben.

The guy recoiled slightly. 'It's patchy. And it was dark, so I didn't see much. But the guy almost… glowed? People don't glow! I must've been hallucinating.'

I gestured to him.

He looked down at himself. He, too, had a slight glow to him. He was surprisingly opaque, too, which meant he'd had some sort of power when he was alive, whether that was mental, physical, or magical.

He gasped. 'I was murdered by a ghost?'

'We believe so, yes,' confirmed Ben. 'Do you remember anything about him? Anything at all?'

'Who *are* you?'

Sigh. I supposed he did deserve some answers. We were asking fairly personal questions in an impatient and untactful way. Which was my style. Clearly Ben was getting worried, too, and not thinking.

'My name is Niamh. I'm a ghost hunter. This is Ben, a witch. We're trying to find the person responsible for your death so that he can't hurt anyone else.'

'A ghost serial killer?' He let out a long, low whistle. 'Wait! He whistled! That was the last thing I heard before I passed out. Then, I woke up like this.' He gestured to his spectral form.

Goosebumps formed on my arms. His murderer had…whistled? So I *had* been hearing the killer, all this time?

Ben glanced at me, his eyes wide. He'd suggested it was tinnitus, but apparently it was something much,

much worse. Was I connected to the murderous ghost in some way?

'Did you see what he looked like?' I asked, trying to keep the conversation on track while my heart was pounding. What did it mean if I could hear him before he killed?

'Now that I think about it, I heard this weird noise for a few days before, too. It was so jarring I couldn't sleep.'

Gulp.

'What was the sound like?' asked Ben.

'Um...disconcerting. Unnatural. Hard to pin down.'

Ben inhaled, keeping his face as neutral as he could. He was connecting the dots, too.

The ghost continued, oblivious to our revelations: 'He had on a bloody apron over the top of some fancy looking suit. Way too formal. Almost Victorian, maybe? Is that possible? I was murdered by a ghost that's older than my grandparents?'

Ben and I exchanged looks.

'It's possible,' said Ben.

It's not what we'd considered, though. It was rare for ghosts that old to still be around, although when they were, they were usually causing trouble or recently disturbed. Looked like our new friend was both.

*

'I'm sorry I didn't believe you about the whistling,' said Ben after our ghost friend had returned to the Other Side.

I fell back on to the sofa, the warm fabric engulfing me. 'I don't blame you. I wouldn't have believed me, either.'

He sat beside me, pulling me into his arms. I curled into him, wishing we could stay there and not have to deal with a crazy, murderous ghost. But it wasn't that simple. We were the only ones who could stop him.

The question of whether or not I was next because I'd been hearing the whistling hung in the air. But something about it didn't make sense. If I was a target, why had I heard it more than the other victims?

*

Ben stayed as long as he could, but eventually, he had to return to work. So I went to find Thomas. He was a Victorian ghost – he might know something. I wandered through the graveyard, the frosty grass crunching under my leather boots. There were still no signs of him. Now I was getting worried. He hardly ever left the graveyard, let alone for so long. And he always appeared when we called him.

Edie had popped in a couple of times around college, but she hadn't seen him either. Neither had Ben, and the library where he worked looked out on to parts of the graveyard. He used to see Thomas playing football with himself fairly often, but he hadn't seen him at all since Tessa's death. Had the ghost hurt him? If the ghost had hurt him, I was going to make his exorcism extra painful.

Feeling hopeless, I went to see Gwendoline. She hadn't been haunting the town as long as Thomas had, since she'd been trapped in a collapsed mine for a couple of centuries, but she was resourceful and knew where to find information.

'Hey Niamh.'

'Thanks for the autopsy reports you gave Ben. That, along with a couple of other bits of information we've gathered, proved we're dealing with a ghost.'

Gwendoline widened her eyes. 'A serial-killing ghost? I didn't even think that was possible.'

I sighed. 'Neither did we.'

Instead of sitting down like I usually did, I paced up and down the park's path, my phone to my ear, as if I was talking on it. 'We know what he looks like, and what he does, but we still don't know his name or his motivations. And the Victorian era is too long for us to search through without narrowing it down, especially when we don't know if he's a local ghost or not.'

Gwendoline hovered along beside me, her hands behind her back. 'I can put the word out, see if anyone knows anything else?'

'Thank you, but be careful. This ghost can't know we're on to him.'

'You think it'd make us a target?'

'It's possible.'

Gwendoline frowned. She was the matriarch for a bunch of ghosts who were lost after their deaths but weren't ready to cross over. She understood my need to protect people. 'I'll see what I can find out. I can't guarantee there'll be anything else, but I'll do my best.'

'Thanks. Have you heard anything from Thomas yet?'

'No. Is he still missing?'

'Yeah. If he'd crossed over, Javi would've said. There's something about this that feels off, I just can't put my finger on what it is.'

'Did you try summoning him?'

'I'm worried it might do more harm than good, especially if someone like the ghost responsible for these murders has found him.'

Gwendoline pursed her lips. 'You're right. You know him better than I do, so if you feel that something is off, I believe you. I have some friends who will help look for him, and search for information. They're discreet and won't alert anyone questionable to what's happening. Just be careful in the meantime, please?'

'I will.'

21

Niamh

'Niamh?'

'Thomas! Oh my god, we've been so worried about you!'

He hovered a few feet away, but didn't look like his usual self. While he was usually translucent, today he was barely visible. He looked shaken, too. As if something – or some*one* – had really spooked him.

I shifted over on the sofa, as if he'd be able to sit beside me. 'What's wrong?'

Thomas floated over, hovering in the vacant spot on the sofa. Tilly trotted in from the kitchen and sat between us. She was too tired from her walk to get excited, but she did seem to like Thomas's presence. Spectre floated in through the wall, settling at Thomas's feet.

'I got your message from Gwendoline. I'm sorry I worried you.' He stared into his hands, rubbing them together. I'd never seen him nervous before. It concerned me.

Although he'd never said why, I always assumed he rarely left the graveyard because he felt safest staying there. It *was* mostly free from the living and the dead, with just a few visits at certain times of the day. Plus, it was quite serene in there. Tall trees, well-kept gravestones from the last two hundred years, a pretty church and library…what more could a ghost need?

'I know…I know who's been murdering people.'

Faking calm to keep him at ease, I turned to face him, tucking one of my feet underneath me and letting the other dangle over the edge of the sofa. 'Did you know them?'

Thomas rubbed his hands together some more, then faced me. 'We weren't friends or anything. He was a little older than me and studying to become a doctor. His name was Dr Randolph Goodfellow.' Talk about an ironic name. Thomas let his words hang in the air before continuing. 'Doctors were different, back then. They didn't know as much as they didn't believe in germ theory, so a lot of their treatments were risky and experimental.' Goosebumps formed on my arms. Where was Thomas going with this? I wasn't sure I wanted to know, but I knew that I needed to if we were ever going to stop Goodfellow. 'He liked to experiment. I mean, a lot of surgeries back then were untested anyway, since we didn't have anaesthesia. But he took things too far.'

'Further than cutting people open when they're still awake?'

Thomas shrugged. 'You did what you had to do to stay alive. Or try to, anyway.' He removed his flatcap, twisting it in his hands. 'He realised that if he took someone's life in a certain way, he could steal their power.'

'Like…magical powers?'

Thomas nodded. 'It was more acceptable back then, to believe. It's only recently it's become less mainstream.'

'How do you know all this?'

'I'm a ghost. I can eavesdrop pretty easily. And I live next to a library. I've got to do something all day and night.'

'Right. Sorry. You were saying.'

Tilly stood up, walked in a circle, then lay back down with her head on my lap. I stroked her neck as her eyes flitted closed again.

'He didn't have powers, originally. But he learned how to harness them. It wasn't just about powers in the way you're thinking. There are other types of power, too: intelligence, beauty, strength, humour, things like that. He discovered he could acquire them in the same way he took magical powers. So he did.'

'How many powers did he take?' Forewarned was forearmed, and all that.

'I don't know,' said Thomas. 'He was difficult to take down, though. It took a witch and a necromancer working together to do it. Whatever happened in there, the house burned down, taking him and his pet raven, Branwen, with him.' He had a pet raven? Why did anything even surprise me anymore? 'They were buried together in the cemetery by the park.'

Of course someone who was well respected in the area would've been buried in a nice cemetery. Little did they realise what he was really capable of. It made me angry someone like him had done so much damage and was still seen as an upstanding member of society.

'Why not the one by your church?'

Thomas frowned. 'Like I care. He was away from me. That was all that mattered.' He hesitated, as if he wanted to say something else but wasn't sure if he should or could.

'What is it? What aren't you saying?'

Thomas pursed his lips. 'This is going to sound paranoid, but…I always thought he'd come back. I don't know why. There was just something about him that felt unfinished.'

'Because of how the witch and necromancer took him down?'

'Because of how powerful and determined he was.'

I shivered. Power and determination went a long way in the natural and supernatural worlds. 'I would've felt the same way.' And did about a certain someone.

A small smile traced his lips, as if knowing it wasn't just him offered him some comfort.

'Do you know what the witch and necromancer did?'

'No, I'm sorry.' He looked down, into his flatcap, as if genuinely ashamed of himself.

I reached out, my hand hovering over his. It was the closest I could get to offering him a comforting touch. 'Hey, it's OK. You've already been a massive help.'

He seemed to perk up at that. 'Really?' he said, his voice full of hope.

I nodded. 'Really. Now that we have his name, we can search the library, the internet, the archives, maybe even the Other Side, to see what comes up. We'll have more answers in no time.'

Thomas grinned. But then it fell again. He glanced out the window, as if everything on the other side of it was out to get him.

'What is it?'

He twisted his cap some more, looking away from me. 'Could I stay here, please? Until he's gone?'

'Are you afraid of him?'

Thomas's face tensed. 'Terrified.'

22

Edie

I got home from college to find Thomas playing with Spectre. 'Thomas! You're OK!' I ran over and hugged him. He hugged me back, resting his head on my stomach. Spectre glared, annoyed he'd lost his playmate.

'Sorry for scaring you,' Thomas mumbled into my coat.

I rubbed his shoulder. 'It's OK. So long as *you're* OK?' I crouched down to get to his eye level. 'Are you?'

Mum walked in from the kitchen, a serious look on her face. 'Ben and Fadil are coming over after Ben finishes work. Thomas has information we all need to hear.'

Well that sounded ominous.

*

Once Ben and Fadil had arrived, Mum and Thomas took no time to fill us in on the crazy Victorian doctor.

I sat on the floor, playing tug-of-war with Tilly and a rope squirrel toy. 'If he's attracted to power, I have to ask: why Tessa?'

'As much as we hate her, she does have skills he could benefit from. Her ghost wouldn't be so clear otherwise,' said Mum.

I grumbled, yanking on the squirrel and pulling it away from Tilly. She glared, waiting for me to give it back. I offered it to her, but she reached for my slobber-free end instead. I didn't want to grab the super slobbery end of her toy, but I did, needing the distraction of playing with her to keep me semi-calm.

'Based on the doctor's desire for power, does that mean we're all at risk?' asked Ben, always the one to bring up the hard questions.

The five of us exchanged glances. Nobody wanted to be the one to say it, but we all knew anyway.

'Well isn't that just marvellous?' said Fadil. He coughed into his elbow before continuing, his voice getting huskier the more he spoke: 'I spent four thousand years mummified in a sarcophagus to be murdered by a psychopathic Victorian doctor a few weeks after being resurrected!' He flapped his arms in the air.

'Let's not get ahead of ourselves,' said Ben, standing up and pacing the living room.

Thomas moved out of his way, opting to stand in the middle of the coffee table. 'We know who he is and what his MO is. Now, we just need a plan.'

'A plan to take down the murderous doctor who has unexpected powers we may not even know about or be able to compete with?' said Fadil. He held his nose to stop himself from sneezing.

'Let's be pragmatic about this,' said Ben, glaring at our melodramatic, germ-infested friend. 'If we let our emotions take control, the situation will be a lot harder to fix.'

'He's right,' Mum agreed. 'As tempting as it is to spiral right now, we have to focus. He strikes me as the type of person who'll be able to exploit our weaknesses.'

'Which means we need to lean into our strengths,' finished Ben.

'Like being alive?' said Fadil, letting go of his nose. 'What strengths do we possibly have against this guy?'

'Each other,' said Thomas. 'And he's a ghost. We know Edie's and Ben's powers work on ghosts, and Niamh's should more now, too.'

'You're right,' said Ben, nodding. 'But we don't know how Fadil's power leeching is affecting Edie. This doesn't feel like the right time to test things.'

'We may not have a choice,' I said.

Ben pursed his lips.

'Maybe we should swap back,' Mum suggested. 'Your powers are more useful than mine anyway.'

'No! We can't swap back at the first hurdle! We swapped in the first place because me with lesser powers is still more powerful than you with wonky powers.'

Mum's shoulders slumped. She knew I was right.

'What about me?' said Fadil.

'What do you mean?' I asked.

'Well, I could give you your power back and just not be able to talk.'

'No,' said Ben. 'We need to be able to communicate. Maybe one day, but right now we may need to make quick decisions.'

Fadil nodded. 'So, what? We just hang around in a group until we know what to do?'

'At least in pairs when it's dark,' said Mum. 'I'm sure Gwendoline will help if we need her, too. If something were to happen, she'd be able to pass a message on pretty quickly.'

'It's December. How are we going to do that when it gets dark so early and our schedules are so different?' I said.

'I'm not sure it's just the dark that puts us at risk,' said Ben. 'So far, he's only attacked late at night, probably to minimise the risk of being seen. So as long as we're home before everywhere gets too quiet, we should be fine.'

'You're right,' said Mum. 'He won't want to risk being caught, so he's only going to attack when there's a lower risk of people being around.'

I pursed my lips. While I understood their reasoning I didn't want to be babysat. I was eighteen, not eight!

'How will he know when his victim is going to be out late, though? Not everyone makes a habit of wandering around at two in the morning,' said Fadil.

'If he's targeting specific people, he's likely to be patient enough to wait to get what he wants,' said Ben.

I shuddered. This guy was getting creepier by the minute.

'While your info is great, Thomas, we need to know how to take him down,' I said.

'Could you talk to Javi, ask him if he can find the witch and necromancer who got rid of him last time?' suggested Thomas.

'Javi!' Mum shouted.

He appeared within seconds. Bowing, he said: 'At your service.'

It was impossible not to laugh at him. 'Would you be able to locate some ghosts for us?'

'I can try,' he said as he returned to standing. Well, floating. 'Who are we looking for?'

We all looked to Thomas, hoping he knew their names. Thankfully, he did. 'Millicent and Percival Hill.'

'And why am I locating these particular spirits?'

'They stopped a serial killer in Victorian times who's returned as a ghost. We're hoping they can give us some information,' said Mum.

Dad nodded. 'I'll see what I can do!' Without another word, he vanished. I swear sometimes Dad liked to pretend he was our very own genie.

'There's someone else who might be able to give you more information on him,' said Thomas, flickering in and out of view. Ghosts only did that when they were afraid. Who *was* this person? Thomas wrapped his arms around himself. 'They didn't necessarily get along, but they studied together. He knows him better than most people.'

'Who?' said Fadil.

We all leaned forwards in our seats, apprehensive to hear who could give us the potentially insightful information.

Thomas took his hat off and twisted it in his hands. 'The alchemist.'

23

Niamh

'No.'

'But Mum!' Edie waved her arms in the air, almost hitting the sofa as she did so.

'I said no.' My voice was calm, even though, inside, I felt anything but. I hoped it conveyed to Edie that what I was saying wasn't open to negotiation.

'It makes sense,' she argued.

I shook my head, pointing at her. 'It does not make sense for this to interrupt your college work so close to your final exams. I will not have anything – natural or supernatural – damage your exam results, do you hear me?'

Edie huffed, folding her arms over her chest. 'It's not going to interfere. How am I supposed to concentrate with all this happening?'

'You'll find a way.'

I was really glad Ben and Fadil had gone home and that Thomas was still upstairs with Spectre. The three of them witnessing our argument would've felt too much like airing dirty laundry and brought back too many bad childhood memories.

'What if I don't want to?' Her folded arms tightened around her.

'What's *that* supposed to mean?' Was she implying she didn't want to study? That she didn't feel it was worth it? Oh no she didn't.

'I don't even want to go to uni anyway! So what's the point?'

'*What?*' If I could've spit fire, I would've. 'You will not miss out on educational opportunities because of this crap! Your studies are more important than that!'

'But all this is so much bigger than my studies! Why don't you get that?'

I rolled my eyes. 'I do get that, Edie. But you deserve a life, too, don't you? You deserve to be educated and happy and have friends and do all the other normal things that kids your age do. Otherwise, you'll just get more and more isolated as you get older. And trust me: that's not a fun place to be.'

Edie's shoulders slumped. She knew I was talking from experience. My whole school had found out that I could see ghosts before I'd done my GCSEs, and it'd ruined my last couple of years of school as a result. I was lucky because I'd had Javi, Maggie, and Manju by my side, standing up for me when people called me crazy. Although sometimes, it was the people who believed that were worse – they saw me as some sort of messiah, or prophet, or messenger, and wanted to follow me around like lost sheep. I was so not a leader, nor did I want to be. My friends had helped keep everyone off my back.

Edie didn't have that, though.

Josh had been her only friend at college, and now he could barely look at her. Barely acknowledge her presence. If she sacrificed her studies for the supernatural, I wasn't sure if she'd ever be able to fully recover. It was a dangerous path to go down. She needed people without powers to keep her grounded. She was already surrounded by too many people who had powers as it was.

'Look, I get it,' I said, trying to reach out to her. She jerked away so that I couldn't touch her. As much as it hurt, I didn't blame her. 'You want to save the world. You don't want anyone else to get hurt. But you can do just as much from college.'

While I only half-believed that, it did seem to perk her up.

'What do you mean?'

I sat on the sofa, the adrenaline from our argument wearing off.

I patted the spot on the sofa beside me. Edie took a seat, turning slightly towards me, but also keeping farther away than she usually would've.

'Tessa is the only victim we know of who hasn't crossed over,' I explained. 'We never know when she'll be able to remember something. It could also make her ghost form a target for Goodfellow.'

'You think?'

'I don't know,' I confessed. 'Right now, we don't know enough about him to know what his end game is. All we know is that he's desperate for power. But the way he sought it when he was alive is unlikely to work when he's dead. Powers don't work the same without a body. If he hasn't figured that out yet, he will soon. Then he'll panic.'

'So you want me to keep an eye out? See if he appears at college? Doesn't that put Josh at risk when he's at home?'

'I don't think he'd show up in rooms full of people, but he might be watching somehow. There has to be some way that he scouts his victims. If we can find that, we might be able to find out more about him or even how to get to him.'

Edie nodded. 'All right, fine. I'll go to college in the morning. But after, I'm going to see Tobias to see what he knows.'

I clenched my teeth. 'I can't go with you. I have a client meeting.'

'That's fine. Fadil can come,' she said. An answer for everything.

'Are you sure he'll be up for that?'

'I'm sure he'll be up for an excuse to get out of the house,' she said. 'And he won't want me to go alone, so even if he doesn't want to go, he'll come anyway.'

And she'd got me. There was nothing else I could say or do to stop her from visiting the bloody alchemist.

'All right, fine. But you don't skip your studies because of Goodfellow. Got it?'

'Got it.'

24
Edie

To help us process Tessa's passing, Mr Hazelock organised for a memorial to be held in the courtyard before college.

It wasn't mandatory, but a lot of people seemed to be turning up an hour or so early, to either pay their respects or be nosy. I wasn't sure which. I was the latter.

While I really wanted to visit Tobias and see what answers he could give us, I'd agreed with Mum I'd wait until the end of the day. She seemed to think I might get useful information from college, so I got up early and went to Tessa's memorial.

She'd been popular. The amount of people who'd turned up really shouldn't have surprised me. Most people seemed to know her name even if they hadn't gone to school with her, or weren't in any of her classes. She was just that kind of person.

She was floating around the courtyard, trying to eavesdrop on conversations while everyone congregated, waiting for Mr Hazelock to speak. She couldn't get to many people, though, because everyone was huddled together to keep warm. It was so cold I could see people's breath when they spoke.

An impromptu stage had been set up at one end of the courtyard, with a microphone and speaker on it. Directly in front of it was a row of seats featuring Tessa's parents, Josh, Melanie, and Laura.

Above, I was almost sure I saw a glowing raven circling the courtyard, but it was too far away for me to see for definite. Was it a ghost raven? Didn't Goodfellow have a raven? I had a ghost cat. A ghost raven wasn't totally ridiculous, was it?

Had Goodfellow sent it to spy on us, somehow? Could a raven do that, let alone as a ghost? I stepped back into the shadows, just in case.

Mr Hazelock stepped on to the stage, stood in front of the microphone, and cleared his throat. 'Hello, everyone. Thank you for coming. I'm sorry we've come together under such tragic circumstances.'

Tessa floated over to him and stood next to him, looking out over the crowd. She nodded, a smirk creeping over her pretty face. Of course she was going to enjoy this.

'Tessa was a remarkable student. She touched the lives of many of us here, as today's turnout shows.'

What Mr Hazelock wasn't factoring in was that many people were glad to be rid of her, something I'd heard a few people allude to while eavesdropping on their conversations. They weren't *exactly* speaking ill of the dead, but they sure weren't saying anything nice, either.

Mr Hazelock continued to talk about how great Tessa was. I ignored him, instead listening to what the people around me were whispering. I vaguely knew some of them, but not well enough to know their names. I'd only seen them in passing. Judging from how they spoke, they'd been in Tessa's classes.

'What's he on about? She was an insufferable know-it-all. No one else ever got the chance to answer questions in class because she always butted in. Hardly ever even put her hand up. And the teachers didn't notice,' said one girl.

Her friend leaned in to her to reply: 'The teachers noticed all right. They just didn't care. She was too far up their arses.'

The first speaker snorted, covering her face with a gloved hand. 'Should we be saying this at her memorial?'

The friend shrugged. 'Who cares? Nobody's listening. They're too busy paying attention to Mr Kiss-Arse.'

I wasn't the only one who'd noticed Tessa's parents in the front row next to Josh, then. The people on the front row were the only ones sitting on chairs. Despite being closer to the ground than most of the other attendees, they were loud enough to make themselves known.

Tessa's mum had a similar cry to her daughter, and she looked a lot like her from the back, too. Our head teacher was probably kissing up to them to either try to get money out of them, or to get his fifteen minutes' of fame on the local TV, who were recording the whole thing from their spot at the front. He'd never been that great of a head teacher when it came to waking up and noticing what people were really like.

He'd barely even punished Tessa for doing permanent damage to my back.

Well, almost permanent damage.

Dominic had taught me how to give my pain to Tessa and steal her good health. It was one of the few things he'd actually helped me with. And at least Tessa wasn't dealing with the consequences anymore.

'I'm sure we can all agree how tragic it is that Tessa's life was cut short, and she'll never be able to fulfil her dreams of becoming a lawyer,' continued Mr Kiss-Arse. Sorry, Mr Hazelock.

Tessa let out a strangled cry. She made sobbing sounds, floating off the stage and out of sight. While she couldn't technically cry, she could still make the noises and express how she felt through body language.

For once, I felt sorry for her. She'd attended her own memorial to gloat, but instead, it was reminding her of everything she'd lost.

Tessa couldn't go far, so I crept away from my spot at the back of the crowd and went into the corridor. Sure enough, she was hovering above a bench, sobbing.

I sat down on the bench near her.

Tessa turned to me and glared.

'What do you want?' she snapped. 'Shouldn't you be off solving my murder?'

'Shouldn't you be more polite to one of the few people who can solve your murder?'

She clenched her jaw and crossed her arms, then floated through the wall behind us and back into the courtyard.

Well, that conversation went well. So much for feeling sorry for her.

I stayed where I was, listening to the rest of the memorial through the wall. As it wrapped up, the corridor began to fill with people again.

Melanie sat next to me on the bench, in the spot Tessa had vacated. 'How did she take it?'

'Not great,' I replied, assuming she meant Tessa. 'She came in here when it got too much and when I tried to talk to her, she stormed off. As much as she could, anyway.'

Melanie shook her head. She was wearing all black, which she didn't usually. How Victorian of her. 'That's just like Tessa. She never did like it when the conversation got too sensitive or serious. She's always been pretty closed off.'

I sighed, looking up to see Josh walking past. Tessa was nowhere in sight. Probably still in the courtyard. It was close enough for her ties to Josh, but far enough that she had her own space.

'Could you excuse me a minute?' I said to Melanie. I got up and went over to Josh, touching his arm to stop him. He flinched at my touch, jerking his arm away. That was never not going to hurt. I understood why he did it. He'd have been even less willing to be near me if he'd known I was responsible for his recent ankle injury. I was a monster. How could I have ever used my powers to hurt him? He'd done nothing wrong, but he kept paying just because he'd been my best friend. It wasn't fair.

'I'm really sorry for your loss.' Even as I said it, I knew it sounded hollow. But I had to show him that I still cared; that I hated seeing him in pain. Because I did. Especially as his pain seemed to manifest as anger at the people around him – and himself.

Josh frowned. 'What do you care? You didn't even like her.' He stormed off before I could reply.

While I still couldn't see Tessa, I was pretty sure I heard her cackle.

*

'How are you feeling?' I asked, walking into Ben's house.

Fadil shielded his eyes, turning away from the front door and going into the lounge without saying anything. The curtains were shut, and it was eerily still inside the house. Usually he had the TV or radio or a podcast on in the background when he was alone. Not this time. 'Being cursed was easier. At least I was just lying there.'

'You've never had a cold before?' I asked, going into the kitchen and putting the chicken soup Maggie had made for him on the side.

'Sure. Four thousand years ago.'

Right. Germs had come a long way since then.

I dug into my bag and took out a couple of packets. 'Doc gave me some recommendations.'

Fadil peered over my shoulder. 'Recommendations for what?'

'Things to help speed up your recovery or lessen your symptoms: probiotics, to boost your immune system. Vitamin C, to reduce the duration of your cold, and Maggie's chicken soup to coat your throat.'

'Coat my throat?'

'Something to do with the stuff in it. Turns out, chicken soup does have health benefits. And Maggie just happens to make the best.' While we continued talking, I put the soup into the microwave to reheat and stuck the kettle on.

'You didn't ask Maggie to make this just for me, did you?'

'No. She makes it at work to use up the leftover roast chickens. Smuggled me a tub out.'

Fadil rolled his bloodshot eyes. 'Thank you, but you shouldn't have. None of you should have.'

'What kind of friends would we be if we didn't look after you when you're ill?' I started making a hot drink for him to take his supplements with. 'Oh and Doc said it's better to get your vitamin C from food rather than supplements, as your body will process them differently. But since you were comatose for a few millennia, he thought it was better to be safe than sorry. He also suggested eating sweet potatoes and strawberries to increase your vitamin C intake. But don't bother with strawberries this time of year. It's like eating squishy water.'

'I've never eaten a strawberry. Or a sweet potato.'

I stared at him for a moment, the kettle whistling and the microwave humming in the background. Sometimes I forgot how new and alien twenty-first century life was for him. 'We'll fix that. When things don't taste like water.'

'I'd kind of like to try that, actually. It seems… strange.'

'Well, that can be arranged. I think Ben is going grocery shopping on his way home. I've passed on the message from Doc.' The kettle finished boiling and I made us both cups of tea.

Fadil sat at the table, cradling his head in his hand. 'Do colds always feel this bad?'

'Depends on the cold. Although given you probably don't have much of an immune system to fight it off…'

He shook his head. 'My throat burns. My nose is blocked one minute, running the next. My head wants to explode. Is this normal?'

'Sadly.' I took the soup from the microwave, divided it into two portions, then put the bowls on the table with a couple of spoons. When Maggie had asked if I'd like some soup, too, it'd been impossible to say no. Hopefully the chicken soup really would be good for my soul as well as his germs. 'This should help your throat, and hopefully clear your nose out a bit.'

He picked up the spoon and raised it in my direction. 'Here's hoping.' Lowering it into the soup, he took his first mouthful. 'Damn, that's good.'

'Duh. It's Maggie's.' I gave him his tea, then sat down opposite him. Caring for Fadil gave me a welcome distraction from the memorial that morning. Until the quiet in our conversation while we ate allowed my brain to return to all the things I didn't want to think about. Yay.

'What are you thinking?' Fadil asked between mouthfuls. 'You look…pensive.'

'Am I monster?'

Fadil looked up from his soup, slamming his spoon back into his bowl. It clattered, some of the soup splashing on to the table. 'No! Why would you ever think that? You're one of the kindest people I know.'

I stirred my soup, preferring to stare at it than eat it. There was something weirdly therapeutic about watching it go around in circles. 'For what I did to Josh. And Mrs Brightman. And everyone else Dominic made me hurt.'

'You just said it yourself: Dominic *made* you do those things.'

'I had a choice though, didn't I? I could've said no.' I stopped stirring my soup and put my spoon down. Lunch didn't seem so appetising anymore.

'He was manipulating you. You didn't know that. But you got out! That's a hard thing to do when someone like that gets under your skin.'

I shook my head. What he was saying made sense. If I'd been in his shoes, I would've said something similar. But I still couldn't stop blaming myself. 'I touched Josh's arm to get his attention, and he flinched. He still barely looks at me. A whole lifetime of friendship, destroyed in ten days.'

We ate in silence for a few moments. It didn't bother me, that Fadil didn't say anything. I wasn't expecting him to have answers, and I appreciated that he wasn't trying to come up with them. Some problems didn't have a solution, but there was something about discussing them that made me feel lighter.

'Should I tell Josh what Dominic did? What he made me do?' Then, something worse hit me. 'How do I know if he's fully recovered? What if he struggles for the rest of his life? What if when he hit his ankle because I drained him, it did permanent damage?' I covered my mouth. 'I *am* a monster!'

Fadil moved my hands from my face and held them in his. 'You're not a monster, Edie. And you can't change the past. If you try, it'll consume you.'

'So what am I supposed to do instead?'

'Find ways to live a better life.'

'Well that sounds difficult.'

'Nobody said life was easy.'

25
Edie

'Are you sure we should be doing this?' said Fadil. I couldn't work out if he didn't like walking in the cold evening – which, to be fair, he'd never really done before – or where we were going. Probably both.

'It'll be fine. What's he going to do?'

Fadil flapped his arms in the air. Or at least, he tried to. His quilted coat was so big that he was almost waddling as he walked, but he seemed to be hyper-sensitive to the cold. He was going to hate it when it got to January and was even colder. 'We don't know, that's the point!'

'He's ancient. There's no way he'd be able to chase after us even if he did try to do anything.'

Fadil rolled his eyes. 'You think he'd need to chase after us? He *peeled my skin off*. He doesn't need to be fast to catch us!'

'Right. Well. In this case, I think he's going to be helpful and you're overreacting. Creepy as he may be, he's never really posed a threat to us.'

That seemed to make Fadil relax a little. Which was good, because we'd reached the edge of the woods where Tobias's house was. No turning back now.

'And he might be able to give you answers about why you can see ghosts now, since he's the one who did the procedure.'

Golden leaves crunched under our boots as we entered the woods. The leaves had fallen off some of the trees, while the other, evergreen trees, continued to stand tall and green.

'I suppose. Maybe I am being melodramatic. Can you blame me?'

I put my arm around him. Well, as much as I could. It was hard when he had so many layers on. 'No, I can't. But the guy's just taken on someone else's dog. A crazy person wouldn't do that. Would he?'

Fadil scoffed, shrugging me off. 'Yeah. To make him look *less* crazy.'

'A crazy person couldn't plan that well. They'd be too busy acting on impulse.'

'You...you and your logic!' Fadil flapped his arms again. It was pretty funny given how gigantic his coat was. I didn't laugh, even though I wanted to, just in case it made him tetchier.

'If you need to wait outside, I understand,' I said.

'Are you *kidding* me? I'm not leaving you to go inside there on your own! Why do you think I agreed to this plan in the first place? We need answers and we need them now, and your mum and Ben are busy. They can't interrupt their routines without looking suspicious, and you and I just happen to be free. And if this guy is old enough to remember the first time Doctor Crazy was around, well, there aren't going to be many other options, are there!' More flapping. Was he trying to look like a bird?

A raven cawed nearby, landing on a tree that was lit up by the moon. I glanced up. It was glowing. A ghost raven. Was it the same one from earlier? Were we being watched? It felt like too much of a coincidence after everything else that had happened so far…

I suppressed a shudder. It was better if Fadil didn't know my suspicions, since he was already panicking. So, even though I hated leaving things out, I kept walking and convincing him that we were doing the right thing. It was dark, but I didn't think Dr Goodfellow would attack us until it was nighttime. There were still people around, leaving school and work. Although probably not in the middle of a forest. Maybe Fadil was on to something…

Well, it was too late now.

We reached Tobias's front door and I knocked before I could talk myself out of it. Or Fadil could try to again.

The door flung open, revealing Tobias looking happier than I'd ever seen him. Dave sat at his feet and looked up at us.

'Well hello, isn't this an unusual visit? Come in, come in.'

Fadil and I exchanged confused glances, then went inside. He seemed unusually chipper. Even his house seemed brighter, like the yellows and the greens were less faded, and Tobias's skin seemed less…grey. Had he been leeching? No, he was an alchemist. He couldn't do that. Could he?

I mean, Thomas had all but told us the guy was almost two hundred years old, so at that point, who knew what was possible?

'How are you doing since the surgery, Fadil? Your skin appears to be healing well!' Tobias gestured for us to sit on the sofa. We did so, and Dave jumped up, settling into my lap. It was cute that he remembered me, even though I was trying to block out the time we'd lived together. I stroked his head.

'Yes, it is, thank you.'

'Good, that's good.' Tobias settled into his yellow armchair, resting one foot on top of the other knee. 'So, what brings you to my cottage? I assume this isn't a social call?'

Why would he ever think we wouldn't visit him socially? It wasn't like he was seriously creepy or anything…

Fadil shifted in his seat, swallowing, rubbing his hands together. 'Is it…is it normal that I can see ghosts, now?'

Tobias leaned forwards. 'Huh. I haven't heard of that before, but that's not say it isn't possible. I mean, it's highly logical, in fact.'

'It is?'

Tobias nodded, his shoulder-length grey hair falling into his face. He tucked it behind his ear and continued: 'Dominic's powers were a part of him. Every part of him. So when you took a part of him – his skin, in this case – there would've been blood cells, hair cells, bacteria, et cetera that had been a part of him for hours or even weeks before the procedure.

And now that they're a part of you, they might take a while to settle in, but they'll likely merge into your system in the same way that another part of someone's body would after a non-magical transplant.'

Fadil shuddered. 'Does that mean I'll be able to do more over time?'

'I can't say for sure. It's possible, but unlikely. After all, you didn't inherit his powers, only his skin.'

'But I got his powers *through* his skin.'

'Let's not forget that being able to see ghosts is a fairly basic skill, albeit one that most families have lost now. It could be tapping into pre-existing powers that were dormant in your system. We simply don't know.'

Fadil leaned back on the sofa, as if he was processing everything he'd learned. I couldn't tell how he felt about being able to see ghosts. I wasn't sure he knew, either. It was a lot to deal with. Although it would make it easier for him to be able to see ghosts since the rest of us could.

I put my hand on his leg to comfort him, feeling bad for encouraging him to try to find answers. He put his hand on top of mine as if to reassure me that it was fine, so I moved the conversation along.

'We actually had some questions about something else, if you've got time?' I said.

Tobias sat upright with excitement. 'What is it?'

'Have you ever heard of a Dr Randolph Goodfellow?'

Tobias's back tensed. His chipper demeanour vanished. His mouth turned into a tight line. 'What about him?'

'We think he's behind the recent murders. Have you heard of him?'

'Yes.'

Short, clipped, not really wanting to talk. Not helpful, but I needed to push.

'Can you tell us anything about him? Anything that might help us stop him?' I pleaded.

His jaw tightened. Instead of answering my question, he got up and started pacing the small room we were sitting in. 'We studied medicine together, a long time ago.' You could say that again. 'He had an incredible aptitude for it. If I remember correctly, he was at the top of our class.'

I wanted to interrupt and ask questions, but he seemed to be reciting a monologue, so I let him continue, as hard as it was to not interject.

He cleared his throat, tapping his leg. Dave jumped off from the sofa and ran to him, sitting at his feet. Wow, that was the most responsive I'd ever seen him. Tobias picked up the dog and hugged him as he continued talking. 'While we were studying, we discovered alchemy. I chose to stick to the grey areas, but he was more comfortable doing whatever he could for his own gain. As we were preparing to go our separate ways, he discovered how to channel a different source of power. Some would call it black magic.' Gulp. 'After graduation, we lost contact, but both stayed local. He opened a practice on the outskirts of town, treating whatever ailments he could. If you could call them treatments. Any form of treatment back then was dangerous, but anything he did was even more so. For the rich, he took their money and did what he could. If someone couldn't pay him as much, he'd take something else instead.'

'Their powers?'

He rubbed behind Dave's ear, turning to look at us. His expression was blank. Eerie. Haunted. 'Yes. At first, he took indiscriminately, unsure of what he could actually take, so figuring the more he experimented, the more he could gain.'

So far, he seemed to be confirming and fleshing out what Thomas had told us. That was good. Well, good in that he wasn't lying to us. Bad in every other way. Very, very bad.

'Was he a witch? I thought only witches could use magic,' said Fadil.

Tobias gave him a down-turned smile. 'Only witches have active powers, but, technically, anyone can cast a spell to manipulate the forces around them. Black magic can sometimes be easier to wield, and lead to more concrete results, which is why it's more attractive to people who are born without powers.'

Wasn't that just great?

Tobias continued: 'As he became more aware of what he was doing and how it affected both him and his so-called patients, he focused more on people who had the types of powers he wanted. I believe his dream target was a vampire.'

'Did you just say "vampire"?' said Fadil. 'They're *real?*'

Tobias gave him a small smile. 'Of course.'

Ghosts, witches, necromancers, why not vampires? Ben had suggested more paranormal creatures existed than we knew about when we'd first met him. Nothing surprised me anymore.

'Did he ever acquire a vampire's powers?' I asked.

'No,' said Tobias. 'Luckily. He was close to unstoppable when he was alive. Can you imagine what he'd have been like with the powers of a vampire?'

Fadil rubbed his hands over his legs. 'What, exactly, *are* the powers of a vampire?'

'That's a good question,' said Tobias. He put the dog in his chair, then sat in front of him. Dave curled up at the back of it and went to sleep. 'As you know, vampires need blood to survive. The type of blood they drink can affect them. More magical blood allows them to heal faster, for example. So does chicken blood. High in protein. The blood of an old person, who's mentally or physically ill, won't sustain them for long. The blood of a child may help them look more youthful or give them extra energy.'

'So they can heal?' I asked, trying to clarify his ramblings.

'Yes, very well. Germs don't impact them at all. If they suffer from any injuries, once they've drunk blood, they can heal. There are always exceptions to the rule, but that's the general consensus.'

A psychopathic murderer who could heal? No wonder he wanted a vampire.

'Can they do anything else?' asked Fadil.

'Most have superior strength. They may be faster, more agile. I guess you could see them as having the abilities of a big cat.'

'That's…great. Just great.' Fadil shook his head.

'Oh, they're no threat to us. Contrary to popular belief, most don't kill their victims. It's too messy. And most victims don't remember when they've had a little blood taken, they'll just blame a good night out.'

'Their memories are removed, too?' I said, trying to follow an entirely new lore I'd only just discovered. Knowledge was power, and all that.

'Sometimes, yes. A vampire's saliva mixes with the victim's blood, eliciting a chemical which causes them to forget the last few minutes. It also makes them woozy, which is why victims often blame alcohol. Some people also wake up with hangover-like symptoms, reinforcing that belief. Vampires often target anyone who's drunk for this very reason, since they're immune to the impact of alcohol.'

'I'm not sure whether to be fascinated or horrified,' said Fadil.

I laughed, so did Tobias.

'Both seem adequate,' said Tobias.

'Is there anything else you can tell us that might be helpful when it comes to Dr Goodfellow? Any tips on how to take him down?' I asked.

'Alas, that's all I know. I'm afraid I don't know who set his house on fire, only that it was quite a pretty blaze.'

Of course he'd say something like that. On that note, it was time for us to leave.

I jumped out of my chair and Fadil followed. 'Well. Thank you for your help. It's good to see Dave has settled in so well.'

Tobias nodded. 'Be careful. Both of you. Goodfellow is not someone to be taken on lightly.'

26

Niamh

Even though I wanted to curl up into a ball and hibernate because my headache was trying to kill me, I had a call with a potential client, so I couldn't. I liked money coming in and was still waiting on Mrs Brightman's money to finish jumping through hoops and turn up in my bank account. Not that I'd want to use that on bills anyway. That felt wrong, somehow. Like it was dishonouring her memory.

So, going against my better judgement, I got into my car and began driving to the client's house, barely able to keep my eyes open. Even with sunglasses on, the sun was glaringly bright. The hum of the car engine caused my whole body to ache. I tried to focus on the radio, but the host's voice annoyed me so I had to turn it off.

My eyes did not want to stay open. They flitted closed over and over. It wasn't far to drive. I could do it.

I cranked up the air conditioning and turned up some rock music from my phone. If I was cold and deafening myself, I couldn't fall asleep, could I?

Sure, it hurt my head. But falling asleep at the wheel was more dangerous than a headache. Wasn't it?

The light in front of me turned to red. I hit the brakes, almost doing an emergency stop and jerking myself forwards at the hard braking. The driver of the car behind pipped his horn at me. Yeah, yeah.

The lights went green and I carried on driving, trying to be extra cautious so that I didn't slam the brakes again. My driving was jerky and I was really glad nobody else was in the car. It was almost embarrassing how bad I was, as if I was a learner again and not someone who'd been driving for over twenty years.

Twenty years? Had it really been that long? Wow, I felt old.

Focus, Niamh!

There wasn't much farther to go. I could get there. Just take it slowly.

Another driver honked their car's horn at me. I checked my speed. I was doing thirty in a forty, but there was no room for them to overtake because of the bollards in the centre of the road. Oops. I'd failed one of my driving tests for being too far under the speed limit. I should've known better.

I sped up, hitting forty. When we got to a clear spot of road, the car that'd been behind overtook me, the driver flashing me a rude hand gesture as he went past. How lovely.

Just past where he'd overtaken me was a particularly bendy stretch of road. It was one of my least favourite spots to drive through, but one of the main ways to get out of Hucknall, so pretty much unavoidable.

Windy windy windy…and a stupid texture on the road that forced you to slow down and felt horrible in cheap cars like mine. I widened my eyes, forcing them to stay as open as possible and barely blinking. The last thing I needed was to crash into the house halfway around the turns. I wouldn't have been the first driver to do it, but I didn't want to be another name on that list. How those homeowners didn't go mad I'd never know.

Made it past the house. Phew. Just a little farther. If I got to the end of the road, it was a win. Then, just a couple more turnings, and I'd be at my destination. It really wasn't far. I could do it.

I reached the mini roundabout at the end of the road, checking both sides multiple times to make sure nobody was coming. It was better to be extra careful when driving tired, right?

I turned left, driving past an old pub I'd always planned to check out but never had, despite it having existed longer than I'd been alive. Just a bit farther. Not far to go.

I carried on down the road, keeping an eye out for anyone coming in either direction, on foot or in a car. I was so busy paying attention to them that I turned early, driving straight into a lamppost.

*

Well wasn't that just bloody brilliant? Maggie and Ben were at work. Edie was at college and she was my daughter – it wasn't her problem. I almost expected

Javi to appear and try to help out, but for once, he didn't.

Angry at myself, I got out of the car and stood near the pub, the smell of lunch wafting over to me and making me want to throw up. Pacing up and down the pavement, I called my insurance company. I was on hold for ages, but they were helpful and sending a tow truck to pick up my car.

Since I hadn't been going too fast, it hadn't done a huge amount of damage, but it was enough that my car would need to go into the garage for a few days. My timing was brilliant.

Mortified, I called the potential clients, explained what'd happened, and tried to rearrange the quote. They were really understanding and told me to take my time, which I appreciated. I was still hoping to see them in a day or two so that I could get them booked in, but it'd depend on if the garage had a courtesy car available.

What was I going to tell Edie? Or Ben? Or Maggie? If I told them the truth, I'd get a lecture and they'd worry about me even more.

But I couldn't lie, either. I'd promised Edie I'd tell her the truth, even if it hurt.

Meh.

That was a problem for later.

The garage gave me a lift home, saying they'd drop a courtesy car off later. In the mean time, I was going to curl up on the sofa with Tilly and Spectre and have a well-earned nap.

27
Edie

'Mum?' I called, walking into the house.

Tilly and Spectre greeted me, so she wasn't out walking. But there was no car on the driveway. That was odd. 'Thomas?' I called. No answer.

Garden? No, it was too cold for that. What was she doing?

I took my shoes and coat off, Tilly dancing around me the whole time, then trudged upstairs. The loft hatch at the top was open, a pair of step ladders underneath the opening. 'Mum?' I called up.

'Just fetching the Christmas decorations, don't mind me,' she said.

Thomas floated down through the ceiling. 'Hi, Edie.'

'Hey Thomas.'

'Here, grab the tree,' said Mum, pushing the dusty box through the hole. I reached up to grab it, lowering it down then resting it just inside Mum's bedroom door. Tilly sniffed it, then walked off. Obviously Princess Westie disapproved of the fusty plastic smell.

'I thought the house could do with some festive cheer,' said Mum, handing me another box. 'Especially after everything that's been going on lately.'

Thomas frowned, then floated downstairs to give us some privacy.

'You mean like whatever happened to the car?' I said. While I couldn't guarantee something had happened to it, no car on the driveway and Mum getting the decorations down mid-December were flashing neon signs something had happened. She was usually a 'put the decorations up the week before' sort of person.

Mum cleared her throat, almost shoving the next box at me and causing me to stumble into the wall. She didn't say anything else until she'd closed the loft hatch and stomped down the ladder.

'I crashed into a lamp. *Don't* say anything.'

Oh my god. What had I missed while I was at college? Why didn't she ring me?

'I wasn't going to! Other than what happened? Are you all right? You look all right?'

She leaned against the doorframe and crossed her arms. 'I'm fine, obviously, but the car took a beating, so it's in the garage. They're sending a courtesy car over. Your dad already gave me a lecture about driving when I'm so tired.'

'Yes, yes I did,' said Dad, appearing beside her with a sombre expression on his face. He gave Mum the side eye. 'You know better.'

'What was I supposed to do? Cancel on a client?'

'You did anyway,' he mumbled.

She glared at him.

'It's not my fault I can't get any sleep! If it isn't for my pounding headache, the relentless tossing and turning, or the racing thoughts, it's that damn whistling!'

'You're still hearing it?' I asked. Was that what was causing Mum's headache? No wonder she couldn't sleep.

'How often are you hearing it?' asked Dad.

'Most nights,' said Mum, shaking her head. 'The tune varies. Some nights, it's just an annoying sound. On the nights he murders, it's impossible for me to block it out. A million times worse than nails on a chalkboard. Based on what one of his other victims said, Ben and I think he torments his victims first to weaken them, then uses the second whistle to either torture them in another way or exert some sort of power over them before he kills them. Maybe to incapacitate them so that they can't fight back.'

'Could whistling really do that?' asked Javi.

'There are a lot of things in our lives that sound impossible but seem to happen anyway.' Mum gestured to him.

'Point taken.'

'And look at what the sodding noise is doing to me. I imagine it'd be louder and more annoying for someone he's right in front of.' She massaged her forehead, a reminder of just how much pain the noise was causing her.

'Do you think you're on his list?' I couldn't help it. I had to ask. Why else would Mum hear his haunting tune? Or lack of a tune?

She sighed. 'Who knows?'

Was that supposed to reassure me?

Instead of answering my question, she grabbed a box of Christmas decorations and marched down the stairs.

No wonder she couldn't sleep. She was terrified she was next. So was I.

I looked over at Dad, who shrugged, picked up the Christmas tree, and followed her. How much energy was he using doing that? Was he even *allowed* to do that? Not that he'd ever been one to listen to rules.

I picked up the last box and joined them in the living room, where Tilly, Spectre, and Thomas sat on the sofa.

'Did you hear it the night Tessa was killed?' I asked. Even though Mum wanted to end this conversation, I so wasn't over it.

Mum nodded, using a pair of scissors to score open a box. 'Yes. I didn't know what it was at the time, but I heard the other tune a few nights in a row before she was killed, too.'

'It doesn't make sense,' said Dad. 'Unless...'

Mum looked up. 'Unless what?'

'Well, you died for a few minutes before Edie resurrected you, right?'

Mum nodded. Dad had been there when it'd happened but he'd been in a trance, so he had no recollection of that time.

He hover-paced as he talked, floating through the coffee table and back again. 'What if you've got a closer connection to the spirit world now, and that's why you can hear it, not because you're a target?'

'That makes sense,' I agreed, taking the scissors from Mum and opening the other box. The smell of dusty tinsel filled the air. I kind of liked it. It reminded me of when times had been simpler. 'It's been going on too long and things haven't escalated. It doesn't make sense otherwise when the others are only tormented for a few days before the tune changes.'

'That's somewhat relieving,' said Mum. 'It at least means he's not on to me yet.' We hoped.

'If it will help you sleep, I can keep an eye out when you're asleep,' offered Dad.

'Are you allowed to do that?' asked Mum.

He shrugged. 'If it'll make my family feel better, I'm not opposed to breaking a few rules.'

28

Niamh

I crashed hard that night after the stress and insomnia of the last few days. If Goodfellow did whistle in the night, I wouldn't have heard anything. It wasn't very often I slept that heavily, but I'd obviously needed it. If I hadn't been woken up by my phone ringing when the sun had only just come up, I might've caught up on some sleep. Bloody typical.

Barely processing, and with my eyes still closed, I grabbed my phone without looking at caller ID. 'Hello?' I said with a yawn.

'Hi, Niamh. It's Mrs Brightman's lawyer here. Sorry if I woke you. I just wanted to let you know that all the paperwork has gone through. Mrs Brightman's property and all her assets now belong to you. The money should be in your account within a few days.'

It was a good job I was still in bed. I wasn't ready to process all of that. So much had happened lately I still hadn't fully accepted she was gone, or allowed myself to feel the pain of losing one of my closest friends.

Sure, I could've summoned her. But, whether I liked it or not, she'd crossed over. She wasn't *meant* to talk to us anymore. We broke the rules enough with Javi and my mother already. Summoning Mrs Brightman just so that I could talk to her again wouldn't help me move on and was unfair on her when she was trying to enjoy her afterlife.

'Thanks for letting me know,' I said.

She said I could go pick up the keys any time, although I was in no rush as I had my own set anyway.

I lay back in bed, listening to Edie and Tilly going through their morning routines downstairs. It was comforting to know some things hadn't changed.

Instead of doing the responsible thing and getting up, I rolled over and pulled the duvet over my head. It wasn't an adulting day. Edie was old enough to sort her own breakfast and I was drained enough to need more sleep.

*

Ben and I had arranged to go out to lunch, so I dragged myself out of bed half an hour before I had to leave, made myself look human, and met him outside the library just past twelve. 'Hey, you,' he said, pecking me on the lips.

I kissed him back, then wrapped my arms around him. If I was holding on to him, I could walk around with my eyes closed and get a few moments of relief. Perfect.

'What's wrong?' he said, hugging me back.

I leaned my head on his shoulder, not wanting the hug to end. I needed the closeness of someone calm and understanding. 'Mrs Brightman's stuff was finalised today.'

He rubbed my back. 'At least it's over now.'

'Yeah, I suppose.' I moved my head to his chest, trying to avoid the zip of his coat so that it didn't dig into my face. 'But it's not really, is it?'

'What do you mean?'

'I've still got to redecorate her house and decide what to do with it. Do I want to sell it? Move in to it? How do I decide? It's such a lovely house, it'd be a shame to sell it. But I like where we are now.'

Ben held on to me as we walked over to the cafe we were visiting for lunch. 'Why don't you focus on something smaller before deciding what you do?'

'What do you mean?'

'Before you sell it, you have to give it a bit of a facelift, right?'

I snorted. 'It needs more than a facelift. It needs gutting.'

'Well then. Why don't you start with the necessary work that needs doing? Focus on the smaller tasks first, then you might figure out what to do as you go.'

'That's a surprisingly good idea.'

He chuckled. 'You don't have to sound so shocked I came up with it.'

'Not shocked, impressed.' I flashed him a flirtatious smile, which he returned.

Occasionally I opened my eyes to see where we were going, but I instantly regretted it because it was too bright, even through my sunglasses, so I clutched on to Ben and used him as a walking aid instead. 'How's your headache?'

'I've become the ginger Jackie O. With a less refined fashion sense.'

Ben laughed. 'I think you look great in those giant sunglasses.'

'Thanks,' I said, unsure if his compliment was sincere. I'd take it anyway. 'Either way, these are the only thing I've got to make the world less bright. Just having my eyes open is painful. Is it always this bright in December?'

'There does seem to be less cloud cover than usual,' said Ben.

'Typical,' I grumbled.

'I'm sorry,' he said. 'Do you think it's because you're not sleeping? Or the sound Goodfellow makes?'

'Both? Lack of sleep causes headaches, right? And that noise goes right through me. It kind of…lingers, if you get me?'

'Yeah, I get you,' said Ben, rubbing my hand.

We crossed the road on to the pedestrianised high street, walking across the uneven cobbles that I was even more aware of with my eyes closed. They really didn't feel nice under the thin soles of my boots. 'How's Fadil?'

'Snotty,' said Ben. 'It's his first cold. At least in this millennia. He's handling it fairly well all things considered.'

'He's resilient that's for sure. How many boxes of tissues has he got through?'

'Roughly one per day. Edie gave him some moisturiser because the skin on his nose was starting to peel from all the tissues.'

'Ouch,' I said.

'Yes,' agreed Ben. We reached the cafe and Ben held the steamed-up glass door open for me. I really, really hoped the cafe was quiet and there were no noises that could make my headache even worse.

*

'Thanks for lunch, I needed that,' I said, kissing Ben on the cheek as we left the cafe. My head still hurt, but the food and company had been a welcome distraction for an hour.

'Me too.' He put his arm around my waist as we headed back to the library. He glanced over his shoulder at the vacant shop in town, a sad expression washing over him. Had he changed his mind about turning it into a bookshop?

'Shall we go take a look?' I said, trying to guide him back to it.

'No,' he said, standing his ground and refusing to turn around.

'Why not?'

He stopped walking and sighed. 'I've decided not to bother with the bookshop. It was a dumb idea. I never should've considered it to begin with.'

I tried to stop him from walking, to turn him around, but he kept going as if driven by a motor. 'What are you talking about? It's a great idea! This town could do with a decent bookshop.'

'Well then it won't be owned by me.'

'But—'

'Drop it, would you?' His tone was stern, like he'd made his mind up and nobody was changing it.

'What's got into you?'

'Forget it.' He let go of my hand, charging off back to the library.

What was that about?

I contemplated following him, but thought giving him time to cool off might be better. Whatever was going on with him, he obviously needed time to process it alone first.

Since we were headed in the same direction, I lingered for a moment, giving him time to return to the library before I walked home.

Once he'd disappeared inside, on autopilot, I walked through the graveyard beside the library. It was oddly quiet without Thomas there. Even spookier than usual, despite the fact there was no one else around.

'Niamh!' said Thomas, bouncing up to me as I walked through our front door. Tilly also jumped up at me to say hello. Spectre stared from above the coffee table.

'Hey, Thomas.'

I picked Tilly up and sat on the sofa, stroking behind her fluffy white ear.

'What's wrong?' said Thomas. He hover sat on the space beside me.

'Ben just went really weird when we were talking about something I thought he wanted to do. I'm confused.'

'Did he change his mind?'

I tapped my foot against the sofa. 'Maybe. But why? What caused the U-Turn? He was so excited!'

Thomas shrugged. 'There's only one person who can tell you what Ben is thinking.'

'Yeah, but I'm not sure he's ready to talk just yet.'

'He might just need processing time, especially if he's changed his mind,' suggested Thomas.

I stopped tapping the sofa and rubbed Tilly's back. 'If he takes too long to process the opportunity will be lost.'

'If he's decided against it anyway, will he care?'

*

Still confused about what had happened with Ben, I went to Mrs Brightman's house. Now my house. It felt wrong to call it that, but it wasn't like she had a use for it anymore. And, based on what Javi had said, she was perfectly happy in the afterlife with her husband. That was comforting but didn't change how much I missed her.

I walked into the living room, examining the top edges of the cream floral wallpaper. It was peeling in the corners, although not as bad as you might've expected from something that old. Chances were the wallpaper was probably hiding a wall that needed replastering, though.

Javi and I had worked so hard to earn enough to buy our own house. It'd been cheaper back then, but still meant a lot of savings and investments to get enough. And now, after all that struggle, I owned two houses.

Mrs Brightman's house was in a slightly nicer area of town than mine, which added extra to the value. If I redecorated, I could get even more from it. A part of me didn't want to sell it, though. I was still too attached to it.

I'd worry about that when I needed to.

I went into the kitchen, searching for some coffee to wake me up. It was tucked at the back of the cupboard, but still decent, so I made myself a cup, then put some in a paper towel and placed it in the fridge to absorb any smells.

Black coffee wasn't my favourite, but I needed the caffeine.

I sat on the sofa, picturing Mrs Brightman sitting in her chair by the window. I'd spent hours on that sofa, talking to her about nothing and everything. It wasn't the comfiest sofa, but that wasn't what had mattered. It was the company I'd really cared about.

I sighed. Moving back to where I'd grown up was meant to make life easier. Instead, it'd messed everything up. I was divorced, one of my closest friends was dead, my daughter was a necromancer, and she was probably going to be a moving target for the rest of her life.

But good things had happened, too. I had to remember that. Maggie and I were friends again. Mrs Brightman may have only been in my life for a short while, but she'd been a close friend and she was happily reunited with her husband. Fadil had come into our lives and was a great friend to Edie, and I had Ben.

Ah yes. Ben. What was going on with him? Why had he changed his mind so quickly about the bookshop?

I took my phone from my handbag and realised Ben had texted me saying sorry. No explanation for his outburst, but at least he could acknowledge that he'd overreacted. Dan never would've done that.

Nope.

Stop, brain.

No comparing Ben and Dan. That was dangerous territory. They weren't even comparable. Ben was way less selfish than Dan.

No, brain! That's enough.

As I was arguing with myself, Ben rang me. I answered right away.

'I'm really sorry,' he said. 'I shouldn't have overreacted like that.'

'You already apologised. But thank you.'

'I know, but you didn't reply and I was worried you hated me. And I wanted you to hear me say it. After I sent the text I realised it seemed like a hollow cop-out.'

My heart fluttered at how cute he was. 'It didn't.'

'I don't normally freak out like that. But I've decided not to open the bookshop. I hope you don't mind?'

I was disappointed, but more for him than me. He'd seemed really excited. What had changed his mind? I really wanted to know, but if I forced him to open up, he probably never would. As much as I hated it, I had to respect his decision.

'As long as you're happy, that's what matters to me,' I said.

'Thank you.' There was a pause. Someone talked in the background. 'Sorry, I've got to go. I snuck off to ring you. See you later?'

'See you later.'

29
Edie

Hard as I tried, it was impossible to avoid Josh and Tessa at college. Even though it was a pretty big campus, we had to cross paths to go to different classes. And we lived fairly close in a small town, which meant we sometimes walked past each other going to and from college, too. It didn't help my mood.

Ever since the memorial, Tessa had worn a sad puppy look. Being dead seemed to be finally getting to her. It was about time. At first, it'd felt like she'd almost enjoyed it. But after the memorial, it was like a switch had been flicked. One that made her realise just how isolated she was. I felt sorry for her, but she'd made it pretty clear she didn't want help with any emotional issues, and my purpose was to stop her murderer. Nothing else. So that was what I was going to focus on, not because I wanted to help her, but because I wanted to get rid of her.

It was a mild day for the middle of December, so I chose to eat my lunch in the courtyard. I couldn't be bothered to walk all the way home when I had a lesson in an hour. It seemed pointless. So I settled in with my sandwich and watched the world go by while I ate.

There weren't many flowers or birds or bugs to watch. It was too cold. But there were plenty of people about. And between those red-bricked walls, they still couldn't stop talking about Tessa and the possibility that the old mining town had its very own serial killer.

Some people thought it was cool. Finally, the town had a claim to fame. Apparently Lord Byron, Ada Lovelace, and Eric Coates weren't enough for them.

Others were afraid they might be next. After all, they didn't know what the murderer's MO was. Or if he even had one.

They also didn't know the murderer was a ghost. It wasn't like I could tell them that part. Given that they couldn't see ghosts, they'd either think I was mad or it'd create widespread panic. So I kept my mouth shut.

'Can I—can I sit here, please?' said Tessa. She sounded unnaturally sheepish.

I nodded, putting my sandwich back into my lunchbox and switching it for my phone, which I held to my ear.

'Is that so people don't think you're nuts when you're talking to me?'

'Yeah,' I said.

She raised her head in acknowledgement. 'Does it work?'

'So far.'

'Huh.'

We sat in silence for a moment, so I resumed eating my sandwich. It wasn't like we had a lot in common. We had even less now that she was dead.

All right, fine. We had more in common than I liked to think. Now that she was dead, my family were the only ones who could help her. I was pretty sure she wouldn't cross over until her murderer was stopped. And she couldn't do that alone.

'Do you remember anything else about what happened to you?'

She lowered her head, shaking it just once. 'I've been trying. But it's like a black hole in my mind. Like I was drugged or hypnotised or something.'

'Probably a defence mechanism,' I said.

She nodded. 'Most things are fragments, like an old, broken mosaic that's been lost and rediscovered. The last thing I remember clearly is sleeping with Andre.' She put her hand to her mouth. She'd *cheated on Josh*? After kicking up all that fuss to get him? Bitch.

'What's that face for?' said Tessa.

'You chased Josh for months, then cheated on him within weeks?'

She shrugged. 'Why do guys married to movie stars sleep with the hot nanny?'

I shook my head. I really wanted to rage at her, but I knew that was inappropriate in public. So instead, I finished my sandwich, biting into it more aggressively than necessary. And hurting my tongue. Ow.

There was no one else around because the next lot of lessons were about to start. So I took the opportunity to look Tessa dead in the eye: 'You're unbelievable, you know that?'

*

I felt sick for the rest of the afternoon. Tessa had made my life hell. She'd chased Josh even before I'd moved back to Hucknall. And after all that, she'd cheated on one of the nicest guys in the world? What a bitch. Josh didn't deserve that. He'd been through enough.

Fadil was sitting on the sofa, playing with Tilly, when I got home. 'Why do you look like you could breathe fire?' His voice still sounded hoarse, but it was a little better. I wasn't sure if that was because his health was improving or he'd been living on chicken soup. Mum had bribed Maggie to make him some more, and she'd obliged, making a vat of the stuff so big it had barely fitted into Ben's freezer. And of course, it was full of vegetables containing vitamin C, too.

I dropped my bag on to the chair by the window and stormed into the kitchen. Fadil and Tilly followed.

Mum was sitting on a stool, leaning over the stove, making some sort of dish I didn't recognise. It must've been one of Maggie's recipes, because there was no way she'd experiment in the kitchen otherwise. She wasn't a confident enough cook. Whatever she was making, though, it smelled good.

Mum span around on her chair and lowered her sunglasses to look at me. 'What's with the scowl?'

I flapped my arms in the air. 'Tessa cheated on Josh!'

'Does he know?' Mum put her sunglasses back on, then turned one of the pans down on the hob. I smelled hints of cheese, bacon, chicken, and milk. Yum.

'No. But she confirmed it! And she was so...*chill* about it! Josh deserves better than that!'

'What do you mean by "chill"?' Fadil turned away from me, sneezing into his elbow. 'Stupid germs.'

Without even looking away from the stove, Mum pointed to a packet of cough sweets by the kettle. I got up and passed it to Fadil, who took one out and sucked on it. The smell of menthol and blackcurrant took over the room, engulfing even the aroma of the food Mum was cooking. But hopefully it helped his throat. And I didn't mind the smell anyway. It was kind of soothing, actually.

Fadil picked Tilly up and put her on his lap. She sat with her bum against his stomach, her front feet resting on his knees. It was a weird, cute pose she did a lot.

I flapped my arms again. I probably looked like a baby bird trying and failing to fly, but I was frustrated and didn't know how else to get rid of some of my pent-up anger. 'Like it was no big deal. She even compared it to celebrity guys who cheat on their hot wives with the hot nanny.' I shook my head.

'Half the time, those nannies aren't even hot,' said Mum.

'Mum! So not the point!'

'Right. Of course.' She picked up the blue stress ball I'd been using to help with revision and threw it between her hands. It was weirdly hypnotic to watch.

'It's a power trip,' said Fadil, the cough sweet rattling between his teeth. 'They feel like they can get anyone they want, and they want to prove it.'

I sat down, tapping my foot against the chair leg. 'Should I tell Josh? I should tell Josh, shouldn't I?'

'No!' said Fadil, at the same time Mum said, 'yes!'

Frazzle.

'Well that wasn't helpful.'

Mum and Fadil exchanged glances.

Mum stopped throwing the ball and clutched it in her right hand. 'You have a moral obligation to share what you know with him. He didn't deserve any of this. It might help him move on.'

Fadil shook his head. 'No way. It's none of your business. And it's not like Josh would listen to you anyway, based on what you've said. He'd probably accuse you of making it up to drive a wedge between them. Especially since you haven't mentioned he's being haunted by her yet, or that you've spoken to her ghost. So he'd question your sources.'

Double frazzle. He was right. As much as I wanted to tell Josh the truth, I wasn't close enough to him anymore. He'd never believe me. It wasn't like I could blame him, either.

Mum met my eye. She frowned. Great. She knew Fadil was right, too.

So it looked like it didn't matter what I wanted to do. I wouldn't be able to do it anyway.

30
Niamh

'What are we looking for, exactly?' I asked Ben as we walked with Tilly past the hedge, through the gate, and into Hucknall cemetery. It was larger than the one Thomas haunted, and much more open.

In the distance, a church sat on the hill, a few cars parked beside it.

Ben crouched down in front of a gravestone. 'This is where Goodfellow was buried. I thought if we could take a look at his grave, it might tell us about how he got out, which might give us information on how to stop him. Or at least, more about who he actually was.' He stood up, examining the next gravestone.

Tilly watched him, waiting to keep walking.

'While I like the idea, this is going to take forever. There are hundreds of graves her, and some of them are easier to read than others,' I squinted through my sunglasses at the grassy graveyard in front of us. Usually, it was a quiet and peaceful place to walk the dog. Right now, it held an insurmountable task. 'It looks like most of the ones around here are more modern. We need to go farther back to get to the old ones.'

Ben stood up. 'How can you tell?'

'These are all shiny. The ones over there look older and more matte.' I pointed to the far side of the cemetery.

'Good call.' He slipped his hand into mine and the three of us walked around the edge of the cemetery, occasionally stopping to examine something that looked older. There was one gravestone that had fallen over and a tree had grown over it, which showed just how old some of the graves were. And how nature will always win in the end.

We got to the centre of the graveyard, where a path took us to a central area with a few trees, or to the left where more graves and the church sat. The older graves looked to be in front of us, so we kept going towards the tree.

'These dates are much more what we're looking for,' said Ben. He wiped his glasses on the edge of his coat, then put them back on. 'This one is 1847!'

Something just ahead caught my eye. I gravitated to it, Tilly trotting along beside me. A few of the graves looked recently disturbed. Some of the headstones were smashed or lying down, and the stone that had been placed to cover the grave itself was smashed. It had once been covered in moss, showing how old it was. The top of one of them had a raven on top. The bottom of it was disturbed, but the raven was not. The name on it? Dr Randolph Goodfellow.

'Found it,' I said.

Ben walked over to us. 'That's a unique design.'

'You don't think it's...twee?' I lowered an eyebrow.

Ben lowered one back at me. 'You're just being cynical.'

'The guy's a serial killer!' I waved my arms in the air, causing my sunglasses to move slightly on my face and expose me to the bright, orange sun as it set over the cemetery. Usually, it'd be pretty. When my head wanted to explode, it was painful. Could I get blackout sunglasses? How many things would I walk into wearing those? Would it be better than living with this headache?

'They didn't know that. They thought he was doing the right thing.'

I snorted.

'They could only go based on the information they had at the time, the same as we are now,' said Ben.

'Or, they were desperate, so they let him get away with things because they had no other choice.'

'Possible. But you're definitely also being cynical.' He crouched down to examine the grave. 'It looks like the grave cover was disturbed recently.'

'Great.'

The graves surrounding it had had their gravestones and covers smashed, too. It looked like too much of a mess for someone to have intentionally disturbed Goodfellow's grave. I wasn't sure if that was better or worse. 'Do you think he was freed by accident? Some idiot teenagers or drunks smashing up graves for a laugh?'

'Sad, but probable.' He stood up, shaking his head.

*

We got back from the cemetery feeling deflated. While it was interesting to see Goodfellow's grave, all we'd confirmed was that someone disturbed a bunch of graves, meaning he was likely freed accidentally on purpose by a disrespectful idiot. Oh, if only they knew what they'd done. None of what we'd found had told us anything new or given us information on how to stop him.

I sat in front of the TV. It wasn't long before Ben, Edie, Fadil, and Tilly joined me. Thomas stayed upstairs, playing with Spectre. I think he liked having another being he could interact with.

It felt like the rest of us were sharing in our frustrations by turning our tired brains off. I had the TV on quiet, and still wore my sunglasses, but the closed captions were on so everyone could follow along even if it was too quiet for them to hear it properly.

During one of the commercial breaks, Javi bounced into the living room, gradually becoming more opaque as he materialised. 'Guess what guess what guess what?' He had that excited child air about him that I'd always loved. It always brightened my day.

Except today. Today, it was jarring and I wanted to punch him. We were talking life and death and he was acting like we were off to a theme park. It wasn't like his afterlife had been short on excitement.

Javi rolled his eyes. 'All right, if none of you are going to ask, I'll tell you anyway. Ladies and gentlemen, I'd like to introduce you to Millicent and

Percival Hill. The witch and necromancer who took down Dr Randolph Goodfellow.'

All five of us froze, our gazes transfixed on the spots beside Javi where the two ghosts had appeared. While I'd asked Javi to try to find them, I'd always known it was a long shot. It wasn't like the Other Side had a yellow pages or an internet he could search. Did it?

The two figures looked the picture of Victorian elegance: Percival wore a sharp suit, complete with a white waistcoat, black bowtie, and perfectly shined shoes. His hair was kept short and tidy, and his posture was so good I straightened up from my own hunched position, feeling self-conscious.

Millicent was resplendent in a green dress with a high collar and probably a perfectly fitted corset designed just for her. Her blonde hair was fixed into a neat bun, enhancing her sharp cheekbones. 'Hello,' she said.

'Hi,' I said.

Javi continued to grin in the background, while Edie, Ben, Fadil, and I were speechless. Since we hadn't expected Javi to find them, we hadn't planned any questions. A great idea, I know.

'Did Dad tell you about what's going on?' Edie asked, leaning towards them from her seat on the sofa.

'Yes,' said Percival. 'Do you know how he was disturbed?'

'We think someone accidentally disturbed his grave at the cemetery, but it's hard to know for definite,' said Ben.

Millicent frowned. 'The only solution we could come up with at the time was to trap his spirit inside his damaged body, then trap that inside the coffin, bury it, and cover it in stone. We'd hoped it would be permanent.'

'That sounds familiar,' mumbled Fadil.

Edie reached out and put a hand on his arm. He patted it.

Ben glanced over at Fadil and frowned. 'Do you mean you cast a blood curse?'

Millicent put her hand to her mouth in shock. 'We would never!'

Oops. We hadn't taken the decision to cast a blood curse on Dominic lightly, but having done it made me sometimes forget the level of power involved in doing it. And just how dark it was.

'It was similar, I suppose you could say,' said Percival. 'A blood curse can only be cast on the living, though. And there's no way we would've been able to get close enough to him to get the necessary hair or blood to perform a curse like that. So, we had to improvise. We combined necromancy and witchcraft, internal and external forces, and exploited him at his weakest, to achieve our goal.'

'I see,' said Ben, pushing his glasses up his nose.

'We also trapped his raven, Branwen, with him. They had an unusual connection, so it seemed safest to eradicate the threat from her, too,' explained Millicent. That explained the bird.

Percival shook his head. 'We didn't think anyone would be able to disturb him once he was buried. We covered it with a stone grave cover and a mortsafe, just in case. We never expected someone to disturb such an intricate gravesite. It was part of why we encouraged the townspeople to do something so ornate.'

'What's a mortsafe?' I asked, not sure I wanted to know.

'An iron cage placed on top of a grave to stop grave robbers,' said Percival.

'Lovely. Glad I asked.' Not.

'A lot of mortsafes have been removed or damaged,' said Edie. Why did my daughter even know that? I didn't want to know.

Ben removed his glasses and wiped them on his shirt. 'Goodfellow's didn't have one, just a broken grave cover.'

Percival frowned. 'Unfortunate.'

'And now he's angry because he was trapped for two hundred years,' said Millicent.

'Wouldn't you be?' said Percival.

'No, I'm just plagued with anxiety and mask it well,' said Fadil with a half-laugh.

Millicent and Percival exchanged confused looks, but didn't say anything.

'You don't need to mask from us,' said Edie, squeezing his arm.

'I'm masking from myself,' said Fadil.

Well. Ouch. Edie squeezed his hand. What could she say to that? Was it possible to mask how you felt from yourself? I wasn't self-aware enough to answer that question.

'I'm sorry, are we missing something?' said Percival.

'Fadil is four thousand years old,' Javi answered. 'Long story.'

'Oh! My!' Millicent covered her face, as if trying to hide her surprise.

'So, I hate to feel like I'm rushing this fun catch up, but how did you take him down, exactly?' I asked.

Millicent clasped her hands in front of her. 'We broke down each of his powers, rendering him nothing more than a vulnerable, psychotic human. Then, after absorbing his life essence, we set the house on fire.'

'Well, that's a surefire way to get rid of someone,' said Fadil.

'That's what we thought,' said Millicent. 'After all, taking his life essence meant he'd be too weak to do anything whether he was living or dead. Obviously, he could recharge over time, but that wouldn't have mattered if he was still trapped. I suppose the most important thing right now is to remember that he can't regain any powers. They have to be tied to a vessel because he wasn't born with them. And if he does choose a vessel, he'll be restrained by the physical limitations of that body, which could be very different to his own. Whether or not he's figured any of that out yet…'

'How many people he's murdered would suggest he hasn't yet, but he might do soon,' I said. 'That or he just really likes killing people.'

'Based on what he was like when he was alive, I think it's likely a combination of both,' said Percival.

Well wasn't Goodfellow shaping up to be a real ray of sunshine?

'Do you know what powers he took last time?' Ben asked.

'When we defeated him, he had strength, intelligence, and witchcraft. Before he died, he was targeting a vampire, which is why we knew we had to act when we did.'

'I'm sorry, a vampire?' I said. As if they were real as well. Why was I even surprised by these things anymore?

Millicent and Percival exchanged knowing looks. 'Your time is really very sheltered, isn't it?'

Fadil scoffed. 'Try narrow-minded.'

I glared at him, but I had to know: 'Why would it have been bad if he was targeting a vampire?'

'Since vampires are immortal, it would've given him the power to heal, which meant that we wouldn't have been able to stop him. It would've completely changed our plan and made him close to invincible.'

Edie frowned. 'Tobias said that, too.'

Millicent flinched. Was there a history there? They would've been from around the same era. Maybe they'd known each other. Alchemists were known for being dodgy…

I wanted to ask, but it wasn't the time. We had bigger things to worry about.

Percival pursed his lips. 'We were almost too late.' He glanced at his wife as he retold the story. 'When we arrived, he was in the middle of stealing a vampire's powers. Because we interrupted, the vampire could escape and fully heal. I believe he's still around now, although I doubt he's local anymore. As we interrupted Goodfellow mid-ceremony, it also meant that he was more vulnerable, which worked to our advantage. We started by removing his active witch powers, as those were the ones that were the most likely to harm us, then, we worked on the others.'

'Couldn't you have drained him by taking his life essence, first?' asked Edie.

'That's a nice idea in theory,' said Millicent, 'but the power he inherited from a witch was a forcefield, which meant that Percival's necromancy skills wouldn't have worked on him until he was more vulnerable. Taking him down mid-ceremony meant he couldn't cast the shield at the same time as his magic wasn't strong enough to multi-task.'

Ben tensed beside me. He didn't know any other witches with his power – it wasn't one that ran in his family – so this was probably somewhere between interesting and horrifying for him. 'He couldn't use the shield and steal powers at the same time?'

'No. He wasn't strong enough. Perhaps, if he'd had more time to hone his skills, he may have learned how to. But he wasn't a native user, nor was the witch he acquired the power from particularly strong, which limited his capabilities,' said Millicent.

'Of course, he didn't know that powers are a sliding scale and some users are more powerful than others,' added Percival.

Millicent smirked. 'Which worked in our favour.'

'Very much so,' agreed Percival, 'because it meant he was unprepared for our powers.'

'He thought that he'd still be able to take us on because he had the shield, but he was unaware that he wouldn't be able to use it unless he broke the procedure he was performing on the vampire.'

'Didn't the procedure stop when the vampire got free?' asked Edie.

'No. They were still tied together until Goodfellow broke the bond, which he didn't want to do halfway through. When he realised what we were doing, he did, but by then it was too late. He was too drained from what he'd done already, making him even more vulnerable as he hadn't been able to recharge from someone else's power.'

'All right,' said Ben, standing up and pacing around the living room, navigating furniture and ghosts. It was quite impressive how he managed it while maintaining his restless pace. 'So what you're saying is that right now he has no active powers, but there's something innately powerful about his spirit, just not in the sense we're used to.'

'Yes,' confirmed Percival.

'He's always had a strong character. A strong will,' added Millicent.

'And he really doesn't like failure,' said Percival.

'And someone like him would construe what happened last time as a failure, which would make him angrier,' said Fadil.

Millicent nodded.

'Well isn't that just great?'

31

Niamh

'Psst! Psst! Neevie wake up!'

'No.' I rolled over in bed, ignoring my ghostly wake-up call. I knew who it was. But I was trying to catch up on sleep. He wasn't helping matters by turning up past midnight. Surely he knew how sleep-deprived I was? He'd only seen me a few hours ago!

'Neevie!'

I opened my eyes. Javi was lying on his side, floating above the bed opposite me. Oh, the times I'd woken to see him lying beside me, that mischievous grin of his the first thing I saw. Damn, I missed him.

Except when he woke me up. It was all right for him. He didn't need sleep.

'Yes?'

'You've got a visitor.'

'I can see that.' He was right in front of me.

'No, another one.'

He pointed behind me.

Who else would want to talk to me who couldn't just appear without Javi's help? I sat up and turned back around. Lindsay, Ben's sister, was floating between my bed and the window. She was a witch, which meant there were many things she could do. But visiting unannounced from the Other Side required help from a necromancer ghost.

'I'll give you two some privacy,' said Javi. He floated through the wall and outside into the night air. No doubt to nose on the neighbours.

'I know we haven't really spoken,' said Lindsay, 'but I wanted to talk to you about Ben.' She rubbed her hands together, avoiding eye contact. Her curly brown hair fell into her eyes, but she didn't move it out of the way. She looked a lot like Ben. If I hadn't known she was his younger sister, I'd have wondered if they were twins. The biggest difference was her lack of glasses and her better dress sense. She wore slim-fitting blue jeans with a black V-neck T-shirt that hugged and hid all the right places. Simple, classic, effective.

I shifted in bed to sit up. She had my attention. 'What about him?'

I hadn't heard any barking or movement, so Edie and Tilly must've still been asleep. I appreciated Javi not waking them up. Edie needed her sleep even more than usual with everything that was happening lately.

'Ben can be really harsh on himself sometimes.' Lindsay hovered up and down, whatever was going on with her brother clearly making her restless. 'He talked himself out of getting the bookshop, you know.'

'I figured something like that had happened.' I mean, I didn't know the exact reason, but a U-Turn that fast usually stemmed from a lack of confidence or a lack of finances. His reaction made me think it was the former. Being self-employed was scary and hard. I didn't blame him.

Lindsay shook her head, then looked up at me. Her hair fell over her shoulders. 'I need you to talk to him.'

'*Me*? Why me?'

'He'll listen to you,' she said, meeting my eye for the first time since she'd woken me up.

'The last time we talked about it, he stormed off. That doesn't sound like someone who's going to listen to me.'

Lindsay pursed her lips. She started hover-pacing the length of my bed. It would've been unnerving if I wasn't used to Javi doing it. It was a sign of a restless ghost. Kind of like when a person did it. But mid-air, obviously.

'Have you tried talking to him?' I asked her.

She laughed. 'I'm his baby sister. He's never going to listen to what I have to say.'

'That sounds like exactly the reason he'd listen to what you have to say.' Not that I really knew anything about siblings. Maggie, Javi, and I were all only children.

'I appreciate you asking for my help, but I don't want to get into another argument with him. He seemed dead set on not opening it. If you feel that strongly, you should really talk to him about it yourself. I think he'll pay more attention than you think.'

He'd beaten himself up about Lindsay's death for a long time. She'd been in her late twenties, and he'd been convinced she was killed because she'd got into dark magic. Turned out, she'd been killed trying to stop Dominic from using his. And while she'd succeeded, she'd lost her life in the process, leaving her twin daughters motherless.

Lindsay opened her mouth to say something else. She stopped, closing her mouth and narrowing her eyes as if concentrating on something.

Javi floated back in. 'Do you hear that?'

The whistling. It was back.

'Is that the noise you keep hearing?' he asked me.

I nodded. It was the murder noise.

'I'm going to follow it.'

Before I could tell him not to – not that he would've listened anyway – he'd floated back through the wall in the direction of the whistling.

Lindsay and I waited, avoiding talking about Ben any further but otherwise falling into a comfortable conversation.

Javi returned ten minutes later, his face taught. 'I couldn't find it.'

'What do you mean?' said Lindsay.

'I tried to follow the direction of the whistling, but it sounded like it was really close and really far away. Like it was coming from everywhere and nowhere. It was so weird.'

'Did you find anything?' I asked.

'No,' said Javi. 'It was impossible to track.'

But the inevitable victim that would be found in the morning wouldn't be.

32
Niamh

'*Another body was found today in what police now believe to be the work of a serial killer.*' The radio echoed through the small bedroom that had once belonged to Mrs Brightman. So much for it being fun background noise.

Maggie had offered to help me clear my old friend's wardrobes and take stuff to the charity shop, since she had a bigger car. While the garage had dropped off my courtesy car, it was barely big enough to fit Tilly in the boot, let alone all the bags we needed to sort through.

Maggie was also incredibly organised, so would make both my life and the charity shop employees' lives easier. And she took payment in coffee, so I wasn't going to turn down the help.

I hadn't told Maggie, but part of our plan to take down Goodfellow involved summoning him to Mrs Brightman's house, since it was old and vacant. If we removed anything of value first, it wouldn't matter if he damaged anything.

But first, we had to organise almost nine decades of someone's life into boxes. It was sad, really.

'Oh my god,' said Maggie. 'Did you just hear that?'

I nodded, pushing my sunglasses up my face. Even though I really didn't want to think about what our Victorian friend had been up to, it was hard to avoid it. I couldn't even buy groceries without people talking about the murders, worried they'd be next, caught walking back to their car in broad daylight. And it wasn't like I could reassure them by explaining that Goodfellow didn't work that way. Especially when we didn't know for certain that he didn't, we were just going based on what little evidence we had.

'Have you found out any more about who's behind it yet?'

I hesitated, taking more time than was necessary folding a handmade wool cardigan. I wasn't sure if Mrs Brightman had made it herself, but I'd seen her wear it before. It had really suited her. I sighed, placing it into the bag. It wasn't something any of us would wear, so it was better off at the charity shop, where hopefully someone would buy and appreciate it.

Maggie frowned. 'What aren't you telling me?'

I was as transparent to her as ever. How couldn't I be? She'd known me long enough. But I really didn't want to worry her by telling her the full story.

'Neevie,' she said in her stern Mum voice. It caused the hairs on the back of my neck to prick up. I couldn't ignore that tone. No one could.

I turned around and leaned against the built-in wardrobe. 'The police aren't going to find who's responsible.'

Maggie gasped.

'It's a particularly nasty ghost. I mean obviously he's nasty. But what he's capable of is on a scale like we've never seen before.'

'So…are we at risk? Is my family?' Her voice went up at the end of that last bit. I didn't blame her. Her family had been through enough.

Um…think. What could I say? What could I do? I couldn't lie to her. Could I offer her some sort of protection?

Noticing my hesitation, her eyes went wide. 'Is there anything you can do?'

'I could put the wards back on your house?'

Maggie tensed.

'What?'

'That…might make things awkward with Harry. I really don't want to do anything to upset him right now.'

Her husband Harry had always been a sceptic. On some occasions he'd been downright antagonistic. But how could I protect her family if I couldn't do something as basic as preventing spirits from entering her house?

Maggie lowered her head. I couldn't protect everyone in her house, but there was a way I could at least protect her. 'What about the amulet? Would you wear that again?'

'Harry found it last time and told me to stop believing in "woo-woo nonsense" and almost broke it trying to take it off me.'

That was quite the overreaction to a piece of jewellery if I ever heard of one. Suspicious. But not entirely out of character. He was a mardy git and he really didn't like Edie or me.

'You could hide it. I mean, the two of you aren't exactly…*close*, lately, right?'

'No, we're not. He comes to bed late, after I'm asleep, and leaves the house before I'm awake. He's like a totally different person.' She frowned. 'I thought he'd be more attentive after what Josh and I have been through, but it seems to have spooked him and made him more distant instead.'

I reached over and held her hands. 'I'm sorry, Mags.'

'It's not your fault,' she said, wiping at the tears forming in her eyes. 'He doesn't deal well with emotions, you know that.'

There was not dealing well with emotions, then there was letting that dissociation hurt people, but I didn't think pointing that out would be helpful. 'A little protection never hurt anyone.'

Blinking back tears, she nodded. 'All right. I'll wear it. I always did think it complimented my colouring.'

'Exactly. If he asks, you can just say you think it's pretty and it suits you, but you don't believe what I say it can do. Whether you do or not.'

'I do, for the record. But thanks. That's a plausible excuse. It's better to be safe than sorry these days, right?'

'Right.' I nodded. 'Abigail is probably too young to be a target, and we can't help Josh and Harry if they don't want to be helped. And it won't be for long, anyway,' I added, feigning more confidence than I felt.

Maggie narrowed her eyes at me, but didn't say anything.

Still faking confidence, I continued: 'We're trying to find a way to take him down, but he's hard to find. We're not sure if a seance will even work. Javi tried to track him the other day but couldn't tell where the whistling was coming from.'

'Whistling?'

'That's what he does right before he kills someone. He whistles. And only ghosts and his next victim can hear him. And me.'

Maggie waved her arms in the air. 'Does that mean you're on his radar? Niamh, you have to be careful. There are rumours he dismembers victims while they're alive!'

'It's not a rumour. He does do that.'

Maggie gasped. 'But I thought ghosts couldn't... interact for that long?'

I shook my head. 'So did we. But then, a year ago, I never would've believed my daughter could bring me back from the dead.'

Maggie stopped mid-trouser fold. 'Wait a minute. You *died*?'

Oops. Forgot I hadn't told her that. And that probably hadn't been the best way to introduce the topic. It was getting hard for me to keep track of who knew what. I was so used to telling Maggie everything I forgot she'd missed just a few weeks in which *everything* had changed.

I filled her in on how Dominic had stabbed me and Edie had brought me back, then on how she was no longer as powerful because she'd chosen to help Fadil.

After I'd finished my story, Maggie paused for a moment, clearly digesting everything she'd missed. So much had happened in such a short space of time, I was still processing it myself. I couldn't blame Maggie for needing a moment, too.

She shook her head. 'It never stops with your family, does it?'

'Wish it did,' I said, sinking on to the floor.

Maggie sat next to me. 'It's not your fault.'

'It's not *not* my fault, though. This is all because of things I can't control, sure, but I always wonder if I could've protected Edie more. Or educated her more. Or just done *more*.'

She patted my shoulder. 'You're a great mum, you know that? You need to stop blaming yourself every time something goes wrong. Things go wrong all the time. That's life.'

'Life sucks,' I grumbled.

'Come on now. You don't mean that.' She turned to look at me. My expression must've been pretty bad, because she added: 'Do you?'

I shrugged. 'Sorry. This is all so small and stupid compared to what you went through.'

'Are you kidding me? You *died*. That's no small thing.'

'And you were tortured by a demon. That's not small either.'

Maggie gazed into the distance, her eyes glazing over. Fiddlesticks. I hadn't meant to cause that. While she'd been going to counselling with Alanis to process what she'd been through, it was still a lot. She'd only been out of the coma and away from demons for just under two months. It wasn't long enough to deal with that level of evil being in her face for ten days with no break.

She shook her head, as if trying to shake herself out of something. 'Sorry.'

I rubbed her hand. 'You all right?'

'I will be.'

She wiped at her eyes with the back of her other hand. We knew Dominic had had something to do with the demons that'd tortured her and Josh, but we didn't know how to find them, or even if they were on this plane. If I ever did find them, I'd introduce them to my own form of torture. Being raised by a narcissist had taught me a thing or two.

'What do you think Mrs Brightman is up to on the Other Side?' Maggie asked. Interesting change of subject. If it took her mind off demonic torture, I was going to go with it, even if it pained me.

'Javi said she's doing good. He wouldn't elaborate, but if she's happy, I'm at least happy about that. But it doesn't undo what Edie did.'

Oh no. I hadn't meant to mention that part. Stupid big mouth.

Maggie frowned. 'What do you mean?'

I shifted in my spot. Maggie sort of knew what Edie was capable of. But she didn't know the full story of what had happened. I'd tried to not tell her things, but I kept putting my foot in it. Well done me.

'What did she do?'

I sighed. I couldn't back out of telling her now. Wiping my sweaty palms on my jeans, I filled her in on how Mrs Brightman had been dying, and how Dominic had tricked Edie into taking the last of her life essence so that she could cross over.

'Oh my god,' said Maggie.

'I'm sorry I didn't tell you. I just didn't want you to judge Edie or me or hold it against us. Dominic was… a horrible person. And he used every tool he could to get what he wanted.'

Maggie put her arm around my shoulders. 'I'm glad you told me. You're not Edie's actions any more than I am Josh's. They're adults now. And even when they were children we could only do so much. They're people, not puppets. We can do our best, but we can't control them. And we shouldn't be punished for their actions, either.'

I pulled her into a proper hug. 'Thank you for understanding.'

'Of course. I've been around you long enough now. I mean, we had a brief snafu, but I think that's understandable. Javi fixed things, like he always does.'

'Damn, I miss him,' I said with a sigh.

Maggie nodded. 'Me too. His optimism was infectious without being irritating.'

'I dunno, it got pretty annoying at times,' I laughed. It still did sometimes, like when he woke me up in the middle of the night.

'That's true. I suppose I didn't live with it.'

I lowered my head. 'And I didn't get to live with it for long enough.'

She squeezed my shoulder. 'But you have Ben now, right? Things are good with you two?'

I rested my head on her shoulder. 'Yeah, they're good. But it's hard to let go of the what ifs, you know? Especially after what happened with Edie.'

'Yeah, I get it,' said Maggie as she stroked my hair. It was soothing. 'I sometimes wonder how Abigail and Harry would be different if she hadn't been possessed.'

I sat upright. 'What do you mean?'

'Abigail's been pretty withdrawn lately, even with Josh and me. She always seems ill lately, too. Germs after germs. And Harry is like a totally different person. Wait. You don't think he's possessed, do you?' She met my eye, a glimmer of fear in it. Then, we both started laughing. 'Who am I kidding? He's always been a mardy git, I was just in denial about it.'

'What changed?'

'I was tortured by demons who used his attitude against me. Even though I see him every day, I still find it hard to look at him.'

'Well. That'll do it.'

I felt bad for her. The demons and Dominic had taken so much from her already. Had they ruined her marriage, too?

She laughed again. 'If you don't laugh you'll cry, right?'

I nodded. 'And sometimes you have to do both.'

Maggie stood up and held her hand out to help me stand. I took it and she pulled me upright. 'I'll have a lunchtime drink to that. What do you say?'

'Where are we going?' I asked as I brushed some dust from my jeans.

'Mrs Brightman's liquor cabinet. I saw an expensive wine in there. This seems as good a reason as any.'

'The dark horse! I didn't even know she drank.'

Maggie smirked. 'Everyone has their vices.'

33
Niamh

'We have a problem,' said Ben the next morning. He walked in without greeting, a sombre expression on his face. Fadil was behind him, looking equally defeated.

'More problems?' I asked, hugging my coffee to me as if it would make me feel better. It didn't, but at least it was warm.

Edie looked up from the sofa, where she was eating her toast. Tilly ran over to them, demanding attention. Fadil picked her up and cuddled her, but it seemed more like it was because he wanted comfort than because he wanted to play. She cottoned on quickly, settling into his arms.

'Goodfellow killed a witch,' said Ben. He glanced out of the window, as if checking for something or someone, but there was no one there. It was a usual grey, dreary December day.

'*What?*' Edie and I chorused.

Ben nodded. 'We were due to go on an investigation last night. I didn't go just in case, but the other witch on our crew never said she wasn't coming, she just didn't turn up. One of the guys went to visit her house this morning and found it empty. Her body was at the

231

end of her street, as if she'd been caught walking to the investigation and he'd found her.'

'I'm so sorry,' I said, walking over to Ben and hugging him. He rested his head on my shoulder. I didn't know much about his ghost-hunting crew, but they seemed to go out together fairly regularly.

'Oh my god,' said Edie. 'Do you think that's what happened?'

'Everything fits.'

'Do you know what her power was?' I asked.

'Super hearing. I suspected she was a vampire but could never prove it and didn't want to ask. It's kind of a personal question. But if Goodfellow's whistling has something to do with his murders, perhaps it has some sort of impact on his victims. It would've made her particularly sensitive to it, too,' said Ben.

Still clutching Tilly, Fadil sat on the sofa, shaking his head. 'Now what do we do?'

'We need to speed up our timeline,' said Ben. 'If he hasn't figured out he needs a vessel yet, he will have now. The mind can trick us into many things, but it can't give us super hearing without supernatural intervention.'

'Well isn't that just great?' said Fadil, rolling his eyes. He sneezed into his elbow, causing Tilly to glare at him. 'Sorry.' As if satisfied, Tilly curled back up in his lap.

'She hates it when you sneeze or cough,' Edie informed him. 'Don't know why.'

'Shame we can't infect Dr Not-So-Goodfellow with my germs,' he joked.

'It would be one way to incapacitate him more easily,' Ben agreed.

I clenched and unclenched my fists. 'Looks like we're going to have to bring our plan forwards.'

*

Summoning a psychopathic ghost with a doctorate in butchery felt like a disastrously bad idea, but if we didn't do something, more people were going to get hurt, and I'd never get any sleep again. Not to mention Edie would never be free from Tessa's torment if we didn't stop her murderer.

We were going to summon Goodfellow to Mrs Brightman's unwarded, unoccupied house. It would keep him away from our houses if anything went wrong.

Of course, if he wanted to find us he probably would. But mentally it made us feel better to summon him away from our homes.

Edie and Fadil drew a salt circle in the centre of the worn living room carpet, while Ben and I moved the furniture out of the way so that he couldn't use any of it against us. We'd tried to convince Fadil not to get involved, but he insisted that there was safety in numbers and he wasn't backing out. He was leeching Edie's powers, now, so in theory, if she needed a boost, we hoped he could provide it. He might also have a little bit of Dominic's spell-casting powers, too. We'd tried to get him to cast a couple of spells before, but nothing had really happened. Would trying it under all the stress make a difference? We were about to find out.

'Ready?' said Ben as the four of us arranged ourselves in a square around the salt circle.

'Not in the slightest,' I said.

'We're as prepared as we'll ever be,' said Edie.

'Doesn't mean we're ready,' mumbled Fadil.

'We are. We've got this,' said Ben. I wished I shared his confidence, but I didn't. Assuming he meant it and wasn't just saying that to give *us* some confidence, that was.

My hands shaking, I reached out and held one of his. It reassured me, which gave me the confidence and calm I needed.

Even though I'd faced off against a poltergeist fairly recently, I was still terrified of them. They were crazy, unhinged, unpredictable. One had killed Javi because we'd been cocky and underestimated him, which was part of why we were taking so many precautions. That didn't make me any less afraid of him, though. The ghost who'd killed Javi had been bothering one family. This ghost was terrorising a whole town and was capable of dissecting people. He was a whole new level of unhinged.

'We call upon Randolph Goodfellow, to commune with us tonight, grant us your presence, come join us in the light,' the four of us chorused.

We'd adapted the spell to specifically attract Goodfellow and nobody else, since sometimes other ghosts intercepted the signal.

His figure flickered into view, like an image on a zoetrope. When he stopped, I was surprised at how clear he was. If it hadn't been for the faint glow around him, he would've looked human. Worse, that glow was fainter on him than it was on most other ghosts. Even without other people's powers, he was still insanely strong. Gulp.

He looked just how his previous victims had described him – imposing, formal, slightly bloody. His posture was tall and stiff; he carried himself proudly. His expression was one of curiosity, as if he wasn't sure how he'd arrived in our salt circle but was intrigued to see how things played out. I just hoped they played out in our favour.

We started the spell I'd only used a handful of times before. It was designed to obliterate any ghost in the vicinity. It was the nuclear option, but it'd never failed me before.

'Save this house from the ghost inside, remove this spirit from where they preside, give them no right to the Other Side.'

We repeated the spell, over and over, but it didn't seem to do anything. He flickered a little, but it was hard to know if that was from the spell or just because he was a ghost. Why wasn't the spell working? What were we missing? Was he too powerful, even for four of us? Surely not?

Please not.

Over the top of our chanting, he began to whistle. It wasn't the melodies I'd become familiar with during my sleepless nights; this one was different. It felt more like a summoning.

Fiddlesticks.

A bird cawed. A moment later, a raven flew into the living room, landing on the salt circle. Branwen. Using her wing, she wiped a gap into the salt circle. How could she *do* that? That was not normal. And we were about to be in big trouble.

Goodfellow wiped his hands together. Stepping out of the circle, he laughed. 'That all you got?'

He flung his arms wide.

The four of us flew backwards. I crashed into the sofa. Edie hit the floor. Ben headbutted the armchair. Fadil smacked into the wall.

While we were all conscious, everyone seemed too weak – or maybe unable – to move. I rubbed the top of my shoulder where it'd hit the sofa.

Goodfellow whistled again. This time, it was a tune I knew all too well. It was the one he used right before he murdered his victims. Gulp.

The sound set my nerves on edge, filling me with an internal buzzing.

But it also washed over me, like it was trying to do something but couldn't.

I glanced around at the others. Their bodies were stiff, as if they were frozen into position. Was that what his whistling did? Was it a way to immobilise them?

Why wasn't it working on me? Was I immune somehow?

Goodfellow walked over to Fadil, kneeling in front of him.

Fadil's lips drew into a tight line. His face was the only part of him that seemed able to move.

'There's something unusual about you, but I can't work out what. I like it, though.' Goodfellow reached out, as if to stroke Fadil's cheek. Fadil's face tensed further. Goodfellow never touched him, and I wasn't sure if it was because he couldn't, or because he never intended to. Either way, it seemed to have the desired effect on Fadil. 'You're a curious specimen. I'd love to get know you more. Perhaps one day.' He smirked, then stood up.

Fadil's body was so tense I thought he was going to start vibrating. Even though Goodfellow was now circling around the room, as if choosing who to pick on next, Fadil still looked terrified. It felt like we all held our breath as he floated around the faded maroon carpet, taking his time, enjoying the sights, tormenting us.

Branwen flew in circles above, watching everything unfold, waiting for the next orders from her master.

Goodfellow jerked, shoving his face into mine. I jumped. Annoyingly. He smirked. Because of course he did. 'You can still move. Well, isn't that interesting?' He glanced around at the others, who were still immobile but able to move their faces. 'Branwen didn't tell me about that, but, I suppose she can't know everything. She is only just a raven.'

'What's that supposed to mean?' I asked.

He glanced up at Branwen, who was still circling above us. 'Branwen monitors people for me. Notices characteristics that may be useful.'

As if things couldn't get any creepier, his bird had been spying on us. Wasn't that just brilliant?

Before I could ask a follow-up question, Goodfellow continued: 'There's something about you, but I'm not sure what.' He leaned back, as if taking me in. I shuddered. 'You must be the matriarch.' He nodded. 'Yes, that's right. You're not the smartest, but people come to you anyway. Was this plan yours?' He tutted. 'You really should've known better. Isn't it your job to protect everyone? Haven't your failures hurt enough people already?'

How did he know that? Had he been watching me? Listening to my conversations? A bird couldn't handle all of that surely?

I curled my hands into fists, not wanting to fall for his bait but feeling every word. He was right. It had been my plan. I'd failed. And now I had no idea what he was planning, but it was like we were all too incapacitated to stop him.

'That was some spell you cast,' said Goodfellow, crouching down in front of Ben. Ben looked like he wanted to do something, like use his forcefield, but he was too restrained by invisible forces. How long would Goodfellow's hypnotism, magic, whatever it was, last? And why didn't it affect me? 'You must be quite the witch. And you have the added bonus of forcefields. Wonderful power. So many useful things you can do with them. The things I did back in the day. That I'll do again.' He smirked.

Finally, he stopped in front of Edie. 'A necromancer. A rare creature indeed.' His lips curled into something between a snarl and a smile. 'Wouldn't you be fun to play with?'

'Leave her alone!' I said, falling for his bait. Fiddlesticks. That was the last thing I needed to do, but I couldn't stop myself. I wasn't going to let him hurt my daughter.

Goodfellow didn't come over to me, but he did turn to face me, smirking again. 'Feeling overprotective now, are we? Little late for that, don't you think?'

I ground my teeth together. Even though I wanted to say something witty or defensive, I didn't. It was like my mind was devoid of any sort of come back. Was that him, or was it me?

Goodfellow returned to Edie: 'I sense your rage, necromancer. It's powerful. You can do a lot with it. *I* can do a lot with it.' He nodded, his expression appearing as if he was half in the moment and half in thought. 'Don't lose it, necromancer. It could be your most powerful weapon.' He grinned, standing up.

The blood was pounding in my ears so loudly I could barely hear anything. If my heart beat any faster I was going to start hyperventilating. What did this guy want with us? Why was he tormenting us? Couldn't he just get whatever he had planned over with?

'Don't worry,' he said, addressing all of us this time. 'I'm not ready for you yet. But when I am, oh, we'll do great things together.'

With one last cackle, he and his raven vanished.

*

Everyone in the room relaxed.

'I can move again!' said Edie. 'What the hell was that?'

'Some sort of hypnotism, I think,' said Ben.

'But ghosts can't whistle,' said Fadil. 'They have no lungs! Technically they have no lips! *They can't breathe air*!'

'They're not meant to be able to touch people, either. This guy is defying all the rules. Because why break one when you can break them all?' I said, not sure if I was joking or being serious. In our current situation it was hard to tell.

'It's weird,' said Edie, stretching her arms out behind her and cricking her neck. 'He didn't feel all that magically powerful. His life essence was more just…overpowering, if that makes sense? Almost like what I got from Dominic but without the side of necromancy and illness.'

'That's interesting,' I said. My hands were still shaking and the blood pounding in my ears. Was it over? Was he really gone? I really hoped so. But also… we'd failed. Who knew what he was going to do next? 'Is everyone OK? That's the most important thing.'

We crawled over to each other, huddling together.

'Sore but fine,' said Fadil.

'Still in one piece,' said Ben.

'Me too,' said Edie. 'Mum?'

'Yeah, I'm all right. Physically, anyway.'

We slowly pulled apart, but stayed close to each other.

'I'm sorry. I wasn't fast enough to put my forcefield up and stop him,' said Ben. He lowered his head, blinking back tears.

'It's not your fault. He caught all of us off guard,' I said, putting my hand on his shoulder. He flashed me a weak smile in response. He was clearly beating himself up for not acting fast enough, which I didn't really blame him for as I would've done the same thing. But it *wasn't* his fault. It was *my* fault because it'd been *my* plan. Trying to exorcise him in a house with no extra protection had backfired colossally.

'Are you all right? I mean, technically he's a poltergeist. And he's *powerful*.' Ben put his hand on my leg.

I held my hands up to show how much I was shaking.

Edie reached out and grabbed them. 'Ignore what he said, Mum. None of it's true.'

'He was just trying to get inside our heads to weaken us,' I said, giving Edie's hands a squeeze. His words *had* got to a part of me, though. I felt like a failure for so many reasons, that encounter with Goodfellow being one of them. 'I still hate poltergeists but I'll be fine.' If I said it, I'd believe it, right? At the very least it'd stop the others from worrying about me.

Edie nodded. 'I thought he was going to kill us.'

'So did I,' said Fadil with a shudder.

'He needs us,' said Ben. 'And now he knows it, too.'

'What do you mean?' I asked.

'It looks like he's known about us for longer than we thought, thanks to his raven spying on us. I knew they were smart creatures, but I didn't think they were capable of that.' Ben removed his glasses and cleaned them on his shirt.

Edie tensed beside me.

'What?' I said, noticing the subtle movement most other people wouldn't have.

'I think I've seen Branwen around a few times lately.'

Fadil huffed. 'Why didn't you say anything?'

Edie waved her arms in the air. 'She's a bird! I thought she was harmless!'

'It would appear she can certainly do something to help him, I'm just not sure what,' said Ben.

'Marvellous. As if we don't have enough to worry about already,' said Fadil.

Edie patted his leg.

'We need to be careful. Now that he knows who – and what – we are, we're all at risk. And it seems like he wants to torture us before taking advantage of what we can do.' Ben put his glasses back on, a solemn expression on his face.

Edie gulped. 'Meaning what?'

'I'm not sure I want to find out,' said Fadil.

34
Edie

I can't believe we failed. Our plan had been solid. Why hadn't we been able to exorcise him? Had we underestimated his power? Or was there something more to it? I wasn't sure, and I was too tired to figure it out.

Spectre lay beside me on the bed, so I absentmindedly stroked his grey fur. He licked my hand in approval. I smiled. He wasn't a very affectionate cat, but then, I was the only one who could touch him. That little lick felt like I'd earned his trust. I really hoped I could take him with me when I moved out one day.

I closed my eyes, hoping I could get some desperately needed sleep. It was too tempting to heal myself and my family using my powers. I really, really wanted to, but it was a bad idea. We needed rest and good food instead.

As I was almost asleep, I heard it. Whistling.

I sat upright, startling Spectre. If the way he'd tensed was anything to go by, he could hear it, too. It was different to the one he'd used on us when we'd been at Mrs Brightman's earlier in the day.

Was the crazy doctor coming for me? Or just trying to drive me mad so that I couldn't sleep?

He couldn't get through our wards. I didn't think. Dad could only bypass the wards because he was on our side. There was no way a ghost who wasn't even technically magical could. Could he?

I got out of bed and looked out of the window. I'd only wake Mum up if there was a reason to. Which I really hoped there wouldn't be.

Right outside my window, lit up by a streetlamp, was Goodfellow. So much for him not finding out where we lived.

He looked up at me, his lips curled into a sneer. He cackled, tilting his head back he was laughing so hard. Lifting his arm out, he began to walk away. Branwen flew over and landed on his arm as he walked off down the street before the two of them disappeared.

The whistling stopped.

My heart thudded in my chest. I couldn't breathe. I grabbed Spectre and barged into Mum's room. She was already awake, on her phone. Tilly was at the foot of her bed, growling. When Mum saw me, her eyes went wide. 'You heard it?'

'He was outside my window.'

'*What?*' She clutched her phone tighter.

'He laughed then walked off with Branwen on his arm. He's gone now.'

I lay beside Mum in bed. Tilly and Spectre curled up with us. 'It's like he's saying he can watch us whenever he wants. For some reason, I can't always sense when Branwen is there. I don't get it.'

'They're only small animals. They won't have a particularly strong life essence. If there are a lot of stronger forces around, it may get drowned out.'

'Could this get any worse?'

'Maybe let's not tempt fate right now…'

*

Knowing Goodfellow or his creepy raven could be watching any of us at any point put me on edge. Even just the sound of Tilly barking, someone knocking at the front door, or a cyclist going past when I was walking Tilly caused me to jump a mile.

Mum, Ben, and Fadil were just as bad. We did what we could to support each other, spending every moment we could to come up with another plan, but we weren't really getting anywhere. Since he was a ghost, we couldn't recreate what Millicent and Percival had done. But was there a way to adapt it?

I tried to continue with college like everything was fine, but my anxiety got worse by the hour as I waited for Goodfellow to do something to one of us. I doubted he'd strike when there were lots of people around, since he'd never been caught, so I doubted he'd want to risk being caught now, either, but I couldn't say for definite. He was a ghost, after all. It wasn't like most people could see him anyway.

Then, on top of that, I still couldn't stop thinking about how Tessa had cheated on Josh. I might've decided not to tell him, but that didn't mean not doing so wasn't eating me up inside. Nor did it stop Tessa from doing her best to keep me away from him. She got in my face while I was walking down the corridor, then sat in between us, right in the middle of the classroom floor, during English. As if he'd sit anywhere near me anyway.

I couldn't work out if she was more afraid of me or angry at me, but I honestly didn't care. Really I just wanted her to leave me alone. I had more important things to worry about.

I was packing my things up at the end of English, thinking of ways to defeat Goodfellow, when something made Tessa jump. She squealed, falling into me. Frazzle.

I stumbled, doing my best to regain my balance and make it look like I'd just lost my footing.

'Oh my god. You feel…corporeal.' Tessa poked my arm. I flinched. She giggled. 'This is amazing! But why can I touch you and not anyone else?'

I rolled my eyes and walked off. That was just great, wasn't it? Now Tessa knew that she could touch me, she could use that against me. As if her being in my face and a constant presence that only I could see when I was trying to study wasn't bad enough.

Tessa used the fact that she could touch me to further try to keep me from Josh for the rest of the day. It wasn't like I ran into him all the time, but she seemed to think I might. Any chance she got, she was pushing me and getting in my face. It was really hard to keep pretending I was just being clumsy when she did it around others.

I got so tired of it that at the end of the day, when it was quiet, I grabbed her and dragged her behind some bushes while Josh packed up his things from art class on the other side of the wall.

'Would you leave me alone? I'm not going to tell him! It's none of my bloody business! I have enough going on already and I'm really tired of you trying to make my life even harder.'

Tessa crossed her arms, resting her weight on one foot. Well, sort of. She was a ghost. So she didn't have any actual weight. I assumed it was a pose she'd learned when she was alive and she was doing it out of habit to show attitude. 'I don't believe you.'

'I honestly don't care what you do or don't believe. Just stop harassing me!'

It was frustrating, having to practically whisper so that nobody saw me talking to air. But I had to say something to her because I couldn't go another minute with her in my face. Even dead, she was still torturing me. I'd had enough.

Tessa pouted, looking away from me.

'You don't like me, I don't like you. Why don't we just agree to leave each other alone? You can haunt Josh in peace, and I can get on with my life, ghost-free.' Well, not ghost-free, but Tessa-free.

'Fine,' spat Tessa. She flew through the wall behind me and back to Josh.

Peace. Finally.

I really hoped getting rid of Goodfellow would get rid of Tessa, too. The sooner she crossed over, the happier I'd be.

35
Edie

To my surprise, Tessa really did start ignoring me. It was heavenly, not having her in my face. Instead, she hovered near Josh, peering over his shoulder. Surprisingly, she wasn't even speaking to him anymore. Had she finally realised it was a waste of time, because the only person who could hear her was me?

On Saturday, I took Tilly for a walk in the hopes that it would make it easier for me to concentrate on revision when I got home. I was almost done with mock exams, but my brain had already decided to give up on me. So I thought some fresh air and some movement might help.

Tilly trotted along beside me, occasionally stopping to sniff a patch of grass. A thin layer of white covered the grass and the ground. It was early, earlier than I'd usually be up, and the wind had a bite to it. The frost made the ground slippery, so I was careful not to lose my footing. I'd wash Tilly's paws when we got in to get any grit, poo, or other things from between her toes.

A couple of times I had to stop her from rolling in fox poo, her favourite perfume. Even though the ground was slightly frozen, that fact didn't seem to deter her from trying to get to the fox poo. It was so gross. But of course, as a dog, she didn't think so.

Other than that, it was a refreshing walk.

Until, on the way home, Tessa's funeral procession went past.

I knew it was hers because she was watching from a few feet away, sobbing.

I stopped, lowering my head as the three black cars passed.

Tessa walked alongside the cars, hunched over and with her head in her hands. I'd never seen her cry so hard. Fragility wasn't something she showed very often. But I supposed when other people couldn't see you, what did it matter?

Tessa covered her eyes, her chest heaving as she almost seemed to hyperventilate. She couldn't, since she didn't breathe, but that was the best way I could describe the way she moved. It looked like she was almost having a panic attack. Could ghosts have panic attacks? I mean, her funeral did seem like a prime candidate for something like that.

She noticed me watching her, met my eye, then turned away and kept walking.

It was the first time I'd seen Tessa look truly broken. And lonely. It didn't sit right with me. Even though she was a massive bitch, she'd suffered for something that wasn't her fault.

Unfortunately, my walk home was in the same direction as the funeral procession. So I had to keep going behind it, at least until the end of the road, where I could go in another direction.

Tessa noticed I was following. 'Coming to the funeral?' she said with a forced laugh.

'No.'

Nobody else was around, and I figured anyone in the funeral cars was too busy crying to notice me. Josh was probably in one of those cars. I pushed the image of him crying in his black suit, sitting beside her parents, to the back of my mind.

Tessa lowered her head. 'I'm sorry. I don't know how to do this.'

'Whatever.'

I wasn't interested in her fake apologies. Tilly and I sped up, carrying on down the street and turning away.

*

Mum was at home, polishing the living room, when I walked in. 'Good walk?'

'Sort of.' I let Tilly off her lead, then went into the kitchen to get the stuff to clean her paws.

Mum followed me, standing in the doorway. 'What happened?'

'Saw Tessa's funeral procession. She tried to apologise to me.' I shook my head as I filled the cup with shampoo and water. 'I'm so tired of her games. Why can't she just leave me alone?' I turned off the tap. 'It's like she doesn't even want our help solving her murder, she just wants to keep bullying me.'

Mum twirled the yellow polishing cloth between her fingers.

'We can't just sit by and let Goodfellow keep killing people, though. Or wait for him to attack one of us. But it feels like she wants to keep suffering, and she's fine if other people keep suffering, too.'

Mum sighed. 'Have you tried talking to her on your terms?'

'What do you mean?'

Mum pursed her lips. 'Hear me out, before you say anything. If you can find a way for Tessa to talk to Josh – which is clearly what she wants or she wouldn't be haunting him – it might give them both some closure. And help you understand what they saw in each other.'

I snorted. 'Why do I care about that?'

'It might help you move on.'

'I've moved on just fine.'

Mum put the cloth down and sat on the sofa. 'You're not the least bit curious what he sees in her?'

'All right. Fine. What if I am? You really think she'd even consider talking to me? Let alone actually do it?'

'If she wants to get the closure she needs, she hasn't got a choice.'

36
Edie

Tessa? Cooperate with me? Mum had to be joking. I didn't see it happening, but I did believe it was key to helping her – and Josh, and me – move on. Even though I really didn't want to do it.

I walked along the college corridor, contemplating the best way to deal with Josh and Tessa. Was there a best way? Or was I going to have to make it up as I went along?

I was paying so little attention I walked straight into Tessa. 'Frazzle. Sorry.'

Tessa kept looking down and turned away from me. That was new. Where had her antagonistic streak gone? Had something else happened?

Josh, who'd obviously been standing nearby, talking to Melanie and Laura, looked over at me. He narrowed his eyes in confusion. I jerked my head into an empty classroom.

'Can you excuse me a moment please, ladies?' he said to Melanie and Laura. My skin prickled at how polite he was to them. He hadn't been like that with me for a long time.

'Sure,' said Laura.

Melanie met my eye for a moment, a question in her gaze. I nodded, hoping she understood that it was about Tessa. She nodded back, guiding Laura away.

Josh and I went into the classroom. I expected Tessa to follow, but she didn't.

It was an art room, so the walls were adorned with students' finished paintings, and there was a rack in the corner where the paint was drying. The tables were covered in paint splashes, and a couple had half-finished drawings on them. I stared at one of a laptop, trying to focus on the detail so that I didn't have to look at Josh's face while talking to him. Being so close to him just reminded me of everything we'd lost because of Dominic.

'What do you want?' said Josh. His tone was curter than I would've liked, but I didn't really blame him.

'Did something happen with Tessa?' I asked.

He rolled his eyes. 'Yeah. She's dead. Obviously.'

I pursed my lips. Of course. He didn't know. I'd thought he might've figure it out by now, or at least wonder, but obviously not.

Something seemed to click in his mind. 'Is she a ghost? Is she here? *Now*?' He seemed to perk up a bit, as if the prospect of interacting with her again made him happy.

My heart plummeted. Maybe he really did have feelings for her. 'She's not in this room, but she is a ghost. And she's haunting you.'

'*What*? Why didn't you tell me sooner?'

'It's not really the kind of thing most people want to know. It tends to freak them out,' I said. Can't imagine why.

'Is she following me, like, everywhere? Including the shower? The *toilet*?'

I pursed my lips. Only Tessa could answer that, although I really hoped the answer was no.

'Can you, like, stop her from haunting me? Or is she tied to me forever?' Now he seemed a little bit spooked. That was the reaction most people had. That or disbelief, but we'd already gone through that stage with Josh.

'That's up to her.' There'd probably be something in the Book of the Dead about it, but I still hadn't translated that much of it. I was too nervous of what I might learn. While I liked knowledge, I didn't always like knowing what I could do with my powers.

And translating it was a lot of effort. It was easier to ask Gran. Or get Dad to ask her. She seemed more willing to give him straight answers than anyone else. Maybe it was a respect thing because he was also a powerful ghost. Who knew? 'I imagine once her murderer is caught, she'll cross over, but I don't know for definite. It depends what unfinished business she has. Can you meet me at the park after English? I think it'll be somewhere quiet you can talk to her.'

'As in, I'll be able to see her?'

'I'll have to translate. She can't make herself visible to you, but I can let you know what she said.'

To Tessa's dismay, probably. But being able to make herself visible was beyond any power she had.

Without any magical powers, she'd have to channel her emotions to be able to do it and that took some ghosts years to learn, if they ever did learn to do it.

He sighed, stuffing his hands into his pockets. 'All right.' He left the empty art classroom without saying anything else.

I hated that things had become so stilted between us. We'd been so close, but so much had happened that I wasn't sure our friendship would ever recover. Things had ended so badly with me and him, and me and Dominic, and I was the villain in both situations. I didn't want to be that for Tessa, too. She'd been a bitch to me, and she'd never be my favourite person, but I hated to see her suffering. No one deserved the kind of death she'd experienced, not even her. It was horrific, and it would destroy her spirit if she stuck around too long.

She had all the hallmarks of a future poltergeist – a tragic death, a broken heart, and a bitchy streak. Although I hoped that her looking so sad meant she was starting to feel the consequences of her actions. It was just a shame it'd taken her death for her that to happen.

*

English class felt longer than usual, and not just because there was a heavy focus on revision rather than on learning anything new and interesting.

Once the hour was up, I practically ran out of the classroom, making my way to the park alone so that I could think, instead of waiting for Josh and Tessa.

Josh had avoided my gaze for the whole of class. That wasn't anything new, but he seemed different since I'd told him about the haunting. More relaxed, almost. I doubted that had anything to do with me. Especially after the way he'd perked up when I'd told him Tessa was haunting him and that he could speak to her.

Did he really have feelings for her? Had he had them when we were together? I really hoped not, but he'd moved on so quickly, it seemed impossible that he couldn't have. Feelings didn't develop that fast. Did they?

I sat on one of the swings in the park, staring at my combat boots. Tessa and I were so different. How could Josh have ever had feelings for both of us? Or was that why he had?

'So, where is she?' Josh had appeared in front of me and was now watching me expectantly.

To most people, he looked the same as he always had: blond hair, blue eyes, wearing blue jeans and a quilted coat. To those who knew him well, he was different. He walked with his head bowed and his shoulders hunched. He struggled to make eye contact with people, especially Mum and me. But it was his eyes that really gave him away. They had a haunted look to them that they hadn't had a few weeks ago.

I looked over his shoulder. Tessa stood as far away as she could, her arms folded as she watched a cocker spaniel running through the park with its owner.

It was a big, open park filled with half-dead grass, a handful of trees around the periphery, and a children's play park, which we were currently in. The spaniel and its owner were too far away to hear us, and there was no one else around, so we could talk freely.

'Behind you,' I said.

Figuring out we were talking about her, Tessa floated over. 'What are you doing?'

'Giving you two the opportunity to talk,' I said.

Tessa's jaw fell. 'Why…why would you do that?'

'She's asking why I'm helping you two talk,' I said to Josh. 'Because it's the right thing to do,' I told Tessa. 'So, what would you two like to say to each other?'

They both started talking at the same time. I put my hand up. 'One at a time, please. I can't translate if you're both talking. Tessa, you go first.'

'What am I supposed to say?'

I'd never known Tessa speechless before. It was refreshing. 'Say whatever's on your mind and that you'd like Josh to know.'

Josh sat on the swing beside me. It gave me flashbacks of all the times we'd sat together on the swings while out with Tilly. I forced the memories down. It wasn't the time. It was a *very* different time. I'd never expected to be on the swings with him as his ex-girlfriend, passing on messages to him from his dead girlfriend. Complicated, much?

Tessa hovered up and down a few times. It was a habit I'd seen from a lot of restless ghosts. They tended to do that or pace. 'I guess…tell him I'm sorry. I was so busy worrying about my own future that I couldn't enjoy the moment enough to really spend time with him or be there for him in the way that he needed.'

Well, I hadn't expected that. After a deep breath, I repeated what she'd said.

Josh wiped at the corner of his eye with his coat sleeve. Was he crying? He didn't usually get that emotional so fast. Should I have thought this through more?

'I know you left the party with that guy,' said Josh.

Tessa looked like a deer in headlights. 'I don't know what he's talking about.'

'Tessa, come *on*,' I said.

'What's she saying?' asked Josh.

I pushed myself off from the ground and began swinging. 'That she doesn't know what you're talking about.' I met her eye and added defiantly: 'but I know she does.'

Tessa's nostrils flared. I smirked back at her.

'What do you know?' Josh asked me.

I raised an eyebrow at Tessa in challenge. 'Would you like me to tell him? Or should he hear it from you?'

'Well, he's going to hear it from you regardless, isn't he?' said Tessa, that inner malicious streak returning. Defence mode: engaged.

'He can hear it from me, or he can hear it in your words. Your choice. I know it isn't ideal, but it's going to mean more to him if it comes from you.'

That seemed to soften her a little. Her chest rose and fell in a staccato rhythm a few times. If she'd still been alive, she'd probably have started crying. 'We'd had an argument. It's not an excuse, but it left me feeling kind of hurt. You said I was emotionally detached, but I felt like you were, too.' She shook her head. 'It was a bad combination, so I sought comfort.'

'She said that you had an argument, which isn't an excuse, but it left her hurt,' I translated. 'You said she was emotionally detached, but she felt like you were, too. That combination left her seeking comfort.'

Josh lowered her head. 'She's probably right. Emotional detachment is easier. I can't get hurt if I don't feel anything.'

'Josh—'

He put his hand up to stop me from saying anything else. 'I don't want your sympathy. I was tortured by demons because of you. Do you have any idea what that's like? I had no idea what was real and what wasn't. The only constant was you. *You*. They kept talking all about *you*. Sometimes they even pretended to be *you*.' He practically spat *you* every time he said it, as if I still disgusted him. Knife to the heart, much?

'He was tortured by demons?' said Tessa. 'When?'

'When he was in the coma,' I said to Tessa.

'That's right,' said Josh, figuring out what Tessa had asked. 'For ten days, demons teased me, tormented me, tortured me. They'd dangle exactly what I wanted in front of me, then rip it away in the worst possible way. I wasn't sure it would ever end. It was like a nightmare I couldn't wake up from.'

'But it did end,' I said.

'How do I know it won't happen again? So long as you're around, I'm in danger.'

How had this conversation about him and Tessa turned into one about him and me? I wasn't going to stop him, though. I had a feeling this was the first time he'd really opened up about what had happened to him. Hopefully it would offer him some sort of catharsis. Even if every one of his words just drew the knife deeper into my chest. He'd already broken my heart once. Why not shatter it again into even more pieces?

'You don't,' I said. 'Just the same as we didn't know it'd happen the first time. What Dominic did to you was incredibly rare and complicated magic. Putting a blood curse on top of demonic torture like that? Nobody we know has ever done that before. And I doubt anyone else would be cruel enough to ever do it again.'

'You don't know that, though. Do you?'

'He's right,' said Tessa in that know-it-all tone of hers.

I rolled my eyes at her. 'Of course we don't know for certain. But it takes a lot of power and he likely didn't do it alone. He probably worked with a demon from the Demonic Realm. Most people aren't stupid, reckless, or dangerous enough to do that.'

'Are you sure?'

All right, now he was winding me up. Did he expect me to have all the answers or something?

I stopped swinging, causing the bark underneath the swing to fly a few inches. I tightened my grip on the strings of the swing. 'Tell me one thing in life that's for sure.'

'The grass is green,' he said.

'What if it doesn't rain for a bit and it dies and turns brown? Looks like that's happening right now.' I pointed over to where the man and his dog had been. There wasn't much green left there. 'Or if it rains too much and becomes a different shade of green? Or it rains so much that it floods and kills the grass that way?'

'All right. The sky is blue.'

'Technically it's not, it's an illusion. And things like clouds, lightning, eclipses, and smog change it. Nothing in life is permanent except impermanence. We can worry about everything that might happen, or we can make the most of the situation we're in. Either way, change is going to happen.'

The tension in Josh's shoulders released, as if my words had got through to him on some level. I really hoped they had. They were all I had to try to comfort him. 'Tessa, I'm sorry for disconnecting. You didn't deserve that.'

Tessa's lip quivered. 'And you didn't deserve for me to betray you. You've been hurt enough already. I had no idea.'

I repeated her words.

'I didn't want you to,' said Josh. 'I had to keep the supernatural a secret, but having nobody I could talk to about everything just ended up hurting more people.'

'Is there anyone he can talk to? Like, a supernatural counsellor?' Tessa asked me.

'Tessa wants to know if you'd be willing to talk to the healer we know. She has a degree in psychology and has been working with your mum,' I said. Alanis seemed to have been a great help to Maggie, although she was much more open to therapy than her son was.

'I'll consider it,' he said.

It was progress. I'd take it.

Tessa almost smiled at me. It was a kind of mutual appreciation for him being open to the possibility of help. It was as close to us being on the same side as we'd ever get.

'Do you mind if I have a minute alone, please?' said Josh.

I went to stand, but Josh beat me to it. 'If you stay within about a hundred yards, Tessa can stay here and still have someone to talk to.'

Josh nodded, then walked off.

Tessa's body seemed to relax. 'I feel better after that, thanks. As much as I don't like you, I know you were the only person who could do that.'

I tightened my grip on the strings holding the swing up. If I held on much tighter, I was going to get rope burn.

'Can I tell you something?' she asked.

'Sure.'

I wasn't sure if I really wanted to hear what she had to say, but who else did she have?

'Mentally, I feel like I might be ready to cross over. But I can't until whoever did this to me is stopped. And I find out why they chose me.'

I tapped the string with my black fingernails. Should I tell her? It wasn't like she was unaware of the paranormal anymore.

'What? What aren't you telling me? Do you know who did this?'

If I didn't tell her, she'd only pester me even more.

'Yes. He's a Victorian ghost on a power trip. He kills people for their powers.'

She frowned. 'But I don't have any powers.'

'Supernatural abilities aren't the only forms of power. We think he targeted you for your intelligence, but we don't think it worked.'

'He wanted my brains? Well, that's a first from a guy.' She faked a laugh. 'You have to be joking. This type of thing isn't real.'

'Wish I was.'

She stepped closer to me, studying me with curiosity. 'Are you really a necromancer?'

'Yes.'

Tessa's gaze intensified. 'You're…still not joking?'

'No. Like I said: there's a lot more than witches in this world. And witches are the least of our concerns.'

37
Niamh

'Niamh, wake up!'

'Huh?' I opened my eyes to see Gwendoline inches from my face, practically screaming at me. I jumped, almost going through her she was so close.

Gwendoline floated back. 'I'm sorry, but I saw Edie's friend Josh in the cemetery by the park. He was doing a seance.'

'Son of a—'

'Goodfellow found him.'

'As if this month can't get any worse.' I hopped out of bed, almost falling over. Gwendoline reached out to help me, but for obvious reasons, couldn't. I righted myself, then grabbed the nearest clothes and began changing into them as fast as I could. 'Can you get Edie and Ben, please?'

'Of course.' She vanished out of sight.

I was grabbing my phone from the bedside table when Edie barged in. 'Mum—'

'We're going,' I said.

Thomas floated in, a concerned expression on his face. Tilly followed, clearly on edge because she knew something was wrong. She kept looking between us, as if searching for answers.

'Can you look after Tilly, please?' I asked Thomas.

He nodded. 'Yes. Anything. Just get him.'

'We will.' Edie hugged him. 'Come on, Mum. Let's go! Who knows how much damage he's done to Josh already? Where's Gwendoline?'

'Getting Ben,' I said. I rubbed Tilly behind the ears, then we dived out of the house and into the car.

*

Of course the green metal cemetery gates were closed when we got there. Because who needs to quickly get into a cemetery in the middle of the night? There had to be a way to get in. How else could someone have gotten in and vandalised the gravestones? And started this whole mess?

'I got this,' said Edie, crouching down in front of the padlock. She mumbled a spell. Her powers buzzed through the air. The gate rattled, but the lock didn't open. Unusual. Concerning.

'Frazzle!'

'Have you used that spell before?' I asked, crouching down to study the lock. Did I need to start carrying a lock-picking kit? I'd never needed one before, but then, I hadn't needed to break into anywhere before. It seemed to be a regular occurrence for all of us lately.

'Yes!' She stood up and huffed. 'But I feel weird. Wonky.'

Oh no.

If we couldn't rely on Edie's powers to open a gate, it seemed unlikely they were going to be any use against Goodfellow. Which was just great timing, wasn't it?

Think Niamh, think!

Should we have asked Ben and Fadil to bring a lock-picking kit?

Was it too late to ask them? Probably. And I doubted either of them owned one anyway.

There were no resident ghosts who haunted the cemetery, so we couldn't even ask them for help or to let us know if there was another way in. And since it was so huge, by the time we got to the other side of it, Goodfellow could have finished Josh off once and for all. *Not* an option.

Worst-case scenarios ran through my head, drowning out my ability to find solutions.

'Why don't you try?' suggested Edie, pulling me out of my own head.

'Try what?'

'My spell. What if it's just my powers that are the problem, not the spell itself? It's worked on tougher locks before,' she said.

'It's worth a shot,' I agreed. She gave me the spell she'd written to get into the bakery below Dominic's flat. I crouched down to the lock, imagining it opening as I said the words. *Click.* 'Yes!' I pushed the gate open.

It was so dark we couldn't see much, but there was a faint outline of three people near a tree, right in the centre. Since most of the cemetery consisted of gravestones and grass, they stood out against the rest of the landscape in a disconcerting way. Especially since two of them were glowing.

It was hard to tell from a distance, but it looked like Goodfellow was beating Josh and Tessa was watching in horror. Every so often she'd reach out, as if trying to intervene, but she'd get flung backwards and stay there few a moments before trying again.

We followed the path to them as fast as we could. It felt like the closer we got, the farther away we were, but I knew that was our minds playing tricks on us. We were getting there. We just had to keep running, and we'd make it to Josh. And we had to make it.

Noticing us, Tessa floated over. 'Where've you been? Never mind, thank god you're here! I'm so glad that other ghost was patrolling and found out what was happening! I tried leaving Josh but I couldn't.' She frowned, looking down at my legs. 'Can't you run any faster?'

'Not sure if you've noticed, but we still travel on the ground. Using our feet and legs. You can basically fly now. It's a little bit slower than your mode of transport,' I said.

'Run faster!'

I rolled my eyes, ignoring her since I was already going as fast as I could.

Running made me breathless, proving just how unfit I was. But I had to keep going, for Maggie's and Abigail's and Josh's sakes. Thinking of them gave me a burst of adrenaline that acted like accelerant, putting Josh just a few feet in front of me. He lay underneath a leafless tree, curled up in the foetal position. Every so often, he let out a strangled moan. The chilling wind moaned too, as if in conversation with him.

Edie caught up with me, but she didn't stop. Her face contorted in heartbreak and horror as she ran closer to her ex-boyfriend and former best friend. I tried to reach out and stop her, in case Goodfellow was using Josh as a trap, but I wasn't fast enough.

Goodfellow's gaze flickered between Edie and Josh. A plan was bubbling behind those sinister eyes, I just knew it. But I didn't know what it was, and I was terrified to find out. He'd already shown himself to be plenty dangerous. What was he going to do next?

Please don't let him hurt Josh. *Please*. He'd been through enough. Maggie had been through enough. All the Morgans had. They didn't deserve this.

What was Josh even doing there in the middle of the night? Gwendoline had said he was trying to do a seance. But in a cemetery? He knew he was being haunted. What difference did being in a cemetery – where Tessa wasn't even buried – make?

A smirk crept over Goodfellow's lips.

Before we could stop him, he disappeared inside Josh's body.

'No!' shouted Edie, reaching out to him.

Tessa gasped, covering her face with her hands.

Josh fell to the floor, hitting his head on the tarmac. His chest still rose and fell, but he didn't move. The two souls were fighting it out for control. Any minute, we'd see the external signs of that, too. Then, who knew what would happen?

I put my hand on Edie's shoulder to stop her from getting any closer. We were metres away, but it felt like miles. The closer we were, the more we risked putting ourselves in danger without a plan. We might've been trying to work out how to get rid of Goodfellow since our last confrontation with him, but we hadn't come up with anything effective. Which meant we were stuck and now had to improvise. And, just our luck, it appeared that our nemesis was already two steps ahead.

38
Edie

No. No no no no no. He could not be in Josh's body. He just couldn't! It wasn't allowed. It wasn't acceptable. It was completely unfair!

But he was. He was *possessing* the one person who probably deserved it least in the whole world. Not that he knew or cared about that. Knowing that probably would've just made Josh an even easier target for him.

I had to do something. But what?

Could I use my powers to stop him? Was I still strong enough? They'd failed a lock-picking spell, so they probably wouldn't be much good against Goodfellow, especially when they hadn't been last time, either. But I had to try.

I glanced around the cemetery for something – anything! – I could use. Yellowing, dewy grass. Trees swaying in the cold breeze. Frosty gravestones. Nothing. There was nothing I could use.

Why did I feel so helpless? I was a necromancer! I had control over the dead. There was no way I was helpless when a crazy ghost was loose on the town. If anyone could stop him, it had to be me.

My powers hurt people, though. They hurt me. They'd hurt Josh. All my powers had ever done was hurt him, really. What if I hurt him again by using them, even if my target was Goodfellow? Could I really risk using them again on him?

Josh still lay on the tarmac. He was now writhing, like a character in a film who was being exorcised. It looked so much worse in real life. If I was going to pull Goodfellow out of his body, stop him from taking control of Josh, this was my only chance.

I tried to concentrate, to latch on to Goodfellow's life essence, but it was like it was out of focus; impossible to grasp on to.

'What do we do!' I really hoped Mum had answers, because I was out.

She looked just as lost as I did, glancing around the dimly lit cemetery. 'Let's try the seance spell again.'

'That's it? That's all you've got?' said Tessa, waving her hands in the air. 'I thought you were a necromancer!'

I glared at her. 'Thanks. Add to the pressure, why don't you?'

Tessa didn't seem to care. She just watched us with frustration and impatience.

Goodfellow as Josh chuckled. Oh no. He'd won. He had Josh. Pushing himself upright, he smiled. 'It's good to feel again.' He stretched his arms out, flexing his fingers and admiring them as if they were works of art. 'I've never had artistic powers before, but I've always appreciated paintings.' He inhaled slowly, taking in the cold, crisp air. 'I can smell the faint aroma of water colours on this boy's clothes. Oh, how I've missed the little things.'

'His name is Josh,' I said through gritted teeth. Not that Goodfellow cared, but I had to say it. I curled my hands into fists, wanting to lunge at him. But what difference would that make? He reacted fast, and he was in a body that was stronger than mine. He was stronger than me in almost every way now that my powers were failing me. I was doomed. So was Josh.

'Leave Josh alone,' said Mum.

'He's really very quiet,' said Goodfellow. Even though he was in Josh's body, Josh looked different. Like he was someone else. Which, I supposed, was technically correct. Someone else *was* in charge of his body, and that would change everything from his facial expressions to his posture.

His facial expressions and his body movements weren't what Josh usually did. They reminded me more of what ghost Goodfellow had done, back when we'd summoned him. I shuddered, thinking back to our last encounter with him. Were we going to relive that, but with the crazy ghost in Josh's body? Hearing his torturing words would be so much worse coming from Josh's lips. Spoken in Josh's voice. I hated feeling helpless so much. But what could we do? Why couldn't we think of a plan!

I ground my teeth together. 'What have you done to him!'

'Nothing,' said Goodfellow. 'Yet.'

I lunged forwards, trying to force my powers to latch on to his life essence and pull him out of Josh, but nothing happened. Instead, I crashed into him. He flicked me aside like a bug.

I landed on the grass with a thud. At least he'd been able to throw me far enough that I hit the grass instead of the circle of tarmac he was standing on. But still. Ow.

Mum ran over, crouching down beside me.

'I'm all right,' I said before she could ask. The ground was soft and a little muddy, so it'd cushioned my landing. My jeans would be filthy when I got up, but that was the least of my problems.

Goodfellow pursed his lips to whistle, but all that came out were a few puffs of air. The one bright side to him not being from our world was that he didn't understand some of the nuances between the living and the dead. Like how, as a spirit possessing someone else's body, he'd take on the physical limitations of the body. Including not being able to whistle. Worked in our favour.

But, if the look on his face was anything to go by, he had no idea why he suddenly couldn't whistle. I wasn't going to explain it to him. Not my problem.

Branches crunched in the distance. Ben and Fadil were making a not-so-subtle entrance. They were at the other end of the huge cemetery. While we could see them, they were too far away for us to warn them.

It was enough to distract Goodfellow, though. He turned to face them, trying to walk in their direction. Except he wasn't meant to be in that body, and I had a feeling Josh was trying to fight him off. So he walked like he was drunk, or taking his first steps. It was clumsy and laboured; every step took way more energy than it should've. He'd swatted me away so easily before, but I supposed that was a quick burst of energy rather than a concentrated effort. They were different skills.

Mum examined the grave near where I'd fallen. Some of the stone on the top was smashed and covered in moss. 'Sorry,' she mumbled to the grave – I assumed her apology was for whomever the grave belonged to – grabbed one of the stones, and ran at Josh with it.

I reached out to stop her, but I wasn't fast enough.

Turned out, neither was she.

Goodfellow span around, ducked from the stone, and shoved her. She landed opposite where I fell, crashing into a small gravestone.

I ran over to check on her. As far as I could tell, she was fine. Still breathing, no blood. Conscious, but dazed.

Ben and Fadil ran faster, coming face-to-face with Goodfellow on the tarmac path between two rows of graves: Victorian on one side, twenty-first century on the other.

Houses loomed over in the distance. What would people think if they looked out of their windows and saw what was happening? I really hoped they couldn't hear us. With everything going on, I'd forgotten so many houses looked out on to the cemetery. I just hoped we were in a spot that was disguised enough by the high walls and tall trees.

Not realising Goodfellow was in Josh's body, only that something was off, Ben didn't put his forcefield up. We were still too far away to warn him.

Goodfellow picked up a rock from beside one of the graves and threw it in the air a few times, smirking. Ben narrowed his eyes, ready to respond. At the split second he put his forcefield up, Goodfellow threw the rock at them. It hit Fadil square between the eyes. He flew backwards, smacking his head on a gravestone.

'No!' I cried.

Mum stroked my hand, lifting her head. 'What happened?'

'Fadil!'

Mum sat up and turned around. 'Is he still…can you still…?'

'I think so, but it's weak,' I said. Tears dripped down my cheeks. 'Mum, what are we going to do?'

39
Niamh

We hadn't seen Fadil's ghost. I was taking that as a sign he was still alive even if Edie's powers weren't working how we'd hoped. I wasn't sure if her powers were wonky because Fadil was leeching, she was afraid to hurt Josh, or her confidence was beaten since the last time we'd faced Goodfellow her powers hadn't helped. It could've been a combination of all of them. All I knew was that we couldn't rely on her powers to get us out of this. Which made facing him even bloody harder. As if we weren't already short on ways to take him down.

Goodfellow watched Fadil, clearly smug at his handiwork. Git.

Ben formed his forcefield around the murderous ghost, protecting us from him and allowing us to run – or in my case, hobble – over to Fadil.

'Do something! Why aren't you doing something!' screeched Tessa. Seeing her glowing figure floating a few feet away, I was reminded of what Javi had done to protect another spirit from an evil ghost. Could she…?

'All right,' I said, 'I think I have a plan. But you're not going to like it.'

Tessa flapped her arms in the air, causing her to float upwards a couple more inches. 'As opposed to *this*?!'

Branwen flew overhead, waiting for her next instruction, while Goodfellow was standing in the forcefield, trying to whistle. Except he couldn't. Because Josh couldn't and he was bound by the restrictions of Josh's body. Ha. At least something was working in our favour.

'What's your plan?' Ben asked.

None of the others had been present when Javi had pulled the other spirit from someone's body, but I didn't have time to explain how I knew it could work. 'You need to go in there and pull Goodfellow out of Josh.'

'I need to *what*?'

'You can't be serious?' said Edie.

'Why can't you do it?' said Tessa.

'Because she's alive?' said Edie. 'The rest of us can't just go into someone else's body. You can.'

'Oh,' said Tessa, floating down to the ground. Or as close to it as she could get. She squared her shoulders, as if ready to go. 'So I just float right on in there and…pull him out?'

'Yeah,' I said, even though I knew it was unlikely to be that easy. If I told her that she wouldn't do it, though, and she was our only hope. I also didn't want to tell her that in case she crumbled under the pressure.

'Here we go!' Tessa flew through the forcefield and into Josh. Ben had allowed her through, but

Goodfellow wasn't going to. Almost immediately, she was thrown out of him. 'I can't do it,' she said, her voice wobbling as if she was trying not to cry. He's too strong.'

'Try again,' I said in my calmest voice.

Ben was still cradling Fadil, using his forcefield to keep Goodfellow away from us. It offered us a temporary reprieve, but it wouldn't stop him, and that was what we really needed.

'He targeted you *because* you're strong. Maybe in ways you've never even considered,' I told Tessa.

Tessa grunted, then flew back into his body again. And reappeared just as quickly. 'Son of a—' She ground her teeth together. 'There has to be someone else who can do this. Someone with actual powers they can use against him. Wait. I know someone. But I don't know how to get to him.'

'I could cast a tethering spell?' suggested Edie.

'We don't have time,' I said. 'Tessa, let go of Josh.'

'What are you talking about?' she screeched at me, as if I was a mad old woman. Offended.

'If you let go of your death grip on Josh, you could go and get us some actual bloody help!' Fine so that was a little harsh but so was she. And we were getting very short on time. We had no idea how long Fadil had left, or how long Ben could sustain his forcefield. Tessa frowned. 'I don't have a death grip on Josh.'

'You can barely leave his side,' grumbled Edie. 'That's on *you*. *You're* in control of how far you can go.'

Tessa wrinkled her nose. She really didn't like hearing this. Tough. Now wasn't the time for her to give up, admit defeat, or let go of the control over her life. Afterlife.

'You wanted control over your life? After your parents dictated everything you said and did? I *get* it,' I said. I got it more than Tessa would ever realise, even if she'd never actually said her parents controlled her life. It was all over the way they spoke about her on the news. I'd had to stop watching it because every interview made me want to vomit. Their behaviour was way too close to home, even if it wasn't identical to how my mother had treated me. 'I'm truly sorry you'll never get that. But you're the only one who can take control of your afterlife, and you're the key to helping us.'

She nodded, her body relaxing. 'Do you know where Thomas is?'

'*Thomas?*' I said. 'Why Thomas?'

'Ghosts talk. And it just so happens he's more powerful than you think, which is why he's been hiding. So, where is he?' said Tessa, crossing her arms impatiently.

Edie and I exchanged surprised glances. Thomas had looked like your average, translucent ghost since we'd known him, and Edie couldn't sense anything unusual from his life essence. If it turned out he was really powerful, it completely changed everything we'd ever known about ghost lore. Because Goodfellow hadn't done that enough already.

But Tessa had no reason to lie, and even if Thomas wasn't as powerful as she said, the chances were, he was more powerful than her and was therefore able to help.

'He's at our house,' I said.

Tessa squished up her features as her figure flickered in and out. A moment later, she vanished.

Edie looked around, searching for Tessa. 'Did it work?'

'We'll soon find out,' I said.

Ben was still keeping Goodfellow at bay using his forcefield. Thankfully. Goodfellow was still trying – and failing – to whistle. Every so often he'd let out a high-pitched burst of air, but that was about it. It was the same struggle I'd seen Josh have over the years, whenever one of us had tried to teach him to whistle. For whatever reason, he just wasn't able to do it.

Branwen circled ahead, watching. Waiting.

'He's still breathing,' said Ben as Edie and I bent down next to him. I put my hand on his neck to check his pulse, just in case. It was still there, but barely. Fadil's blood was gushing out on to the grass below. We were lucky it was going on to the grass and not a gravestone, really. That would lead to a whole lot of questions.

'That's good, that's good,' said Edie.

Goodfellow pushed against the forcefield. What looked like a bolt of lighting flew from the forcefield and hit his hand. He jumped back, gasping.

Ben smirked.

'Since when can your forcefields do that?' I asked. Not that I was complaining.

Goodfellow stared at his electrocuted hand, pouting. What was he, twelve?

Ben grinned triumphantly. 'Found a new spell recently. What do you think?'

'I like it. Definitely a contender for new favourite spell.'

Ben chuckled. 'Where's Tessa?'

'Helping. I hope,' I said.

'I can feel him slipping,' Edie whispered, her eyes flitting to Fadil. 'We have to do something.' She shook her head, tears glinting in her eyes. 'But I can't use my powers. They don't work.'

'I think I know what to do,' said Thomas, appearing in front of us with Tessa. 'Don't worry about Tilly – Gwendoline is with her.'

Me? Worry about the dog as much as I worried about my daughter? Yeah, that was me.

'I did it!' said Tessa, a huge grin on her face. The grin also made it look like she was expecting praise, a pat on the back, a medal, a letter from the king… whatever reward she could get. It pained me to reinforce her negative habits, but I didn't want to seem ungrateful either.

'Thank you, Tessa,' I said, smiling.

She looked at me as if to say, 'is that it?' but we had bigger problems to deal with.

Goodfellow cleared his throat. 'You know, I don't have all night. You can't hold me here forever.' He pointed upwards to his raven, who was still circling us. We didn't think she could impact Ben's forcefield like she had the salt circle, but we couldn't be sure.

Branwen wasn't going to target the forcefield, though. She flew at Ben, launching herself at his head. He ducked, dropping the forcefield. Fiddlesticks. Ben moved away from Fadil so that the bird didn't hurt him, but being away from all the gravestones just made Ben more exposed. He crouched down, waving his arms around to keep the bird away from him, all while mumbling different spells. Nothing seemed to work. And since I was used to dealing with ghost *people* who weren't directly attacking me, I didn't have anything that could help, either.

Goodfellow laughed, watching as his pet fought my boyfriend. Git.

Spotting an opportunity where Goodfellow was distracted, Thomas dived for Josh's body and disappeared inside it. Was he going to try to take Goodfellow down from the inside, like Javi had with another ghost?

Branwen's cawing as she pecked at Ben echoed through the graveyard. Ben yelped, doing his best to fight her off. She was too fast for him to get his forcefield back up and protect himself. Was it possible to exorcise a ghost bird?

Thomas fell out of Josh's body, landing on his side, mid-air. He turned back to Goodfellow/Josh and glared.

'Are you all right?' I asked.

Thomas lowered his head. 'I don't think I can do it. It's not working.'

'What were you hoping to do?' I asked.

'You think you can do anything to stop me? Look at you!' Goodfellow waved his arms in the air. 'You're all weak. Pathetic. Powerless. There's nothing you can do.'

Thomas shook his head, as if trying to shake the thoughts away. 'No I'm not!' He dove back into Josh's body. I'd never seen him so involved or determined before; he'd always been a passive observer. Not this time.

'Get…out…' Goodfellow as Josh snarled. His body convulsed as it dealt with the three spirits battling inside of him. His movements were disjointed; frenetic; desperate. He fell to the floor, his body twisting in almost unnatural angles.

That didn't stop him. He rolled on to his front and crawled towards us. It seemed to take an almost insurmountable amount of energy for him to make it a few inches. Thomas's head stuck out of Josh's body, then disappeared inside of it again. Then, Goodfellow's. Josh's. Thomas's. Goodfellow's. They were fighting it out. Josh seemed to be helping Thomas in whatever way he could. He was literally fighting for his life.

'We can't just wait to see who wins!' said Tessa. 'Do something!'

'You keep ordering us to do something. If you're so bloody worried why don't you?' I grumbled.

Pouting, Tessa crossed her arms and knelt down by Fadil. At least she could be useful by keeping an eye on him. And consoling him if his spirit did leave his body. Which it wouldn't. That was not allowed to happen.

'I think I have a plan,' I said. Whether or not it would work, I had no idea. But it was all we had. I just had to hope Goodfellow was too busy to hear it. 'Ben, can you trap them with your forcefield? Keep the pressure up as much as you can? Maybe make it suffocating? Like, painful?'

Ben was still cowering under Branwen's attack. If he couldn't free himself from that, my plan would never work. He gave me a thumbs up while mumbling something. A moment later, Branwen flew backwards and out of sight. Well, that was one of them down. At least temporarily.

He stood up, brushing himself off. 'Knew one of them would work eventually.' Gulping in a few deep breaths, he walked over and put his arm around my waist. He looked drained from the amount of power it'd taken him to sustain the forcefield and fight Branwen off, but there was something in his eyes that suggested he was far from done yet, no matter how he felt. Which was exactly what we needed.

'What about Josh!' said Edie in reference to my plan.

'He's been tortured by demons. He can handle a little bit of pressure to get rid of a ghost,' I said. All right, it was harsh, but we needed to make his body a hostile environment for Goodfellow. He'd had it easy compared to Josh, which was why I knew Josh could take it.

Thomas, meanwhile, seemed determined to take down Goodfellow for whatever reason. So I knew he'd go along with our plan.

Ben nodded, standing up and holding his hands into a circle to create a glowing, pearlescent bubble around Josh and the three spirits wrestling inside of him.

I put my hand on Fadil and gestured for Edie to do the same. 'Now, focus on Goodfellow's life essence. Channel it into Fadil, the same way you did with me and Dominic.' I really hoped my words gave her some form of confidence.

'I—I can't,' said Edie, tears in her eyes.

'Yes you can! Now isn't the time for self-doubt.'

'What if it isn't self-doubt? What if my powers just don't work anymore?'

'They do, Edie. They do! With or without the spell, you're still more powerful than I'll ever be. And Fadil is right here, which means you can use some of the power he's still borrowing from you to heal him.'

She squeezed her eyes shut, as if having an internal battle.

'He's fighting me!' said Ben through gritted teeth.

Thomas flew out of Josh's body again, landing just outside of the forcefield. He shook his head. 'It's not working! He's too strong and Josh is too weak!'

'There must be something we can do instead! This can't be it!' said Edie, squeezing her face up to hold back her tears.

Thomas floated over. 'Edie, hold my hand and focus on me. Focus on my energy and channelling it into Fadil.'

Edie looked confused, but took his right hand anyway. Then, he pointed his left at Josh/Goodfellow.

Edie inhaled so deeply I thought she was going to start levitating. The air around all of us changed. It felt tense, like something was building. A tornado began to form around us, trapping us with Goodfellow and the forcefield that was exhausting Ben to maintain.

I really hoped nobody looked out their windows while all this was going on. How would we explain it to someone who couldn't see ghosts? What would they see?

Thomas closed his eyes, his grip like iron on Edie's hand. There was a faint golden glow coming from where they connected, and another from Edie's other hand into Fadil. I couldn't be sure, but it looked like whatever they were doing was working.

Josh fell to the ground, leaving Goodfellow floating above him. Tessa ran over to him, trying to cradle his unmoving body. There were no signs of his spirit, which meant he was still alive but unconscious. Now we just needed him to stay that way long enough for us to finish off Goodfellow and get his body some medical attention because he looked seriously beaten up.

Ben diverted his forcefield to focus solely on Goodfellow, leaving the pressure on him so that there was no escape.

Not that he didn't try.

He wriggled. He chanted. He cursed. He banged against the forcefield, fighting through the jolts of electricity. Nothing worked. Ha.

Branwen, who'd made an annoyingly timed comeback, pecked at the edges of of the forcefield. The glowing white magic rippled, but it never gave way.

Panic radiated from the doctor, but it didn't change that he was getting weaker. Instead of looking almost human like he once had, he was getting faint. So translucent I could almost read the tall gravestones behind him.

Fadil gasped, sitting upright and almost head butting Edie.

'Oh my god you're OK!' Edie wrapped her arms around his neck, squeezing tightly.

'Not if you suffocate me I won't be,' Fadil choked out.

Edie's cheeks flared as she let go of him. 'Sorry.'

He smiled, ruffling her hair. 'Thank you.'

Her smile grew as she rested her head on his shoulder.

Phew. Ben glanced over his shoulder and smiled, too. Even Tessa looked happy to see him upright again, and she barely knew who he was.

'Edie! We need to keep going!' said Thomas. He pointed to Goodfellow, who was flickering again, as if trying to regain his power. Could he recover that quickly? I wouldn't put anything past him.

'Niamh, can you write an exorcism?' said Thomas. I'd never seen him take charge before, but I kind of liked it. It suited him. He was a surprisingly calm, confident leader for someone who looked ten.

'You want me to exorcise him in a cemetery?'

'We're all too drained. You're the only one with enough power left.'

I'd exorcised dozens of ghosts. Maybe even hundreds. Why did this one feel more challenging?

'Can I help?' asked Tessa from her spot beside Josh.

'Can you write a spell?' I asked.

'Erm, no?'

'Then you can recite it but it won't make a blind bit of difference,' I said.

She rolled her eyes. 'Why am I so helpless here?'

'You're not. It was your idea for me to come here,' said Thomas, his words and expression far beyond his years. Apparent years. Ghost age. Ugh. 'I needed that pep talk you gave me. Thank you.'

Tessa turned away with embarrassment. That was not something I'd have expected from her, especially with the way she'd been compliment-seeking moments ago.

Right. Focus. I needed to write an exorcism. One that only affected Goodfellow. Using his full name would be more powerful. That was a good start.

Ben shrank the forcefield even smaller as I wrote the spell. Goodfellow's figure was fading fast. He was a faint, glowing orb, meaning he had very little left. He was the weakest he'd ever been. It was now, or never.

'Randolph Goodfellow, you're not a good fellow, so it's time for you to say hello, to the dark place where you belong, the realm you should've been exorcised to all along.'

Not bad for something I made up on the spot. I needed to give my spell-writing skills more credit.

The glowing orb shattered into millions of pieces. We all turned away as if it could hurt us, but it was still trapped inside the forcefield. And not technically corporeal for most of us either. When we turned back, he was gone. No Goodfellow. No glowing orb. Just an empty forcefield.

Ben released it, lowering himself on to the tarmac and resting his weight on his gloved hands. He was panting, trying to catch his breath, but otherwise, he seemed fine.

Fadil crawled over to him, engrossing him in a bear hug. After everything they'd been through, a hug felt like the perfect remedy.

Edie and I ran over to Josh.

'I think he needs a hospital,' said Tessa, frowning. 'He looks really bad.'

'I could—'

'No, Edie! No more powers tonight!' I said, perhaps a little too aggressively. But she'd used her powers enough for one night. I wasn't having her risk her physical or mental health by relying on them. They hadn't even worked when she'd tried to use them on her own. What made her think they'd work now? Now it was time for the doctors – real doctors, not crazy Victorian ones – to work their magic.

40

Edie

Tessa stood up and walked a few feet away, a wistful expression on her face. Behind her, a glowing white circle, that looked both huge and tiny, near and far, appeared.

She noticed it, a small smile on her face, then turned back to Josh: 'Do you think he'll be all right?'

'He will,' I said, sounding more confident than I felt. He *had* to be all right. There was no other option, not after everything that'd happened.

Branwen cawed ahead. We looked up to see her circling between the light and Tessa.

'I always liked birds,' she said. She put her arm out. Branwen flew over to her and landed on it. Well. Did that say more about the raven or about Tessa? I wasn't sure.

'She's so beautiful,' Tessa stroked her back. Branwen let her. Somehow, they'd formed an instant connection.

'Her name is Branwen. It means "beautiful raven," I think.'

Tessa laughed. 'Of course.'

She shook her head, that wistful expression reappearing. 'There was so much I wanted to do with my life. And I thought I could have a future with Josh. Maybe achieve some of those things with him by my side.' Pausing, she gazed at him longingly, as if envisioning the life they could've had. The life she'd wanted but would never have, all because of something completely out of her control. As much as I hated her, it wasn't fair. Even she deserved more than that. 'Josh is a good guy. But he deserves better than what I could give him.' She shook her head. 'Thanks for your help. Maybe you're not so bad after all.' After flashing us a surprisingly friendly smile, she walked into the light.

*

I really wanted to curl up on the grass and sleep, but if I felt like that, Josh must've felt even worse. He was barely conscious.

So instead, Ben and Fadil went home, and we took Josh to A&E. He slowly woke up on the drive there, but he didn't say anything in the car. I didn't try to talk to him, either. Just thinking about what he might say made me anxious. I didn't have the energy to listen to, let alone respond to, a potentially snarky remark.

A distraught Maggie was already waiting for us just outside the hospital doors when we got there. She ran to us, embracing Josh in her arms. 'Oh my god!'

'Ow,' Josh cringed in his mum's vice-like grip.

'Sorry,' she said, pulling away.

The two of them walked into the A&E department to check in.

Mum put her arm around my shoulders as we followed them. There was no way we were going home until we knew Josh really would be fine. He'd woken up, and was walking and talking, which were good signs, but I wasn't sure if that was because he was fine to walk or he was being stubborn. It had been a long night, but it wasn't over yet.

A&E was busy, with barely an empty seat in sight. Despite that, it was weirdly quiet. I supposed people were too injured, sick, or worried to talk much. An old TV was in the far corner, on a low volume, the closed captions unable to keep up with the live weather forecast.

Maggie and Josh stood at the reception desk, talking to a couple of nurses. Well, Josh was leaning on it, clearly in pain. Maggie held on to him, trying to keep him upright. One of the nurses pointed to a couple of vacant plastic chairs. Sighing, Maggie and Josh went and sat on them. Mum and I walked over.

'What's going on?' I asked.

Josh stared at a spot on the dirty white lino floor, refusing to look at any of us. Even sitting so hunched over looked painful for him.

'They don't think Josh's injuries are severe enough for us to be rushed through. So we've got to wait. Four hours,' said Maggie.

'*What?*' I said, probably a little too loudly. But whatever. Four hours? Seriously?

Maggie sighed again. 'That's just what the wait is.'

'Do you need me to sort Abigail for school in the morning?' offered Mum. It was already past three in the morning, and a four-hour wait would mean that he was seen right as Abigail was waking up.

'Thanks, but she was already in our bed when you called, so she heard the whole thing and insisted on coming too. Harry took her for a walk to get her a drink while we waited. She was getting jittery.'

'Her big brother just got beaten up. Of course she's on edge,' I said.

Maggie nodded, putting her hand on Josh's back.

He inhaled through his teeth. 'Sorry. Sore.'

Maggie frowned, removing her hand from her son. 'Can I get you anything?'

'No, thanks,' he replied.

'Water would probably be good,' said Mum.

He shrugged, as if to say *whatever*, still staring at the floor.

An internal door flung open. Abigail and Harry walked in. Abigail seemed bigger than the last time I'd seen her, even though it hadn't been that long. But she was five. I blinked and missed a growth spurt. She ran to us and put her arms around my waist. I hugged her back. I'd missed her.

Harry didn't share his daughter's sentiment. 'Of course you two are involved in this,' he spat at Mum and me. A few people looked up from their phones or the books they'd been reading. This was probably the most interesting thing that'd happened all night. And of course we were at the centre of it.

'Whoa there,' said Mum, putting her hands up. 'We're in a hospital. Let's keep things calm.'

'Calm? My son is in A&E in the middle of the night because he was stupid enough to go out and let someone beat him up.'

Abigail, who was still holding on to me, tensed. I rubbed her shoulder, hoping it would offer her some comfort. Why was her dad being so aggressive in public? He wasn't usually like that. He was all about keeping up appearances.

'He didn't *let* someone beat him up,' I said. 'It was a —'

'Very aggressive person,' Mum said, saving me from myself. Phew.

I almost blurted out 'psychopathic ghost,' before realising we had an ever-increasing audience.

A nurse on reception eyed us warily, both hands under the desk. From the angle of one of her arms, I was convinced her finger was hovering over a panic button, but I couldn't be sure. Were they a thing in hospitals?

Ignoring us, Harry tilted his son's head, forcing Josh to look at him. Josh flinched, clearly in pain, but Harry didn't seem to care. 'Look at the state of you. Don't you know how to win a fight? Are you really that weak?'

Josh cringed, turning his head towards Maggie. Bruises were forming on his face, neck, and just about everywhere else that was visible. It looked painful.

'Leave him alone. None of this is his fault,' said Maggie.

Harry scoffed. 'Of course it's his fault! He's the one who got himself beaten up!'

'We'll discuss this later. In *private*.' Maggie glanced around the room. The people who'd been eavesdropping returned to whatever they'd been doing before the argument had kicked off, guilty expressions on their curious faces. I would've been annoyed at them, but I'd have done the same if someone else in the room had got into an argument.

Instead of replying verbally, Harry stormed off, leaving us, and probably the rest of the onlookers, speechless.

41
Niamh

'What the hell happened with Harry tonight?' asked Edie on the drive home. It was half eight in the morning. We'd refused to leave Maggie, Josh, and Abigail, even though Maggie had tried to get rid of us. Without her husband – and with him being so angry – she needed the moral support. We'd also been able to keep Abigail occupied so that Josh could sleep in the uncomfortable plastic chair.

When the doctors had finally seen him, they'd confirmed what we'd originally thought – most of his injuries were cosmetic. He did, however, have a fractured arm and bruised rib, so he'd have to wear a cast and take things easy for a few weeks. At least it was his left arm that was damaged, so he could still write and paint. Mock exams were almost over, so I was hoping they'd let him out of the rest because he'd been through enough stress lately. If anyone could convince them, Maggie could.

'That's a good question,' I said, shifting gears. 'Maybe he's been under a lot of stress at work so isn't sleeping well?'

'Yeah, but he's always come across as pretty boring, maybe a little mardy. I've never seen him that angry before. Shouldn't he have cared about how Josh was?'

'You would've thought so,' I agreed. 'It was definitely unusual.'

Edie hesitated. 'Do you think something else is going on?'

'Like what?'

'Could they be having marital problems?'

'How can they not be when he's talking to his wife and kids like that?' I said. 'I'll talk to Maggie when she's home and the kids are asleep.'

Edie nodded, as if to confirm she agreed with the plan.

*

Thomas was on the sofa, stroking Spectre, when we got home. He was showing his full power, just as visible as someone who was alive. He'd been hiding his powers all this time. And we'd never even noticed. Turned out we knew even less about our world than we'd thought.

Tilly ran over to greet us, jumping up as if she hadn't seen us in forever, when really it'd only been a few hours. I let her out while Edie prepared her breakfast, then we returned to the living room where Thomas was waiting for us.

'So. You're a necromancer,' I said, sitting on the sofa. Tilly hopped up to sit beside me, then lay down, watching our floating friend as he talked. Spectre got up and relocated to above the bookcase, observing the events from afar, as he seemed to prefer to do.

Thomas got up so that Edie could sit down, then he floated back and forth across the room. 'I'm sorry I didn't tell you sooner. I was afraid.'

'Of Goodfellow?' asked Edie.

'Of a lot of things.' He crossed his arms, keeping his head bowed as he continued to pace. 'I was killed for my powers when I hadn't even hit puberty. And I knew that whether I was living or dead, I'd always be a target.'

Edie frowned, shifting in her seat. 'You were murdered?'

Thomas nodded. 'While people believed back then, that didn't mean they always knew what to look for. Children died young. Illness was common.'

'But you died so suddenly. Didn't you?' I asked.

'Yes. I was playing in the graveyard after church. My parents were talking just around the corner.' He shook his head. His football appeared above him and fell to his foot. He kicked it, it flew through the air, disappearing again. If he was holding on to it when he'd died, then he could treat it like an item of clothing, or an extension of himself. So he'd be able to control if it was visible or not, just like himself. That must've been how, sometimes I could see it, and sometimes I couldn't, just like sometimes I could see ghosts, and other times I couldn't, depending on what the ghost had decided.

'Do you want to talk about what happened?' I asked.

Thomas pursed his lips. 'You know, I never have. And there are times where it feels like it happened to someone else. Sometimes, it feels like it happened yesterday. Minutes ago, even. I replay every second, wondering what I could've done differently.'

'You were just a child. It wasn't on you to protect yourself.'

'You're right,' Thomas agreed. 'I was angry at my parents for a long time, but they couldn't have done anything. It happened too publicly.' He lowered his shoulders, staring at the floor and crossing his arms around himself. 'Like I said: I was playing after church. My parents were by the main entrance, talking to friends. I kicked my football and it rolled around the corner and down the hill, so I chased after it. Goodfellow and Tobias were at the bottom. Tobias stopped my football and threw it back to me. I caught it and turned to run back up the hill.' He removed his flat cap and began twisting it, as he often did when he was anxious. 'Goodfellow started whistling. It was a horrible tune. And somehow, it made it impossible for me to move.'

'But neither of them have powers. Do they?' said Edie.

A small smile crept over Thomas's lips. 'That's what they want everyone to think. Goodfellow really doesn't have magical powers, but Tobias is my cousin. His father was human, so Tobias isn't as powerful as me, but his mother – my aunt – was a necromancer.'

Well damn. I hadn't seen that one coming.

'How does the whistling work if he doesn't have powers?' asked Edie. It had been bugging me, too.

'It's a hypnotism thing, that's all I know,' said Thomas. 'Some people are more susceptible to it than others. And guess who was at the top of that list.'

'That sucks,' said Edie. It looked like she, Ben, and Fadil had been lucky, still able to talk when he'd used the same technique on them. 'But, I mean...ghosts don't breathe. How could he whistle?'

'*That's* the part of this story that bothers you?' said Thomas, unable to hide his smirk.

Edie waved her arms in the air, making Tilly jump. 'It goes against everything we know about ghosts!'

He gestured to himself. 'And me hiding who I am for two hundred years doesn't? Sometimes things in life don't have the answers we want, and we have to accept that. Just the same as humans can sometimes do things we don't expect or that we can't explain, ghosts can sometimes, too.'

Edie stared at him, deadpan. We were never going to get a satisfying answer. At least not from him. But at this point, I'd seen ghosts do weirder things than whistle, so I was going to let it go for the sake of my sanity.

'So what about your cousin? How did he get tangled up with Goodfellow's plan? Assuming they were working together?' I asked, trying to get the conversation back on track.

'They were. Tobias has always been obsessed with finding ways to become more powerful because he didn't inherit as much of the family powers as I did.

He was envious that I could do more despite being so much younger than him. Over time, that envy ate him up inside. Goodfellow fed that and got him onboard with his plan.'

'So…what happened? If you want to share, that is,' said Edie.

'They took me under the cover of some trees, where Goodfellow drained me. I don't remember how, I just remember staring into Tobias's grey eyes as he watched. Silently. I wanted to fight them off, but since I was paralysed, there was nothing I could do. Magically I was stronger than them, but physically I was only ten. And I was terrified. Even though I had more powers, I had no idea how to use them. The people who could help me were just around the corner, but I couldn't scream. And everyone was too busy talking to walk around the corner and come find us. I was so drained that by the time my spirit left my body, I could appear as nothing more than a faint orb.'

Edie covered her mouth with her hand. 'Oh my god.'

'Since I was only an orb, I didn't see what happened next. You don't have any senses when you have so little left. It took me years to recharge. But from what other people told me, when I could speak to them again, they carried my body to where everyone gathered, making sure my death was as public as possible. It meant my parents' hands were tied – so many people had seen me lifeless they couldn't resurrect me. It'd raise too many questions. Believing in ghosts was one thing. Necromancy was a step too far. Family friends insisted Goodfellow take my body and do his best to preserve it for my funeral. Instead, he experimented on me to see if he could get anything else out of me. Nothing worked. They never got my powers, only my life.'

'So all that was for nothing?' said Edie.

Thomas nodded. 'Yeah. My parents were elderly by the time I could talk to them again, although they always visited me in the graveyard, even when I was just an orb. They tried to convince me to cross when they did, but I couldn't. A part of me knew Goodfellow wasn't done yet and I couldn't cross until I knew he was gone for good.'

'Does that mean…you're ready to…' stuttered Edie, her voice cracking. I reached out and held her hand, feeling emotional at the prospect, too.

'You don't need me anymore.'

'Yes we do!' argued Edie. 'We always need you.' Tears dripped down her cheeks. Thomas walked over and sat on her lap, hugging her. She hugged him back, resting her head on top of his. I wished I could join in, but the most I could do was hug Edie and hope Thomas understood I'd hug him, too, if I could.

That light, the one I associated with happy endings, appeared in the distance. It was a bright white, appearing both close and really far away. We'd only seen it the night before for Tessa, and now we were seeing it for a friend we'd known for so long we'd taken his presence for granted.

Two figures stepped from the light and stepped towards us. Millicent and Percival Hill. They beamed at Thomas.

'Thank you for helping my baby,' said Millicent. Oh my god. *They* were Thomas's parents? Well, I hadn't expected that. But it explained why they'd worked so hard to stop Goodfellow.

Percival put his arm around his wife and grinned. They stepped back, letting us say our goodbyes.

'I've done what I set out to do. Isn't that what life – what the afterlife – is all about?' said Thomas.

I swallowed back my tears. I had to stay strong for Edie. 'It is. Thank you, Thomas, for all of your help. You've earned this. More than most people ever do.'

He smiled. 'Will you say goodbye to Ben and Fadil for me, please?'

'Of course.' I couldn't hold back my tears any longer. The floodgates opened. And of course we'd ran out of tissues, so I couldn't even wipe them away with anything other than my sleeve.

'Thank you for everything you've done for me. I couldn't have got this far without you,' said Thomas.

'Are you kidding? *We* couldn't have got this far without you,' said Edie.

He smiled. 'That's great teamwork, right?'

'It is.' I wiped my face with my sleeve again. It was already soaked. 'You'd better go. You and your parents have got a lot of catching up to do.'

Millicent and Percival didn't say anything. They'd lived in our world; they knew that even though death was an everyday part of what we did, it didn't may the goodbyes any easier.

Thomas hopped off Edie's lap. 'If you ever need me, I'm just a seance away.'

*

I went over to Maggie's as soon as they were home. I was too restless to do anything else, and almost four decades of friendship had taught me that she wouldn't say that she needed moral support, but she most definitely would.

Josh and Abigail were asleep upstairs, leaving a tired but restless Maggie to her thoughts. Not a good combination.

As soon as I walked in, she hugged me. I hugged her back, unable to close the door behind me because she hadn't even given me the chance.

'Thank you for helping my son,' she said, stepping back while trying not to cry. She held her finger under her eye to catch the tears, a habit she'd acquired from years of wearing mascara and trying to stop it from bleeding.

I stepped forwards and closed the door. 'Always. How is he?'

'Bruised. Abigail is insisting on looking after him, so they're curled up together in my bed.'

I smiled. 'That's really cute.'

'Yeah. The police want to talk to him about what happened. What's he supposed to say?' She shrugged helplessly, wandering into the living room.

'Well, he knows he was beaten up by someone. So that, I guess.'

Maggie shook her head. 'It's scary that the police will never catch this guy, so some of the victims' families will never get closure.'

I nodded. It sucked. 'I wish we could give them that, but it's never that easy.'

'Nothing ever is,' said Maggie, adjusting the clip that was holding up her hair. It was her too-lazy-to-style style. 'Have you had breakfast?'

I chuckled, grabbing her and getting her to sit down in the kitchen. 'You've had a rough night. I should be the one asking you that.'

'No. I haven't had time.'

'I'm no chef, but I can rustle something up. What do you want?'

She gestured to a carton of eggs by the stove. 'Scrambled egg. You always did make really nice scrambled eggs. And the largest coffee ever.'

'That I can do.' So I stuck the kettle on and fished a jug out of the cupboard. I knew where everything was because Maggie's system hadn't changed since she'd moved into her own place in her early twenties, and if anyone ever tried to change it they felt her wrath.

'Are you OK to do stuff? I mean, your headache——'

'Has finally gone.' I couldn't remember the last time I felt so good, actually. Lack of sleep not included, of course. Everything was back in colour and surround sound. I could finally enjoy every moment again. Ironically, I couldn't wait to curl up in bed and catch up on some long overdue sleep.

'That's amazing.' Maggie smiled. 'Thanks for staying with us, by the way.'

'You don't have to keep thanking me,' I said. 'I'm just doing my job.'

Maggie snivelled. 'You always do so much. More than you have to. I'm so sorry I cut you out like that.'

I stopped what I was doing and put my hands on her arms. 'You don't need to apologise, Mags. You were traumatised. I get it.'

She shook her head. 'I still find it hard to tell what's real, but Alanis is really helping.'

I smiled. 'That's good. Hopefully Josh will be more willing to talk to her now.'

'If he's not, he's still going and he can sit in her house stroking the bloody cat for an hour every week until he's ready to open up if that's what it takes. I thought I'd taught him better than to adopt toxic masculine stereotypes like bottling up emotions. Apparently not.'

I rubbed her arm, then resumed making her food. She'd feel better once she'd eaten. Although it wouldn't change how she felt about what she'd just said. 'Speaking of toxic masculinity…'

'Harry?'

'Yeah,' I said, sticking the eggs into the microwave. 'What the hell was that all about?'

'I'm not sure. It's not the first time that's happened. Harry hasn't been acting like himself lately.'

I froze. 'Do you think…?'

'No. Don't be silly. I thought you said most of the ghosts from First Pit had gone, and the ones who stayed were nice ghosts.'

'You should keep the amulet a bit longer, just in case. You can never be too careful.'

Maggie's body tensed. 'Careful of *what*?'

'I just think it's sensible to be protected, that's all. After everything you've been through, I think it's better to err on the side of caution.'

Maggie took a deep breath. 'Yes. All right. Yes.'

The microwave beeped. 'Fiddlesticks. Forgot to stir it. I'll make you some more.'

'It's fine. I'll eat it as it is. If I have to wait much longer I'm going to start chewing on my arm.'

'Don't do that. If you do that, who's going to save my failed cooking experiments?'

'The bin. That's where most of them belong.'

I glared at her, but she was probably right. There was a reason she was a chef and I cooked the same three recipes.

42

Edie

I didn't expect Josh to be back at college for a while, so I was surprised when I found him in English a couple of days later. Everyone cooed over him, asking if they could help him with anything, which he hated.

I stayed back, figuring he'd blame me for what'd happened like he did everything else. So when he fell into step with me after class, I was pretty surprised. He walked with a limp, and his left arm was in a sling, but he seemed determined to keep going. I admired that, but I did worry about him overdoing it. Still, it wasn't my place to say anything. Not anymore.

'Hey. Sorry for my dad the other day. He's not normally like that.'

'That's OK. It isn't your outburst to apologise for.' I was pretty sure Harry wasn't going to apologise for it any time soon. And it wasn't Josh's fault.

Everyone seemed to give us a wide berth as we walked, which was good, as it wouldn't have taken much for someone to barge into his injured arm in such a crowded corridor.

'No, but he did cause a scene in public, and for a minute I thought he was going to tell the whole room…you know.' That was the most detail he could go into when we were surrounded by so many people. You never knew who was listening or might hear something they shouldn't. If Goodfellow and Branwen had taught us anything, it was that.

And after what Josh had said to Tessa about keeping our secret, I knew he wouldn't out anything supernatural in public. It was a small olive branch, and perhaps one that didn't have much to do with me, but I'd take it anyway.

'Me too. I'm just glad he didn't.'

'So am I,' he said.

We continued on for a minute. There were some things I really wanted to know, but I was afraid to ask him. What if I pushed him too far and he closed the door again? Something told me he wouldn't, but the paranoia was still there. I shoved it down and asked what was bothering me: 'Why were you there in the middle of the night?' I didn't need to specify where.

Josh sighed, shaking his head. 'It sounds dumb, now, but I thought it might help me talk to Tessa. I took one of those board thingies, but the bird picked it up and flung it over the fence.'

'It's not dumb,' I said. 'The veil can be thinner in graveyards. Although the board thing is dumb. You know that's a copyrighted board game, right?'

He blushed, laughing. 'No, I didn't. Lesson learned.' He shook his head in disbelief for a moment. 'I feel so stupid now. I caused all those problems and I could've just asked you to help me.'

'It's not always easy to ask for help. Especially after everything else that's happened.'

'Yeah,' he said with a sigh. 'I wanted to get you and your mum something to say thanks, but I wasn't sure what.' Out of breath, he stopped and leaned against the wall.

I stopped, too, enjoying what was the first real conversation we'd had in weeks. Until he'd started walking with me, I hadn't realised how much I'd missed it. 'You don't have to do that.'

He shrugged, then cringed and scrunched his face up.

'Are you all right?'

'Be fine,' he said through gritted teeth. 'After the way I behaved, I really didn't deserve your help. But you did it anyway.'

My insides twisted. 'I'll always help you if I can. It's part of my job.' As his friend, which I hoped I would be again some day, and as a necromancer. 'None of what happened was your fault. Or mine.'

Josh shook his head, as if trying to clear it. 'It's just really hard for me to tell what's real and what isn't, still. The demons told me so much that's turned out to be true, it's made me doubt a lot of stuff. Tessa was totally unrelated to all that, so I guess that's why I gravitated to her. But then she ended up being unintentionally involved, too.' He inhaled deeply, then winced. Probably hurt his ribs filling his lungs so much. They were pretty bruised from what Maggie had told us. 'I guess I'll never be able to fully avoid it.'

'Once you know about it, it's kind of hard to,' I agreed. 'You see it everywhere.' Sometimes, I really wanted to avoid it. Then I remembered that it was the reason I had Fadil and Spectre in my life, and why Mum had Ben. The good came with the bad. 'I'm really sorry Goodfellow targeted you. You've been through so much.'

'Was that his name?' Josh shuddered. 'I felt how strong he was. How angry he was. I really thought he was going to kill me. Then everyone else who was there, too.'

So had I.

'It was nice to be able to fight back this time. I felt like Thomas did most of the work, but at least I wasn't completely helpless.' He paused for a moment, looking off to the side, as if in thought. 'Just how powerful is Thomas, exactly?'

'I'm not sure. We only just found out what he can do.'

'Another one, huh? What are the odds?'

'Pretty slim, actually,' I said, moving out of the way so that a group of people could walk past and get outside. The wind had been cold and sharp when I'd arrived that morning; I was in no rush to get outside and feel it again.

'There's something special about you Porters, and I don't just mean in a supernatural sense,' said Josh.

My heart fluttered. Had he just complimented me? Was he so dosed up on codeine he wasn't thinking about what he was saying?

'Thanks,' I said as butterflies filled my stomach. I tried to suppress them, but it didn't work all that well.

If Josh noticed my inner struggle, he didn't say anything. 'Has Tessa crossed over now it's all over?' Way to kill the compliment.

'Yes. Believe it or not, she took Goodfellow's raven with her.'

Josh lowered an eyebrow. 'The crazy doctor had a pet raven?'

'She scouted out potential victims for him. They must've had some sort of special link or way of communicating. I mean, ravens can talk, but he had to train her to identify potential victims somehow. He whistled to summon her, as well as to torture his victims.'

'Ghosts can whistle?'

'Apparently,' I said, half-laughing. 'It was new to us, too.'

'I guess some things we'll never know,' said Josh.

'Sadly,' I agreed with a frown. I hated not knowing things, but the most important thing was that Goodfellow was gone. Was that the end of our drama? At least for now? I really hoped so. I needed a break.

'Are you done with exams now? It sucks you had to do all this on top of them,' said Josh.

'Yeah. Although I'm not really feeling all that festive after everything that's happened,' I confessed.

'Me neither,' he said. 'But Mum seems determined to celebrate, if only for Abigail's sake. At least it's for a good cause.'

'It's Abigail's favourite time of the year, and you've all been through a lot this year. You can't really blame her, right?'

'Yeah, I guess.' Josh nodded. He watched as a few more people walked past. The corridors were getting quieter, now. Just how long had we been talking? I wasn't complaining, but I didn't want to hold Josh up, either.

'Have you finished your uni applications?' he asked. Maybe he did want to keep talking? I wasn't complaining.

'Not you as well.' I rolled my eyes, slipping back into our old ways. I probably should've been more polite since we weren't friends anymore, but I was too drained to play pretend.

'What? What did I do?' He looked genuinely confused.

'Sorry. Mum and Mrs Mitchell have been on at me to apply. I really didn't want to go, but I can't help but think about all that Tessa's missing out on. Maybe I should leave the door open for a little while longer, just in case.'

Josh pushed himself away from the wall and started walking again. We carried on to the end of the corridor and out the front door. The wind was just as sharp as I'd expected. I shuddered.

'Exactly. It never hurts, right? It's not like you have to decide your whole future right now, even if they do make it feel like that sometimes.' Josh pulled his scarf tighter around his neck.

I scoffed, rolling my eyes again. 'Yeah, they really do. But who knows what's in store for us?'

'Not me,' said Josh as we climbed down the stairs. It's a little scary.

Fadil stood just to the left of the stairs outside college, coffees in hand.

'Thanks. You haven't been waiting long, have you?' I said, taking my usual order from him.

'No. Saw you two talking and didn't want to interrupt.' He smirked at me. Even though he'd never met Josh properly, he knew pretty much everything about my history with him.

'You look better,' I said, ignoring the look on his face.

'I am, thanks.' He rubbed his head. 'Doc said you wouldn't even know I'd had a head injury. And as horrible as having the lurgy was, I think it might've helped me acclimatise.'

'That's good,' I said.

Josh stood awkwardly beside me, his free hand stuffed into his pocket as he rocked on his heels.

'Oh, sorry! You two haven't properly met yet.' How had I forgotten to introduce them? I was such an idiot. 'Fadil, this is Josh. Josh, this is Fadil.'

Josh shook Fadil's hand. 'Fadil…you're…from Egypt, right?'

Fadil nodded. 'That's me. Ben's cousin from Egypt.'

Maggie had probably told him about Fadil, which was fair enough. He was already a part of our world, and he was keeping our cover. He'd go along with Fadil being Ben's cousin. If the last few days had taught me anything, it was that.

'Are you planning to stick around for a while?' Josh asked Fadil.

'Yeah, I think so.' Fadil sipped his coffee. 'I think Ben's going to need me.'

43

Niamh

While I was with Maggie, Ben asked me if I could meet him after work. I agreed, excited to see him. Everything had happened so fast the night before we hadn't had the chance to process it all or even just share a quick hug.

After getting home from Maggie's, I had a few hours before I had to meet Ben, so I had a nap with Tilly.

The quietness of the house, knowing all of my loved ones were safe, and the sheer exhaustion of the last few weeks, pulled me into a sleep so deep I hadn't experienced anything like it in months, if not years.

When it was time to wake up, a part of me really didn't want to move, but I knew that I could rest some more after seeing Ben. So I forced myself out of bed to walk Tilly, then went to meet Ben outside the library. It was glorious, finally being able to enjoy everything again without light or sound causing me pain. Everything seemed so bright after wearing sunglasses for so long, it was like waking up inside a children's cartoon.

Even though the sun was high and bright, I could enjoy how it illuminated the Christmas penguin wearing a top hat in the market square, a tradition that'd begun a few years ago in place of a Christmas tree. I liked it.

And it seemed silly to have two trees anyway, when there was a perfectly decent tree directly opposite, in front of the local pub. Its multicoloured fairy lights twinkled in the sunset. Everything felt so much lighter and brighter than it had in a long time.

I turned around, noticing the graveyard Thomas had once haunted. It seemed so empty without him there. I imagined him hovering in the gates, waving. Even though we could still talk to him whenever we wanted to, it felt wrong to summon him when he'd stuck around for two hundred years already and spent all of them terrified of Goodfellow and the alchemist. And with nobody to talk to about it. He deserved some peace in his afterlife.

Ben walked out of the Victorian library with a bounce in his step I'd never seen before. He kissed me in greeting, taking his time with me. I melted into him, feeling comfortable and safe in his embrace. It wasn't often he said hello in such a passionate way, but I was here for it.

Then, without saying anything, he grabbed my hand and began started walking down the road. No, not walking. He was practically running.

'How's your headache?'

'Gone! Finally!' I said, grinning. 'It's heaven. I've never enjoyed the sound of car engines and birds singing so much!'

Ben stopped and kissed my cheek. 'I'm so glad you're feeling better. Everything is looking up. Your headache has gone, Fadil didn't pass his germs on to me, and he's feeling better. I have a freezer full of chicken soup—'

'Sorry about that.'

'No, don't apologise. I don't have to think about what to cook for a week! And…'

'And what?'

He started moving again. He was practically jogging while still holding my hand. I could barely keep up as we scurried along the cobbled street. People moved out of our way as we ran past, navigating the bustling street as people did their weekly grocery shops, collected their pensions, or posted a parcel.

We stopped outside the shop Ben had wanted to buy. He took a key from his pocket and unlocked the front door.

Oh my god. Had he bought it?

Grinning, he held the door open for me. I stepped inside. It was spacious, although it definitely needed a face lift. Or three.

He closed the door. 'I put an offer in!'

I hugged him, excited at his future business. 'Congrats, business owner.'

'It still hasn't sunk in yet,' he said. 'But using my powers to help stop Goodfellow, to save Josh, made me realise I have a way to help the living and the dead. I can turn this into a safe haven for the ghosts and help Gwendoline manage them. So she's not worried about terrifying the children around the new estate. I'll never get acclaim or be well-known like some heroes, but I'm OK with that. It's not about the praise; it's about knowing I can make a difference to people's lives. And afterlives. This way, I can stock supernatural books for those who are interested, have somewhere safe for ghosts to hang out as long as they need, and still spend time around books. I might start selling coffee as a way to lure people in, too. And reduce how much money Edie spends in coffee shops.'

I laughed. 'It's an expensive vice, but it's healthier than some.'

Ben grinned. 'So, what do you think?'

'What do I think? Are you kidding? It's amazing! Do you know how you want to decorate it yet?'

'No. I was hoping you might be able to help. You know more than me about this stuff.'

I kissed him. 'Of course I'll help. Whatever you need.'

'I'll pay you—'

'I didn't ask you to.'

He smiled, kissing my cheek. 'You don't have to do that.'

'With a little help from Edie, Fadil, and you, we can have this place ready in no time.'

'I have to do DIY, too?' His expression suggested he hadn't done very much in comparison to Edie and me.

I chuckled. 'Yes, you have to do some, too. Don't worry, I'll stop you from hammering your finger or drilling into your thumb.'

'Until you said that, I wasn't worried about doing either of those things. Now it's going to be all I can think about.'

I ruffled his hair. 'Maybe you'd be safer with a paintbrush. Leave the painful objects to the professionals.'

'Did I ever tell you about the time I dislocated my toe on a can of paint?'

'So we'll also move the paint and just give you a tray and a brush…'

'I think that would be wisest, yes.' He ran his hands along the dusty, white wall. The paint was starting to peel and half the lights had broken bulbs in them. It would require some work, but that was OK. We were up to the challenge. I'd single handedly turned around far worse locations as a contractor.

'Seriously, though, thank you. I wouldn't have decided to do this if it hadn't been for you. And a couple of supernatural visitors.'

Lindsay must've paid him a visit after all, then. Apparently it'd half-worked. And the other half had been because of Goodfellow. Who'd have thought there'd be an upside to a supernatural serial killer? It didn't bring back the people whose lives had been cut short, but if we only focused on that, it'd consume us. If all the death I'd experienced in my life had taught me anything, it was the importance of looking for a light in the darkness.

'Yes, they do like to interfere, don't they?'

Ben nodded. 'They're usually right, though.'

'Annoyingly so.' I walked over to him, snaking my arms around his waist and pulling him into a kiss. We curled into each other, enjoying each other's presence, and one of the calmest, happiest moments since we'd met. Finally, it felt like things were improving.

Pulling away from our kiss, I said: 'I do have one question.'

'Oh? What's that?' Ben asked, resting his hands on my hips.

'When it comes to doing this place up, where do you want to start?'

The Ghost Hunter's Haunting

Being able to see ghosts is one thing. Being tormented by them at school? Doesn't exactly make it easy to pay attention in class.

And right now, a ghost I don't even know really wants my attention. Why now? If only I knew. More importantly, what does he want? And how the bloody hell can I get rid of him without my entire school finding out?

Meet teenage Niamh, Javi, and Maggie in *The Ghost Hunter's Haunting*, a companion prequel to the *Afterlife Calls* series. Available exclusively to mailing list subscribers.

Get your free copy today: https://www.kristinaadamsauthor.com/the-ghost-hunters-haunting/

NB: This book was previously called *The Mother's Lesson*, so you may still see it called that in some places.

The Ship's Spirit

The sixth *Afterlife Calls* book is coming soon. It's still in its really early stages, so all I can tell you right now is that it's a play on the old ghost ship trope. Niamh and Ben had hoped for a romantic getaway, but these things never go according to plan, do they?

To be the first to find out more, make sure you're on my Very Important Readers list. And don't forget to grab your copy of *The Ghost Hunter's Haunting*, available exclusively to mailing list subscribers: https://www.kristinaadamsauthor.com/the-ghost-hunters-haunting/

Acknowledgements

After putting so much into the first four *Afterlife Calls* books, I thought this one would be easier to write. Oh, how wrong I was. It's hard to admit when an idea doesn't work sometimes, but my original plan for *The Mean Girl's Murder* didn't, which meant I had to strip it back to basics and start all over again. The finished second version is what you've got in front of you. If it hadn't been for the support of certain people, and my always supportive readers, I never would've gotten to this point.

Chelle, thank you for your pep talks and moral support over the years. I still can't believe we've known each other for as long as we have. Your kind words, sounding board, and skincare discussions light up my day. (And nights if I've got insomnia.)

Alexa, what would I do without you? You know what it's like to be an indie author, and we bond over the ups and downs of being self-employed while dealing with our pasts, presents, and futures. It's a challenging ride but having you to listen without judgment is more important to me than you'll ever know. You also understood what I was trying to do/say with this book and series, and using you as a sounding board really helped me bring that vision to life.

Ellie, you've always been in my corner, cheering me on. You really help on those days when I'm not sure if I can keep going.

Millie, you're such a cute little ball of fluff and you always make me smile. All right, except for the days when you refuse to walk. But our family walks are some of my favourite times with you and Carl.

Carl, you've been by my side for so long now I'm not sure I know what I'd do without you. You keep me upright when I feel like I'm going to fall. You're my best friend, my soul mate, my life partner. I love you.

To my amazing ARC readers, thank you for being patient with me. I love your enthusiasm for the series and how much you share that love with other people. Thanks to Tammy for pointing out the last-minute typos I'd missed, too!

And finally, thank you, dear reader, for joining, Niamh, Edie and the rest of the gang for their journey so far. There's lots more to come from them. Once I've had a bit of a rest. Stay tuned.

And if you haven't already, come say hi on Facebook! You can find my author page here: https://www.facebook.com/KristinaAdamsAuthor. And my

readers' group here: https://www.facebook.com/
groups/kristinaadamsreaders

Also by K.C. Adams

Afterlife Calls

The Ghost Hunter's Haunting (free prequel)
The Ghost's Call
The Mummy's Curse
The Necromancer's Secret
The Witch's Sacrifice

Writing as Kristina Adams

What Happens in…

The Real World (free prequel)
What Happens in New York
What Happens in London
Return to New York
What Happens in Texas (free blog series)
What Happens in Barcelona
What Happens in Paphos

Spotlight (*What Happens in… spin-off about Cameron and Luke*)
Behind the Spotlight (runs alongside *What Happens in London* and *Return to New York*)

Hollywood Gossip (*What Happens in… prequel spin-off about Tate and Jack*)
Hollywood Gossip
Hollywood Parents
Hollywood Drama
Hollywood Destiny
Hollywood Heartbreak
Hollywood Nightmare

Nonfiction for Writers
Writing Myths
Productivity for Writers
How to Write Believable Characters

Printed in Great Britain
by Amazon